BLOODMAGIC

BOOK TWO OF THE BLOOD DESTINY SERIES

HELEN HARPER

CHAPTER ONE

I SENSED IT WAS ABOUT TO HAPPEN BEFORE I FELT IT. THE entrance to the little cellar was small and cramped and there was no other way to manoeuvre the next barrel out without awkwardly bending over and yanking it onto its rim. I snapped my hand round my back to catch the offending fingers that seemed to think that pinching my backside was acceptable, but instead just succeeded in letting go of the beer keg and feeling it drop heavily onto my suddenly protesting foot.

Shrieking suddenly in pain, I sprang backwards, colliding with my would-be attacker. He let out an exhaled ooph and staggered backwards while I spun around on one foot, trying to ignore the sharp throbbing hurt in my other one. I grabbed hold of his grubby shirt collar and shoved him against the wall. It was Derek, one of the regulars.

"What the fuck are you playing at?" I leaned closer to him and snatched his fingers with my right hand, squeezing them hard, and keeping hold of his shirt with my left.

He breathed out again, a cloudy breath of stale beer covering my face. I moved my face to the side in disgust and tightened my grip further.

"Jaysus, sweetheart, you need to chill out," he gasped.

The heat inside me rose. Taking liberties with roving hands was one thing, but calling me sweetheart was something entirely different. "Chill out? Chill the fuck out? Watch me chill you out, *sweetheart*." I let go of his hand and reached over to snatch the half-empty glass of ice and whiskey that he'd been clutching in his sweaty paw, scooping it up in one swift motion and then upturning it over his head. I dropped the glass dramatically on the floor and it shattered into several pieces. Derek wrenched away from both me and the wall, hands immediately running up to his head in an attempt to shake off the ice and droplets of booze from his face and hair.

He lashed out with one hand but I was faster than that and easily sprang out of his reach, even within the confines of the small cellar.

"You fucking bitch."

I smiled, deciding I preferred that to sweetheart. Derek, meanwhile, turned back towards me, fist raised. I put my hands on my hips and raised my eyebrows, daring him on. This was going to be fun.

'What exactly is going on here?" A calm voice edged with steel interrupted my plans. Bugger.

"This arsehole," I spat the word, "thinks that my body is fair game. I was merely abusing him of that notion." I turned to face Arnie, who was looking at me unhappily.

He threw a dishtowel at Derek and motioned to me to back off. "Oh come on, Arnie, it was him! I didn't…"

"Enough." He gently pushed Derek out and back to the bar, and shut the cellar door so that the two of us were alone. The offending keg offered little room but he kicked it away to the side and peered at me in the dim light. "You can't do this, Jane."

"Can't do what? Defend myself?" I was getting hotter by the second.

"Can't assault our best customers," he replied calmly.

"Assault? But he..." I tried to protest but Arnie just put a finger to his lips. Falling silent, I opted for glaring at him instead.

"You're a barmaid. It is part of the job – unsavoury, I know, but you should have learnt how to deal with situations like this by now. And this is a job which, I'm afraid, you no longer hold."

I was momentarily dumbstruck. I hadn't done anything – well, hardly anything anyway. I opened my mouth to speak but no words came out.

"I'm sorry, Jane. If you can't keep your temper, then I can't keep you. I'll pay you till the end of the week but you need to go. Now."

The bottom suddenly dropped out of my world. Shit. I needed this job. Without proper identification and references, it had taken me ages to find someone who would take me on. And even then the best I could manage was this dive of a bar. I tried to backtrack. "Arnie, I'm sorry, I blew things out of proportion. I'll apologise. I'll even let him feel me up if that'll help. You can't do this: I need this work."

He shook his head at me sadly and stepped out of the cellar. I sat down on the upturned keg and massaged my swollen foot, trying not to let the prick of tears behind my throat get the better of me. I'd worked my arse off for that bastard – unsociable hours, basic minimum wage, no benefits other than the odd pack of pork scratchings. It wasn't fair! I had the right to defend myself for fuck's sake. I kicked angrily at the fallen keg and it thudded dully against the wall before rolling back and crunching over the broken shards of glass. Bending over, I turned it upright but caught my knuckle on one of the splinters. It pierced my skin and sent out a small shiver of pain. Bastards. Bastard Derek and bastard Arnie and bastard Anton and...I pulled out the glass fragment with my fingernails and watched a drop of iron rich blood ease its way from my hand and splash onto the floor. It was that stupid blood that had made me end up here in the sticks of Scotland in the first place. Bringing my knuckle to my mouth, I sucked the wound and allowed the heat inside me momentarily take over, blanking out my more rational thoughts.

After a minute or two, I sniffed and squared my shoulders. Worse things happened at sea. If I could get through John's death, get through being thrown out of my home by a homicidal werebear, get through living in close quarters with the very shifty and very scary head of the Brethren, then I could get through losing a lousy job like this. I pulled the pieces of my shattered pride back together and steeled myself to face the music.

Standing up, I limped through the cellar door. Derek was looking at me triumphantly, with a sneer all over his ugly pock-marked face. I threw him the nastiest look I could, feeling some remote satisfaction at the fact that he was still dabbing at his neck with the dishtowel. The other bar patrons were staring at me in a hushed silence, but looked away awkwardly when I turned to them challengingly. Without warning, the jukebox's random music selection kicked in with the entirely inappropriate notes of Shania Twain's *Man I Feel Like A Woman.* I tried to avoid rolling my eyes. Arnie wordlessly handed me a brown envelope and raised his eyebrows so, sighing heavily and over-dramatically at the injustice of the world, I reached down behind the bar to grab my bag. Then I left.

My brief wave of bravado deserted me when I got outside and felt the cold night air wash over me. I really didn't know what I was going to do now. Trudging back to my little bedsit, I mulled over the possibilities. I could stay here, in Inverness, and try my luck at getting work in some of the few places I'd not already tried. The nearest pack was over in Aberdeen and, while I didn't have a large enough ego to imagine that every shifter in the country was doing nothing other than trying to find one supposed little rogue, I wanted to keep as far away from them all as possible. But that meant my options were fairly limited in terms of where I could go. Thrusting my hands in my pockets to stave off the cold, I hunched my shoulders. I searched inside myself to find a spark of fire that I could warm my own insides with, but there was nothing there. Fat lot of good all this dragon blood was if it was always going to be completely uncontrollable and never there when I needed it.

I stopped to cross over at a set of traffic lights and realised that gazing steadily at me from the gloom of the other side of the road was a dark shape. I stiffened immediately, tensing. Whoever it was, they were wearing an old-fashioned trilby and overcoat, but their features were hidden in the shadows. I wasn't in the mood for any fun and games. Squaring my shoulders, I stepped off the kerb to confront them, and almost got run over by a huge lorry thundering through and driving too fast through the quiet street. The driver slammed on his horn making me almost jump completely out of my skin. I gestured rudely after him and looked back at the shadowy figure. However, in the time the lorry had taken to pass me by, the other pavement had become completely deserted again. A wave of unease ran through me and I hurried home.

* * *

BACK IN THE relative comfort of my little room, I sat down heavily on my bed cum sofa and rubbed my eyes. This was not good. The morning paper lay unread on the table so I picked it up and flicked through to the classified section. There were scant few jobs being advertised. I ran my finger down the column. An office junior post – paperwork, yuck; a cleaner's position at one of the big chain hotels – they'd demand background details that I couldn't provide; a couple of labouring positions and very little else. I'd have to hit the streets tomorrow and try to cold call the local businesses to see if I could drum anything up. I leaned over to the small kettle and flicked it on to brew a cup of strong coffee, then reached for the battered laptop that had cost me far more than I could afford. Turning it on and heading straight to the Othernet, I cursed myself for my weakness.

When I'd been part of the pack, I'd hardly ever had cause to bother with the Othernet, the supernatural world's equivalent of the internet, but now that I was an outcast I found it hard to keep away. I found myself scouring its sites daily, checking that everything was safe in Cornwall, hoping for some news somewhere that would tell me how Tom and Betsy were getting on now that they had joined the ranks of the Brethren. And, on occasion, looking for gossip about Corrigan. I told myself that it was just self-preservation. He'd sworn that he would find me in his last Voice communication so it was important that I kept track of where he was. Just in case he was in the area and I had to run away and hide of course. I browsed around for a while but there was nothing new to be found. The Ministry of Mages were hunkered down trying to deal with the waves of applications that they were receiving now that they had opened up their recruitment procedures again and apparently there was some trouble over in Wales with some sprites hustling sheep. Nothing about the Brethren, other than an old photo of some of them at some kind of shifter ball that I'd already seen a dozen times. Corrigan was there, wearing a tuxedo that almost seemed to be sprayed onto his muscular frame, with some shapely brunette hanging off his arm and Staines was typically lurking in the background. There was no sign of either Tom or Betsy.

I resisted the urge to click on the link for the Pack's own website. The last time I'd done that there had been a photo of me staring back with a caption asking for anyone who had seen me to call the London number with information. It hadn't even been a terribly good photo; in fact it had been taken in the great hall after John and I had felled a particularly nasty spriggan who had been attempting to steal away a couple of local children. It had been a long chase and I was hardly looking coiffed and groomed. The photo itself had been cropped to leave out John but if you looked closely you could see his hand loosely wrapped my shoulder. That was just painful to look at.

Irritated with myself for still caring about the pack in the first place, I closed the laptop with a thump and lay down with the coffee by the side of the bed. I may not always have enjoyed the restrictions that came with being a member of the pack, and may often have craved more independence, but now I just felt lonely. They'd been my family; I'd have died to keep them safe and I knew that most of them at least would have done the same for me. And now I had no-one.

CHAPTER TWO

DAWN SEEMED TO BREAK PARTICULARLY EARLY THE NEXT DAY. I'D had a restless night, tossing and turning, worried about what I was going to do next. I'd decided, around 3am, that I'd give myself two days to find work here in Inverness and then if nothing turned up I'd head elsewhere. Maybe I could travel to a bigger city like Birmingham and lose myself in the anonymity of life there. There would be a pack for sure, but I was confident I could keep out of their way in the masses of humanity. If there were more people then there would be more jobs. I might even be able to make a few friends and put down some semi-permanent roots. This nomadic lifestyle that I'd been leading so far was starting to grate on me.

After a freezing cold shower in the communal bathroom, I pulled on the smartest clothes I could find and hit the streets. Without a National Insurance number, the Job Centre was out but I might always be able to find some small adverts looking for help in a few of the newsagents' windows. Deciding to venture to the busy Victorian Arcade first to try the little tourist shops there, I set out with a renewed confidence and vigour in my step.

The first few places I tried were polite but firm. It was out of season and they had no need for anyone else, especially someone

just wandering in off the streets. Trying to keep my spirits high –
no-one would employ a grumpy cow after all - I moved onto the
book shop, named Clava Books.

Unlike the other stores on the arcade, Clava Books was dingy
and looked as if it had seen better days. A bell on the door
jangled as I went in. A muffled voice called out from the back
that they'd be with me in a minute so I took a moment to browse
the little shop's offerings. Dotted around the uneven wooden
floor were piles of books placed haphazardly around. I almost
caught one leaning edifice with the corner of my foot and just
managed to pull back in time before the whole thing went
toppling to the ground. It didn't appear to be the most organised
shop in the whole world and I wondered idly if there was much
business to be had at all in the arena of old books that had seen
better days.

There were numerous Gaelic tomes on the shelves, some
incredibly dusty, as well as a sprinkling of the usual coffee table
photo books of the highlands of Scotland. I picked one up and
flicked through, stopping at the pages of Clava Cairns, a 4000
year old group of burial cairns. No doubt this was the bookshop's
namesake. Kind of creepy, if you asked me, to name a shop after a
cemetery. Admittedly there was a rather beautiful full page photo
that had been taken at night, with several people holding flames
aloft and staring towards the back of a group of higgledy-
piggledy stones. *Druids perform the Winter Solstice welcoming
ceremony* read the caption underneath. On reading that, the
vestiges of a thought flickered at the back of my mind. Before I
could fully form the words, however, my musings were
interrupted by a series of clatters and thuds from towards the
back of the shop.

Eventually an older woman with graying hair tied up in a neat
bun, emerged from a dark wooden door. "Aha!" she said, with
warmth in her voice. "So you're interested in the Cairns, are
you?"

I gently closed the book and placed it back on the shelf. "Of course," I murmured. It was important to appear as if everything about this shop was fascinating if I wanted to get a job here.

I clearly didn't do a very good job of looking interested, however, because she gazed at me with a somewhat skeptical expression on her face. "Have you visited the Cairns yourself?"

"Erm, no," I admitted. "But they are high on my to do list," I quickly added with a hopeful smile.

"So it's work you're after, is it?"

I started. How had she known that?

"It's written all over your face, dearie. Sorry, you don't like being called dearie, do you?"

Okay, now I was getting freaked out. Were my thoughts really that transparent?

The old lady smiled benignly and patted my hand. "I'm Mrs Alcoon," she said, warmly.

I couldn't help smiling back despite her formality. "Er...I'm Jane. Jane Smith." I'd kept my surname since moving to Inverness; Smith was obviously a common enough name to arouse absolutely zero suspicion. Using Mackenzie as well would have just been inviting trouble, however, so I stuck with the plain moniker I'd given myself when I'd found work at Arnie's pub.

Mrs Alcoon raised her white eyebrows briefly before murmuring, "Really? Jane? Funny, you don't look like a Jane."

I coughed slightly then cleared my throat, stirring myself to at least appear confident even if I was more than slightly alarmed by the elderly woman's prescience. "What can I say? My parents just lacked some imagination." It occurred to me that if my name really was Jane, I'd be feeling rather insulted by myself right about now.

Mrs Alcoon raised a shoulder in a brief shrug as if to dismiss the matter. "Well, Jane, you've arrived just in time. As it turns out, I do need some help. Not full-time, you understand, but a little helping hand here and there would definitely be welcome. Perhaps a few mornings a week? Cleaning the shop, attending to the customers, running a few errands?"

This was going considerably better than I'd expected. "I… um…yes." I cleared my throat again. "Yes, please."

She smiled at me again. "Then let's brew a pot and have a cuppa and discuss your remuneration."

She led me off into a small kitchen off the side of the main shop area. The tiles were cracked with dirty grouting lining their uneven finish but there was a little fridge, a few cupboards and a kettle and toaster. I supposed you didn't need much else to get by. There was also a little table with two wooden chairs against it in the middle of the small room so I took one and sat down. I was still feeling rather shocked that this was going so well and I half expected old Mrs Alcoon to suddenly burst out laughing and tell me that she'd just been playing a joke on me. To her credit, however, she busied herself with flicking on the kettle and pulling out a couple of chipped mugs and a teapot, humming away to herself tunelessly. Turning her back to me, she started pulling things out of the cupboards and getting herself organised.

Once the kettle had boiled, she filled the little teapot and brought it over, along with some surprisingly tasty oat biscuits. The proferred pot unfortunately wasn't coffee but instead some kind of potent herbal tea that made my eyes water and my tongue sting. I swallowed it down, however, to be polite; Julia had taught me well. It turned out that Mrs Alcoon had been considering taking someone else on for a while, to help keep the shop running. I did wonder if she was actually making any money at all, given the lack of customers that had so far ventured across the threshold but I wanted to work here, not to point out the lack of business that I'd so far seen so I refrained from voicing my question out loud. She needed someone to come in four mornings a week and help out, and I promised that I would help "spruce the place up a bit as well," as she put it. We agreed upon the princely sum of one hundred and twenty pounds a week – which was actually not much less than Arnie had been paying me at the pub and would definitely cover my main costs, though it meant I'd be continuing to scrimp and scrape – and she set me to work straight away cleaning down the shelves.

The rest of the morning passed quickly. Although no would-be customers entered the little shop's doors, there was plenty to keep me occupied. In fact, it was fairly satisfying work. The dust was thick in many of the little nooks and crannies and the many tomes, often as old and dusty as the building itself appeared, regularly caught my interest. The lack of passing trade met my first impressions; Clava Books wasn't exactly full of the glossy bestsellers that would tempt most people to venture inside. Mrs Alcoon, meanwhile, disappeared into another little room at the back from where I occasionally heard the odd clank and thud of things being dropped or moved around. The peace – and immediate trust that she'd placed in me – was reassuring.

By 2pm I'd managed to clear the worst of the dust away, leaving just a few motes dancing around in the weak winter sunshine.

"Goodness, you've done a grand job," she exclaimed, emerging from the door at the back of the shop. "I'll have to find you more things to do next time."

I felt a brief wash of worry that the old lady didn't need me in the slightest and had just hired me out of pity. Then I wondered whether I could afford to be bothered by that and if I should just accept the charity that was being offered.

It's perfect, however," she continued, " as I need to run out tomorrow morning and pick up some supplies. This way you can stay and keep the shop open – otherwise I'd have to shut it up." She smiled without a hint of self-deprecation at all. "And that wouldn't be good for business."

Was she reading my mind again and soothing my worry that I was nothing more than a charity case or was all this just coincidence? I smiled halfheartedly back at her, feeling a nervous flicker of bloodfire in the pit of my belly.

"So where do you come from, Jane?" she enquired with the air of someone who was barely interested.

I stiffened further. Why did she need to know that? I tried not to let my thoughts show on my face. "Oh, I've lived all over," I said airily. At least I hoped it was airily and not with the growl that I really wanted to answer with.

"Ah, a wandering traveller! Part of me wondered whether that brilliant red hair of yours suggested a Scottish heritage. Your accent doesn't fit with this little corner of the world, however."

I smiled weakly again and watched as she picked up a few sheaves of paper and peered at them over her glasses before rearranging them slightly and then placing then back down in a messy pile on the shop counter. Her hands gave away her age, with papery white skin covering the visible blue lines of her veins within. Taking her in a fight shouldn't be a problem, although I knew well that appearances could be deceptive. I'd bested the strongest looking muscle bound shifters down in the pack with ease and had almost been garroted in the same week by a seemingly harmless looking pixie. I'd have to be careful here.

Mrs Alcoon's eyes, for their part, betrayed nothing but warmth as she continued. "Myself, I'm a home bird. I like the idea of travelling and seeing the world, but truthfully I'd rather just stay at home. I've lived here in Inverness all my life, in fact." A sudden shadow crossed her face. "You do have somewhere to stay, don't you?"

"Oh, uh, yes, just on the other side of town. It's very, um comfortable."

"Mmm," she murmured. "Well, that's good then. Are you here on your own? No family?"

The fire in my belly crept up just that little bit higher. "No. No family. They are all…" I paused for a moment, trying to quickly, before giving up. Since leaving Cornwall, no-one had asked me about my background so I had nothing prepared. "I don't want to talk about it really. It's all just a bit complicated."

She pursed her lips slightly and bobbed her head. "Aye, families are complicated things."

"And you?"

She shook herself. "Yes, dear?"

"Your family? Your husband?"

"Oh goodness. No, he passed away years ago." She touched her hand to her throat for a moment and I felt guilty for asking, but I'd needed to deflect her attention away from me. "We have no children either. I'd always wanted them, of course, what woman doesn't? But it wasn't to be."

The melancholy look on her face prevented me from stating very firmly that there were plenty of women around who did not want squalling children running at their feet. It was clear, however, that there was no danger here. I was just being jumpy. She was probably just very good at understanding people. Probably.

I puzzled it over all the way home, stopping to pick up a couple of rolls and some cheese at the local cooperative shop. I havered slightly over some delicious looking quince and lime chutney, but the price was beyond my reach even in my surprisingly new gainfully employed status. Eventually, painfully small shopping spree over, I decided that I was reading far too much into her comments. I was hardly known for keeping my emotions to myself, after all. Way Directive 49 said that shifters should keep their more passionate emotions in check when in public. I'd never been very good at that one.

Once back at my little hovel, I pulled out my one and only plate from a drawer next to the stainless steel sink and broke open the rolls with my fingers. The blunt knife I used to cut through the cheese was far from perfect, but it did a good enough job and soon enough I was munching away, leaning back against the wall that the bed rested against. My gaze fell briefly on my laptop in the corner but I decided that it was time for new beginnings. I wasn't part of that world any more and it was time that I stopped thinking that way. Draco Wyr, Corrigan and the rest of the Otherworld be damned.

CHAPTER THREE

As soon as I arrived at Clava Books the next day, Mrs Alcoon left on her mysterious errands. I was still somewhat baffled at her total trust in a complete stranger but I felt determined to fulfill her expectations. Casting my gaze around the shop, I tried to decide where to start. There was little evidence of a cataloguing system, although perhaps the old lady wouldn't take too kindly to my moving things around drastically. I could start cleaning the floor, I figured, if I shifted the piles of books around, but surely that would put off any customers who might decide to suddenly appear. I threw a skeptical glance at the door; it really didn't seem as if anyone was going to come in, but of course maybe yesterday had just been a slow day. Perhaps if I washed the windows instead, the place might look more inviting.

I found some old newspaper under the till and a wrinkled lemon in the little fridge in the kitchen off to the side and set to work. Glass, however, had never been my strong suit and it seemed as if I was creating more mess by just moving the dirt around a larger surface area. Hmmmm. I sat back on my haunches briefly and surveyed my efforts. "Could do better, Mack," I murmured to myself. Perhaps it wasn't lemon that you were supposed to use. Maybe it was vinegar?

All of a sudden a gloved hand pressed itself against the window from the outside. I was so startled that I gave out a little shriek and sprang backwards tipping over a pile of books on the floor next to me.

"Fuck!" I swore, peering out through the grubby pane to see who had interrupted my work. Whoever it was, however, had since passed on. There was a woman entering the little café opposite the bookshop and a pair of teenagers gossiping over some gadget they held in their hands on the corner, but none of them were wearing gloves and no-one else was around. Someone just wandering past, I supposed. Cursing at my clumsiness, I started to pick the mess of books up and put them right.

I'd almost finished putting the pile back to how it had been before when I reached out for the third last book. It looked similar to all the others, with a cracked leather cover and some faded gold inlay around the edges, but when I picked it up something about it felt different. It wasn't a buzz exactly, or a hum, or a physical vibration, but my fingers tingled and I was opening it to flick through before I'd even realised what I was doing.

There was a beautiful illustration on the first page with vibrant colours that belied the book's age. It was of a landscape, with rolling hills and a dark turquoise blue river. I could just make out a stone painted structure in the background, and what I took to be a pomegranate tree in the foreground. I gingerly turned the page, trying to avoid disturbing the old paper too much, and in the next instant threw all caution – and the book – away from me as if it had scalded me. Because the next page, the title page, wasn't written in English but instead proclaimed itself loudly with a single Fae rune.

My heart was suddenly thudding. A Fae book? Here? In the depths of rural Scotland? I stared at it now lying on the other side of the room as if it might rise up and attack me and tried to think. It wasn't beyond the realms of possibility that it had ended up here by accident. This was a bookshop, after all, and it housed old, in fact ancient, books within its walls at that. And it probably wasn't so unusual that it was here in north Scotland either; what with the Celtic connections and everything, there were bound to be Fae creatures lurking around. I swallowed, trying to avoid the fire inside me rising in increased ire, pushing away the unwelcome thought that if I hadn't been trapped inside a faerie ring back in Cornwall while my home was being attacked by Iabartu's minions then Julia, and the others, might still be alright. And Anton wouldn't be in charge, and I'd still be there and...

Enough. I tampered down the flames and watched the book warily as if it might suddenly attack me. Did Mrs Alcoon know what it was? Did she even know it was here? There had definitely been something off about the way she'd seemed to read my mind. Perhaps it hadn't just been the uncanny wisdom of someone with experience at reading others. Perhaps she was...

"A witch?" A smooth voice asked from above me. "Or worse?"

This reading of my mind trick was becoming tiresome, I briefly thought, and then instinct took over and I was on my feet in a heartbeat. I'd stopped sheathing my daggers to my forearms – it would have been a bit difficult to explain that away in the bar where the uniform had been a white short-sleeved t-shirt and I'd just gotten out of the habit – but I wasn't completely complacent, or stupid, and I used sharp silver needles to hold my hair in place at the back. Flipping them out with a flick of my wrist, I poised to stab them somewhere, anywhere, in the direction of the voice. The front door of the shop hadn't jangled so whoever this was hadn't entered by any conventional routes - and they were making my skin crawl. This was most definitely an otherworldly presence. It was wearing a trilby hat that covered most of its face, although I could just make out a dark smooth skinned jaw, and overcoat. This was the thing that had been watching me from the side of the road the day I'd been fired by Arnie. It had been stalking me. The bloodfire that I'd controlled just moments before suddenly raged inside me, licking up my stomach and chest and throat.

"Whoa," the suddenly clearly male voice stated without a trace of tension, "you might want to calm down there a little bit, Red."

The old nickname registered briefly and, hot blood thudding in my ears, I suddenly lashed out. The figure leaned back in a blur of effortless motion and completely avoided my furious swipe.

"Have you become rusty since leaving the Pack?"

So the nickname had been no coincidence. But this was definitely no-one I knew from my former life so he had to be someone – something – entirely more dangerous. It occurred to me that he may well have planted himself inside the little shop for the very same reason, my traces of Draco Wyr blood, that the demi-god bitch, Iabartu, had killed or maimed almost everyone I'd cared about for. Not gonna happen this time, buster.

I thrust forward again, this time pivoting on the ball of my foot at the last possible second to aim for his more vulnerable flank. To my abject fury, he bent his body back away again in a move a ninja warrior would have been proud of.

"Really, given what I've heard you're capable of, I find this rather disappointing. I'd expected a more," he paused, "impressive display."

I snarled but kept my distance this time, trying to clear my thoughts and focus on the job in hand. Focus the fire, focus the fire, focus the fire. I wasn't going to give in to the temptation of letting the dragon part of me, whatever that entailed, take over. I needed to stay as human as I could because letting go would mean facing up to what I really was inside and I just wasn't prepared to do that yet. I'd come close last year with Iabartu and I had no desire to go that way ever again. Even if it meant I couldn't defeat whatever otherworldly *thing* was in front of me.

Focus the fire. The mantra ran through my head again and again as I fought to compose myself and control my blood to allow me room to think. The flames dampened down although the heat inside me remained.

"There now," he softly cooed.

The bristles on the back of my neck stirred at the patronising tone of voice and I almost, just almost, lost my shaky control. I forced a deep inward breath, reminding myself that completely flaking out and losing my temper would not help me control this situation. I looked him up and down, realising that I still hadn't seen his face clearly from under the shadow of his wide-brimmed hat. I might not be able to quite connect with his body but…

Tensing ever so slightly, I pulled one teeny tiny tendril of flame up from the pit of my stomach and allowed its heat to swirl gently through my veins, before using its power to snatch forward with the very tip of one of silver needles.

He hissed in sudden surprise but I'd achieved my immediate goal. I'd snagged the edge of the hat and managed to take him unawares and pull it off his head. I found myself staring into a pair of deepset indigo eyes that flashed silver in a mixture of shock and fury. Damnit. My would-be attacker was Fae.

The obvious tension in his heavily coated body and in the muscles tight against his high cheekbones betrayed the Fae's own emotions. I felt some momentary satisfaction that he had had to control his own temper at my actions and resisted the urge to chant, 'na nanana na' at him. Instead, I scooped his hat off the floor and twirled it thoughtfully on a finger, returning the silver needles to their hiding place at the same time and keeping my eyes carefully trained on him. Silver would do me little good amongst the Fae; I'd need to find some iron instead. Life would be so much easier if all otherworld nasties had the same weaknesses. There was a limit to how many different types of metallic weapons I could realistically carry with me. The Fae's eyes followed the circular motion I made with his hat as I forced myself to inject a lazy nonchalant drawl into my voice.

"Well, someone's strayed far from the Unseelie Court. Why are you darkening my door, Fae?" I winced slightly at my own over-done cliché, but it did the trick.

Hissing again and baring back his lips in a surprisingly

animalistic grimace that revealed a set of very sharp and very white teeth, his eyes returned to my face and deepened to almost black colour. Neat trick.

"I am Seelie, human. Do not think that you can compare me to the dark ones."

Oh, well. I'd had a fifty-fifty shot at guessing right. With his midnight dark eyes I'd have sworn he was Unseelie – a member of the Dark Fae - although his golden hair did, to be fair, suggest otherwise. "And do not call me human, Fae," I retorted calmly back. "I assume you are here because you know what I really am."

"I know what you are not."

I'm not interested in having this conversation with you. "And what is that?" I said, aiming for an air of almost boredom.

"You are not of the Pack, despite their Lord Alpha's naïve convictions to the contrary. And, you are right, you are not human." He leaned in close to me and took a deep breath as if inhaling my scent. "So what are you?"

I cocked my head, considering. I was relieved that he apparently didn't know the truth after all. The records I'd found secreted away in John's magically sealed drawer back in Cornwall had given away the truth – that, no, I wasn't human, that instead running through my blood were the genetic traces of the Draco Wyr, an ancient dragon race whose blood contained mysterious magical elements. There was the power of the fire that rose inside me whenever I was angry or challenged, and the addictive qualities that had been revealed when Anton had tasted my blood during the Brethren's evaluation challenges and when Iabartu had tried to take me down to use my blood for her sinister and nefarious purposes. She'd almost destroyed the entire pack in her hunt to catch me because she'd seemed to think that she could use it to control others. I was hardly going to reveal the truth of my origins to an untrustworthy Fae, Seelie or not, when total destruction might be the result. Besides, I still didn't really know all that much about the Draco Wyr anyway; my Othernet research hadn't really pulled up many answers.

"I have no idea," I eventually replied, shrugging as if I had no answers. "I have some witchy qualities perhaps but, other than that…"

The Fae glared at me for a second and then rocked back slightly on his heels. His face took on a look of intense concentration and his eyes held mine, daring me to look away. Gold flecks danced across the pupils of his eyes and his voice deepened to a deep murmur. "You will tell me everything."

"Errr…no, I won't, because I don't know anything."

His eyes bored further into mine. "What are you? I won't hurt you, little one."

Little one? This was becoming annoying. He reached out an elegant hand, gently brushing my cheek with the tips of his fingers before I could manage to move away. His eyes reflected even more golden highlights, if that were possible. He smiled at me and softly repeated, "Tell me."

"Fuck off. And don't touch me, how do I know where you've been? I could catch some nasty Fae disease off of you." I was being rude now but I didn't care. I enunciated slowly in case he was hard of hearing. "I…do….not….know….what…I….am….so….I….can't….tell…you."

His face hardened and there was something else there too, some emotion that I couldn't quite define. Surprise? Perhaps even a trace of respect? I couldn't work it out.

"I know you're lying, Mackenzie."

"It hardly seems fair that you know my name and I don't know yours."

"Names have power, even you must be aware of that."

I sighed expressively. "I don't need your true name." Honestly, all the Fae placed far too much importance on what was just a tag. "It would just be polite for you to introduce yourself. I don't know what I am, but even if I did, you are a complete stranger to me. Tell me your name, and it doesn't have to be your real name for goodness' sake, and why you are here talking to me – and stalking me - in the first place, and I might be able to tell you more about what I know."

There. I was being calm and reasonable. And I had to find out how much he actually knew and how he'd found me in the first place. Knowing who he was meant that I could find out more about him once I got back home and logged onto the Othernet too. Knowledge always equals power and right now the Fae was ahead of me by a mile because he at least knew who I was and where I'd come from.

He assessed me for a moment, eyes reverting back to their original shade of indigo. Then something seemed to flicker across his face as if he'd made up his mind. With a sudden sweep from the waist, he sketched a deep bow and held out his hand. "My name is Solus."

I ignored his outstretched hand and just waited. He sighed quietly and withdrew it. "You broke my sister's cruinne and I became...curious. I wanted to know who on the middle plane was capable of such a feat. My sister is not without some considerable power."

I must have looked blank because he explained further. "I believe you call them faerie rings?" There was a trace of distaste in his voice.

Oh. I glanced briefly down at my hands, which were still clutching the silver needles. That had probably been my blood. But getting trapped in that ring had meant that I hadn't been there to help Julia or the others. I felt the heat inside me rise once more and my teeth clenched.

"That ring almost cost me everything."

"I'm sorry," he stated simply. "They are usually the work of Lesser Fae, however my sister is...immature. It doesn't change the fact that you managed to break through it, however. It appeared to be the result of some kind of blood magic so I waited and watched until traces of the blood that had such power showed itself again. Two days ago it did."

That must have been when I'd cut myself on the shards of

glass after Derek's attack. I frowned. Solus had been on the street moments after that though so…

He interrupted my thoughts. "Time moves differently for us. Even you must know that."

Oh, yeah, I did know that.

"I wanted to know who had the power to destroy our magic. It is wise for us to be on our guard when our powers are challenged. So when your blood showed up I watched you. It wasn't hard to find out your true identity either. It appears I'm not the only one looking for you."

My stomach briefly squirmed at the thought of Corrigan before I pushed it away. "And now you've found me."

He watched me carefully. "Yes, now I've found you. I have no interest in the Pack's desires so have no fear that I will reveal your location to them. However I do still want to know what you are."

I believed he'd been honest with me but I still couldn't trust him or his actions if he found out the truth.

"I don't know," I said. "I am not without some ability and, yes, I did break through your sister's cruinne. I apologise if it caused her problems but it was an emergency and I had no desire to be stuck there for centuries just for her amusement. But I really don't know what I am."

"You're lying. I can smell it coming off of you in waves." His conciliatory tone had vanished in a wave of irritation. "But I don't give up easily. I WILL find out what you are." He looked up for a moment as if he was sniffing the air and then gazed into my eyes again. "I'll be seeing you, Mackenzie."

Suddenly without ceremony or so much as a by your leave, he vanished, leaving me standing bewildered and slightly scared in amongst piles of books. Bugger it. Now what?

CHAPTER FOUR

Moments later, Mrs Alcoon strolled through the door with a tartan shopping trolley trailing behind her. I was still stunned by the Fae's sudden appearance and disappearance, and what it would really mean for me, but somehow still managed to register the quaintness of her accessory. I hadn't thought that anyone actually ever used those trolleys in real life but, clearly, I had been mistaken.

She smiled brightly at me. "There now. That's all the foraging done for the time being." Her gaze fell on the few remaining books that lay scattered around the floor, including the Fae one that I'd thrown to the other side of the shop. Her smile dimmed slightly. "Goodness, have we had a visitation of pixies then?"

I eyed her warily. There was definitely more to this old lady than met the eye. Could she sense that Solus had been here? I wondered whether to broach the subject outright with her, but before I could think of what to say, she'd bustled her way to the back with her trolley behind her squeaking on its ancient wheels. I picked up the books, ignoring the thrum of the Fae one which I thrust out of sight under several others but where I knew I'd be able to find it later, and tidied up the pile. I could hear her humming away to herself from the kitchen with the same tuneless notes she'd used before, and then the click of the kettle being switched on.

Wandering into the kitchen after her, I aimed for small talk instead. "So did you pick up anything interesting then?"

"Oh, yes, dear. I've got some nettles and some St John's Wort. Makes wonderful tea, you know, and it's great for the nerves." She peered at me curiously. "Looks like you could do with some."

"Err…I'm good, thanks." The memory of her last brew was still lingering on my taste-buds and I was in no rush to try anything else. I paused and searched for an opening. "So, you are a bit of a herbalist, then?"

"Oh, I dabble, dear, but I'm no expert." She smiled again and I wondered just how far her dabbling took her. Into witchcraft as well, perhaps? Mrs Alcoon continued, "Although I was wondering if there was something that maybe you could help me with this afternoon."

"Of course," I murmured, curious to see what she would actually ask for.

"I promised an old friend who's feeling sick that I'd make her up a little something to ease her troubles. The trouble is that I really need some blisterwort if I'm going to follow my recipe correctly. With my creaking bones it's difficult to get hold of. It really only grows on the outskirts of town and it's a bit of a hike. If I showed you what it looked like, and where to go to fetch it, do you think you'd manage to pick some for me? You need to walk up towards Clava Cairns to fetch it." She suddenly looked a bit worried. "You did say that you wanted to see them, didn't you? I don't want to impose on you, Jane dear."

I swallowed hard. That was the third time that she'd called me dear in the last five minutes. But it was no biggie. Honest. I wasn't getting worked up over something so petty. No sirree, not me.

"I do want to see the Cairns," I reassured her. "And it's no imposition. I'd be more than happy to, especially as it's for a sick friend." I watched her carefully as I said the last, but her expression didn't flicker.

She reached over and briefly touched my shoulder. "Thank you so much. The fever she has isn't life threatening or anything like that, although it can be dangerous to animals, but she is suffering terribly with hot flushes."

"Actually I could do with the exercise." I realised as soon as I said it that it was true. The unsociable hours I'd been keeping when I worked at the pub hadn't been particularly conducive to maintaining a health regime and I wanted to make sure that I was in shape for the next time Solus decided to pay a visit. And in case this little old lady wasn't quite the harmless old woman she portrayed herself to be. Appearances could be deceiving and I wasn't going to let my guard down. There were just a few too many coincidences that hinted that the otherworld had at least its fingertips on her, if not actually a full grip. Besides which, I'd helped Julia out in finding clippings in the forest in Cornwall plenty of times in the past. I was pretty sure that I knew what blisterwort was and that I could find it. It might just be worth taking a short trip via home first however, just to see what particular qualities this herb actually possessed.

I said my goodbyes and grabbed my coat and backpack, re-tying my hair in its bun and attaching the needles safely within, then heading outside just in time to be almost blown away by a chilling gust of wind that attacked my face and hair and virtually undid all my attempts to look neat and tidy. "Fuck," I swore, turning up my collar although it offered scant protection, and hurrying back to the bedsit. If nothing else I'd need to find some warmer clothes if I was going to go tramping around the Scottish countryside in search of a plant.

I was halfway home when I thought I heard someone calling my name. Not Jane, either, but Mackenzie. I turned around, alarmed, but the windswept streets were almost completely deserted, even though it was barely midday. I'm just imagining things, I told myself. I hunched my shoulders over further and battled onwards against the wind. Siberia has nothing on this place, I thought grimly, pushing forward. Then I thought I heard it again. Just a ripple of a voice, however, saying something indistinctly. I whipped around again, ignoring the blast of wind now against my back. My eyes darted around the streets. This was getting bad. Was it the Fae, or something else? I frowned and then turned forward again. There was a little alleyway, or a vennel, as the locals called it, up ahead. I'd been here long enough to know a little of the lay of the land, and it would suit for darting into to see if anyone really was following me. I forced myself to maintain my original pace and not appear too overly concerned.

My eyes were starting to smart from the oncoming wind and I blinked away a few tears, shaking my head to try to maintain my vision. My nerves were jangling and on edge, and I could feel the flames rising. Inverness was becoming just too dangerous, I decided. I'd see what this was behind me, sort it out and then find somewhere else to go where little old ladies didn't seem to frighten me and where Fae couldn't find me. Easy.

A few moments later I reached the vennel and quickly shot in. It would have been nice to enjoy the respite it gave me from the gale force winds but instead I kept my senses open and focused.

Mackenzie.

There. It was faint, but I definitely heard something. And it was definitely my name. I resisted the urge to peek round the corner and instead pulled out the needles again. Bring it on.

It's been a while but I will find you, kitten.

I almost dropped the silver. Shit, shit, shit, shit, shit. That wasn't a voice, that was a Voice. And not just any Voice, either, it was Corrigan's. My panic systems went into overdrive and before I knew it I was poised and ready for flight. I felt as if a screeching alarm was going off in my head. Get out, escape, run now, Mack, run now, it screamed at me.

My heart was thudding in my chest and I felt like I couldn't breathe. Suddenly, nipping into this alley seemed like a ridiculously bad idea. I'd be trapped here and he'd find me. I had no lotion to mask my scent and he'd find out I was human, or at least he'd find out I wasn't pack, I amended to myself, and rip me apart as a result. And then he'd go after Tom and Betsy, and the rest of the remaining pack members in Cornwall and he'd destroy them bit by bit, limb by limb. He had enough strength to that with barely raising a sweat, I was sure. He'd massacre them and then go off for breakfast with all his Brethren buddies and think no more of it. I'd be a footnote, a warning to anyone who ever dared to think they could infiltrate the pack without a were. It wouldn't matter that I might be part dragon. I was dead and so was everyone I'd ever cared about.

Then I realised that the only thing I could now hear was the sound of the wind whistling through the streets and the occasional rumble of a car in the distance. Think, Mack, think, I forced myself. His Voice had been faint. Most alphas couldn't use their Voice far out of their local vicinity but Corrigan had contacted me once from London while I was in Cornwall and that had been as a clear as a bell. This time, however, I'd had to struggle to work out what he'd been saying. He couldn't be anywhere nearby. And he'd said he'd find me. That meant that he still didn't know where I was. I felt the tension almost immediately release itself from my body. He was probably just teasing me, trying to keep me on my toes. I'd not been expecting to hear him; he'd kept pushing at me with his Voice after I left Cornwall but since passing the north-east of England I'd heard nothing and had assumed that I was either out of his range or that he'd given up. Between Solus and my suspicions about Mrs Alcoon and now this, today was shaping up to be one of the worst I'd had for a long time, and I'd not even had lunch yet.

* * *

ONCE I WAS HOME, I changed into a warmer jumper and pulled out a pair of fingerless gloves from a box under the bed. I tried to find some iron weaponry that I could take with me in case Solus decided to show up again, but I had scant few belongings and hadn't thought to prepare myself against a miniature Fae invasion. All my efforts had been concentrated against defending myself against the Pack, and Corrigan. I decided that I'd run this errand for Mrs Alcoon and then definitely take my leave of Inverness and its cold winds. I felt a brief of twinge of guilt because I did like the old lady. Still, I'd only worked for her for two days so I was pretty sure she wouldn't be too devastated at her loss. Besides which, the uncanny way she seemed to read my mind and the Fae book – even if Solus had planted it there – most certainly hinted at things I'd probably be best to stay away from. I was sure she was harmless but, given my past history with the otherworld, it would be wise to avoid anything even remotely connected with it. I didn't know whether Solus would be able to track me if I moved but, even if I completely discounted Mrs Alcoon, there was the threat of Corrigan to take into consideration as well. If he was still in London then his power must be getting stronger for him to project his Voice this much further - and that spelled danger with a capital D. And if it wasn't that his power was stronger but rather that he was nearer in location to me – well, I had to move on. I could probably sneak across the Channel to France somehow without a passport and then take things from there.

I buttered one of the leftover rolls from my previous night's dinner and sat down on the bed with the laptop while I crammed the food into my mouth. Logging onto the Othernet took a few minutes thanks to my slow internet connection so, while I waited, I flicked on the stained kettle to sort myself out a caffeine hit then drummed my fingers against the keys impatiently. I was in a hurry to get up to the Cairn and find these herbs and then pack up my belongings and get out of Dodge.

As soon as I was in, I typed Solus into the search engine but nothing came up. I tried Fae and of course ended up with thousands of entries. Clicking on the first one, a website helpfully entitled Faepaedia, I scanned through its contents.

The Fae are a strong race of daemons that have power over many demsenes. Their true origins have been lost as time has gone by, however they boast of considerable magical powers. Human in appearance, the Fae can transport themselves between planes without the cumbersome requirement for portals. Also known as the Sidhe or the Tuatha De Danann, their homeland has been dubbed Tir Na Nog, a plane that is usually inaccessible to other beings.

Upon Tir Na Nog exist two sections of Fae society: Seelie and Unseelie. The Seelie Court is headed by the Summer Queen, whose palace is located at the Shining Hall, while the Unseelie Court, whose ruler is the Winter King, can be found at the Soul Barrow.

In lore it is believed that the Seelie Fae are 'good' and Unseelie Fae are 'bad'. The reality is considerably more complicated and both Seelie and Unseelie are known for causing havoc and destruction. Seelie Fae, however, tend to be less inclined to truly malignant mischief. Both Courts are considerably at odds with each other, despite the role of the Unseelie Fae in protecting all of Tir Na Nog and the balance that each provides the other. Darkness cannot exist without light and summer does not exist without winter.

Hmmm. Nothing particularly new or unsurprising although Solus had seemed offended when I'd suggested that he was Unseelie. If this othersite was accurate, then surely it was actually the task of the Unseelie Fae to decide whether or not I was a threat, not the Seelies. I pondered that for a moment and then shrugged. I couldn't find anything about Solus himself and, while the absence of evidence was not evidence itself, it did suggest that perhaps I shouldn't be getting my knickers into too much of a twist. He was probably just a Solitary Fae rather than a member of the Trooping Fae, the aristocracy of the Faeries. But it wasn't paranoia if they really were after you. I glanced around my little bedsit and estimated that it would take no more than thirty minutes to pack up my belongings and go. My rent was paid up until the end of next week; I'd just have to swallow the loss in income. It would probably take a couple of hours to get up to Clava Cairns, say an hour to find enough blisterwort for Mrs Alcoon, a couple of hours back and perhaps to pass on my apologies and goodbyes to her - and then I could be on my way out of town by early evening.

I found some images of the little plant so I would know exactly what I was looking for. Opening up one of the image sites fully, I scanned through the information there detailing the herb's medicinal qualities. Apparently it was good for settling nausea, nerves and high temperatures, as well as reducing the impact of red fever. The site cautioned against using it while pregnant, however. I snorted slightly and closed the laptop lid, leaving it on top of the bed where I could grab it quickly later along with the rest of my stuff. Then I hooked up my trusty old backpack and left.

CHAPTER FIVE

I<small>F</small> I <small>HADN'T BEEN IN SUCH A RUSH TO GET BACK SO</small> I <small>COULD SAY MY</small> goodbyes to Inverness then I'd probably have run up all the way up to Clava Cairns in my jogging gear. At least working up a sweat might have staved off the cold somewhat and it would have given me the chance to start to recoup some of my earlier fitness levels. As it was though I was itching to get this last errand done and out of the way so I could get on my way. I hopped onto the local bus to cut down on some time. Typically, however, despite the almost complete lack of passengers, the bus seemed to stop every ten metres at every single bus shelter along the way. I could feel my irritation rising and annoyed heat coiling itself around my intestines. I was tempted to march up to the driver and demand that he move just a little bit faster but I had the sense that if I tried anything like that he'd deliberately take his time and fall behind schedule.

After twenty-five minutes of continual stopping and starting, a greasy looking guy clambered onboard, huffing and puffing as he lurched up the aisle. There was the distinct reek of stale alcohol emanating out from his pores and I tried to breathe through my mouth and lean away from him as he passed. The memory of Arnie's pub was still a little raw and the stench coming off the man reminded me of everything about the place. Not that I missed it of course but at least then I hadn't been bothered by dangerous Fae or slightly clairvoyant old women or threatening Voices.

Just when I thought I was out of the danger zone and he'd passed me by, however, he spun around and jabbed a finger in my direction. "You! You are burning, little girl."

I shied away and glared at him, trying to ignore the sudden thudding beat of my heart. "Get away from me, little man," I hissed back at him. "I don't know you and I don't know what you are on about."

I desperately tried to work out what he was. Definitely not Fae or pack but he could sense my blood. Vampire? But, no, it was still too light outside despite the midwinter gloom that hung over the sky. He could be a warlock, I supposed. Would my silver work against him? I cast a nervous glance up at the driver and wondered if I could disable the guy without appearing to have really hurt him. We were nearing a bend so when the driver's attention was completely on the road I could direct a hit at his shins and make a dash for it. The bus doors were automatic but I could probably wrench them open without too much difficulty. This depended on the whisky-sodden creature in front of me though. If he possessed some serious power – and to sense my blood fire he probably had a fair amount already – then a little kick wouldn't do much to get him out of the way. I started to reach up to loosen the silver needles from hair, just in case. They couldn't do any harm and it was just possible that silver could be a deterrent for him.

As I did so, however, he spoke again, with a hacking cackle that hinted at a few too many cigarettes burning up his lungs over the passage of time. "Ow! You're just too hot for words. Will you marry me?"

He dramatically fell to his knees and held out a hand. The bus driver called out from the front in the tone of someone who'd seen all this before. "Jack, stop bothering the young lady and get to a seat."

The tension immediately fell away from my body. He was just a drunk, trying his luck. I'd never have made this kind of mistake when I was back with the pack in Cornwall. In fact I usually prided myself on being able to read people's body language and intentions. All this paranoia and looking over my shoulder was doing me absolutely no good whatsoever. I was jumping at shadows and harmless locals. Jack, for his part, staggered to his feet, and with the expression on his face of someone who had been terribly wronged weaved his way to the back seat of the bus where he promptly lay down and began snoring loudly. The bus driver shrugged at me apologetically in the mirror.

I sighed deeply and pinched off a headache. Goddamnit. I really was reading too much into things – into everything. Solus was real but perhaps my over-active imagination was working over-time making me stupidly jumpy at everything else. Mrs Alcoon was probably exactly what she seemed: a little old lady who ran a failing bookshop and had a penchant for nasty herbal tea. In fact even Corrigan's Voice had been so faint earlier today that maybe I'd even imagined that too. I had to get a grip on reality. Once I re-located somewhere else, somewhere I was sure I'd be safe, then I'd have to do my best to stop freaking out at every little thing.

Fortunately, a few minutes later, the bus pulled up at the stop that I wanted. It was still a couple of miles' hike to the Cairns themselves, but the path was well worn and clearly marked so I knew it wouldn't take me long. I shifted my backpack to a comfortable position, and tied the straps in front to avoid too much unnecessary bounce and took off at a jog.

The path wound itself around some low lying hills sprinkled with lavender coloured gorse bushes and sprigs of white heather. Occasionally I'd catch the scent of the flowers, but mostly what I smelled was good old-fashioned fresh air. I filled my lungs deeply and stretched out my stride, regulating my breathing to match my gait, and enjoying the moment. For the first time in a long time I managed to completely empty my mind of my stress, worries and loneliness and just savoured the moment. A couple of hikers stopped to let me past along the route, nodding greetings as I whipped past them, but for the rest of the trip I was alone. It had been far too long since I'd felt this close to the natural world and I appreciated every moment.

I rounded a bend and then, far too quickly, the Clava Cairns were in front of me. At first glance there wasn't a huge amount to see – some standing stones were sprinkled here and there in a pretty clearing, while smaller rocks were piled together to form largish circular mounds. The contrast of the mossy grey cairns against the brilliant emerald green of the grass and trees was fairly striking, but the grey skies and cold wind rather marred the effect. I moved closer to the nearest circle and peered at it. There was a raised lip of stone all around the outside, and I noticed that the rocks seemed to have been chosen for their colour. Interesting. The rocks further away from me were definitely redder and larger while the ones by my feet appeared smaller and whitish. I wondered idly whether that was by accident or design. One was never entirely sure with these kinds of ancient burial grounds. One thing I did know though was that whatever bodies the Cairns had entombed, they would definitely be human. Any being connected with the Otherworld used cremation to dispose of their dead; the risk of anything using some form of twisted necromancy to make nefarious use of the bodies left behind was just too strong. I shuddered slightly at the thought. At least necromancy was a power that seemed to have fallen through the mists of time. Much like the Draco Wyr, my traitorous mind whispered before I pushed that thought away without examining it any further.

Leading through two of the cairns were corbelled passage graves. I wandered slowly through one, scuffing the soles of my feet against the rough ground and a few fallen leaves as I did so. It was almost possible to imagine the humans who had come through the same passage to lay their fallen dead reverently inside. Old buildings had always had that effect on me. Once inside the unroofed structure, I trailed my fingers gently across the stones, following the inner circle around. I couldn't feel any twinge of anything otherworldly but something about the arrangement of the stones triggered my vaguely ritualistic motion. I was glad that the roof was no longer present at least – I always found small spaces somewhat claustrophobic. After a few moments, however, I pulled myself back out to the greenery to find Mrs Alcoon's blisterwort.

It's not a showy herb, unlike some others I could think of, so it took a bit of time to find enough plants to root up to make my journey worthwhile. I carefully placed them inside a small cotton bag that I'd brought just for this purpose and then, with a somewhat lighter heart, headed back down the way I'd come. It was only early, in fact barely three o'clock, but already dusk seemed to be approaching. I scowled to myself at the irritating vagaries of nature that curtailed my daylight hours and then straight away laughed aloud at my nonsensical spite. The sound was whipped away almost immediately by the wind, but the suddenness and spontaneity of it made me smile further to myself. Okay, things might be pretty bad on the surface – I had the Lord of the Pack himself after me (and if he found out I was human he'd probably pull me apart slowly and painfully), no friends or stupid faeries to contend with, but I had my sense of humour and my freedom, and the relative excitement of the open road stretching away from me. And let's face it, things could always be worse.

CHAPTER SIX

THE LIGHT WAS ALREADY FADING FROM THE SKY BY THE TIME I made it back to the arcade. Most of the shops were shutting up for the day, even though it was still relatively early. If the bright delights of the Scottish trinket shop, posh looking gentleman's outfitters and old fashioned sweet shop weren't enticing customers in, then there was little chance that Clava Books was faring well, I thought grimly. Then I tightened my lips and hardened my heart. It wasn't my problem; I had bigger things to worry about. Staying around Inverness would just bring more trouble down on my head ~ and, by default, Mrs Alcoon's also. I couldn't be responsible for everyone in the world, I just couldn't... So why then did I feel so guilty about running off?

As I neared the little bookshop, I could see the lights were on. I noted with some satisfaction that the windows at least looked clear and the place was just a bit more inviting and less grubby. From the outside anyway. The bell jangled as I walked in, feeling a bit nervous about the conversation I was about to have.

"Mrs Alcoon? Hello?"

There wasn't any answer so I figured she was round the back in the little kitchen or her office. I glanced at my watch. There was just over an hour to drop off the herbs, speak to her, grab my belongings from the bedsit and catch the last bus. I steeled myself and called out again.

"Mrs Alcoon? Are you there?"

The shop remained silent. Cursing slightly under my breath, I headed for the kitchen and popped my head in. An empty cup lay in the little aluminium sink with some green gunk that I took to be some more odd tea leaves lingering in the bottom of it. I turned around and went for the office door, knocking first. For fuck's sake, where was she?

I knocked again and cleared my throat. "Umm...Mrs Alcoon? I need to talk to you. I have the blisterwort too." I pushed open the office door gently and peered inside. She was sat in a chair behind a neat desk upon which lay a beautiful leather bound notebook and a couple of old books. A desk lamp lit the windowless room, leaving a soft glow. This was the first time I'd been inside the office and I was rather surprised at the tidy appearance. The front of the shop didn't look anywhere nearly as organised as this. I was caught for a split second by a reminder of John's little office and then pushed the thought away before it could take further root.

"Mrs Alcoon?"

The old lady shook herself, her eyes deglazing somewhat. "Why, hello Jane. I see you made it back in one piece then." She smiled at me warmly.

"That I did, Mrs Alcoon, that I did." I was feeling much more relaxed in her presence now, the incident with Jack the drunk doing me much more good than harm in reflecting my own over-enhanced insecurities back at me. Another flicker of sadness that I was about to leave ran through me. I pushed it away and instead pulled the herbs out of my backpack. "Here, I've got the blisterwort that you were asking me for."

"Oh, that's simply wonderful! And so much of it too! Thank you for going to all that trouble."

I felt a warm ripple of pleasure run through me at her words. It was nice to be praised for a change. Mrs Alcoon reached out to take the green leaves from me, brushing my hand as she did so. Before she could take hold of the blisterwort, however, she pulled back and looked at me with a serious glint in her blue eyes.

"You will be safe from him here, Jane. And the other means you no harm."

Uh, what?

The old lady shook herself. "I'm sorry. Sometimes I...see things. I don't entirely know what they mean but I get flashes of, well, I suppose some might call it the future."

I knew it! The pleasure waves vanished and my bloodfire leapt up instead. My eyes narrowed slightly and my body tensed, and I waited for her to elaborate further.

She continued. "You think I'm terribly odd, don't you? With my funny tea, and my demand for strange herbs from ancient graveyards. I'm not surprised." She sighed heavily. "In another generation I might have been burned at the stake for being a witch, I suppose. My grandmother had visions just like this – all the time. I can remember they gave her terrible migraines. Of course, I don't think what I have is strong enough for that. Just odd glimpses now and then. Like now."

I suddenly wasn't quite sure what to think. I felt tense and wary and wondered what she was going to come out with next. So she couldn't only read minds – she could see into the future as well, some kind of soothsayer or clairvoyant. The familiar swirl of heat rose further inside me. It didn't possess the nervous flicker or angry flames that it often did so clearly my paranoia wasn't entirely crazy and misplaced after all.

"You think that you see into the future?" I questioned, my jaw clenching.

She giggled slightly, an odd sound coming from an older woman, though why I thought that I have no idea. "Oh, I don't know that it's the future, dear. Just perhaps potential outcomes. Like with the blisterwort for my friend. She's not that sick, I just have the feeling that there might be something coming on. An illness of some kind. And that this might help. It's all so silly, really. It felt strong with you, though, stronger than I've ever felt before. There's a man – with dark dark hair and," she cocked her head slightly, "a kind of feline grace that's unusual in a man of his size."

I almost snorted at that last part but just managed to contain myself.

"You're hiding from him," Mrs Alcoon said, "that's why you're here in Inverness. And you are going to leave because you're worried that he'll find you here. He won't though." She looked serious now. "He wants to find you, but he won't ever come here. I felt that very strongly. And there's another one, with golden hair but I can't see him as clearly. There is a strange sort of mist surrounding him. He means you no harm, though, that I am sure of. You should be flattered at the attention from both. They are terribly handsome."

She winked at me saucily as she made that last comment, which I found almost as disturbing as the fact that she was suddenly telling me that she had otherworld powers. I had a pretty good idea to whom she was referring, with both of the 'men', and I definitely found neither of their attentions flattering. I also didn't know whether I could trust her vision or trust her.

"I'm not crazy, if that's what you're thinking," she said, suddenly worried. "Some of the locals here think I'm a bit odd, maybe a few think I'm loopy, but I'm really not. I'd like you to stay, Jane. It's good for me having someone around and, I think, it's good for you too."

I just stared at her, tongue-tied. I wanted to believe her and, it did all make a kind of sense. I knew I'd been worrying about her and what she really was but I was also pretty sure that anything otherworldly about her was just a hint. I'd surely have sensed it otherwise. My mind flashed briefly back again to Jack the drunk on the bus and how wrong I'd been there. That had been different, however, because that was my paranoia imagining things that weren't there rather than things that were. She had a little bit of power that had been passed down from her family and that was all.

Trust. I hadn't trusted anyone since I'd left Cornwall. I couldn't tell her what I really was – that would only put her in danger – but I was starting to think that I could actually trust her with who she was. And maybe it was time to stop running and looking over my shoulder like some frightened rabbit. I'd been a nervous wreck lately. I'd never have let a Fae like Solus frighten me away a year ago. Trying to hide from a Fae was also a particularly pointless thing to attempt anyway. I tugged at my hair thoughtfully, wrapping a strand around my finger. People were normally scared of me, not the other way around. As they should be - my temper was legendary. And I was a dragon to boot. Well, almost.

Here I had a job and a roof over my head. I flicked a glance over at Mrs Alcoon looking at me both patiently and benevolently. Maybe I finally had a friend now too. And I couldn't spend the rest of my life running away. Besides which, she had said that Corrigan wouldn't come here. For some strange reason I did feel as if I could trust her. I closed my eyes for a heartbeat, mentally balancing up my options. Then I smiled at Mrs Alcoon, with what I hoped was conveyed to her as genuine warmth.

"You're right. I was going to leave. Perhaps you've just convinced me to stick around for a while longer."

"That's simply fabulous. I am so happy to hear that, Jane."

I took a deep breath, and a very big chance. "Actually, it's Mackenzie, not Jane. Mackenzie Smith. You can call me Mack, though, if you want to." Please do in fact, I don't like Mackenzie, I thought to myself. No such luck though.

"Mackenzie? What a lovely name. Very Scottish, you know. And it definitely suits you better than Jane. That one just didn't sit right with me. Now, come along." She took me by the arm. "Let's have a cup of tea."

"Actually, if you put the kettle on, there's just something I want to get first. To ask you about."

Okay, so there were a few lingering traces of paranoia. Figuring it would be better to completely clear the air of everything first, I stepped out into the shop front and headed for the pile of books where I'd buried the Fae text. Would Mrs Alcoon recognize it? Would she try to explain it away as some kind of Cyrillic book? I pulled it out from under the other books and somehow without disturbing the entire tower, then followed Mrs Alcoon into the little kitchen where she had already turned on the kettle and was spooning more dried green stuff into the teapot. I would really have to bring my own coffee tomorrow. It felt good to be thinking about tomorrow.

As before, the vibrations of the book made my skin tingle. I thrust it out to her. "I found this when I was cleaning up earlier. I don't recognise the language," I lied. "Do you know what it is?"

She took it and opened the cover with care, then her eyes widened and she put the book carefully on a shelf behind her. "Now you are probably really going to think I'm crazy."

I looked at her askance.

She explained. "It's from the Wee Ones. At least that's what my grandmother told me. There are several books like it kicking around here. They never seem to be there when you look for them but, when you're least expecting it, they suddenly appear as if out of nowhere."

Much like the Fae themselves, I thought sourly. Still, I wanted to know exactly how much she knew so I pressed her further. "The Wee Ones? Who are they?"

"Faeries, dear. Sorry, I mean, Mackenzie. They really do exist. Or so I'm told – I've never actually seen one." She looked at me with intelligence behind her eyes. "Oh, I see. You don't think I'm crazy, do you? You already knew it was a Faerie book. You DO actually recognise the language."

I nodded, feeling a bit bad at being caught out trying to test her. Might as well tell the truth then, I figured. "Yes, I knew. I just

– I just wondered why you had it. Or them as you say there are more of them."

"It's more a case of they have me rather than the other way around. Those books have a mind of their own, I swear it."

The kettle hissed and spat steam, chugging its way to the boil. Mrs Alcoon washed out the cup that was in the sink and dried it with a small teatowel then reached into the cupboard for another.

"Now before I get the tea ready, why don't you tell me what you know about Faeries, Mackenzie. How did you know it was a Faerie book?" There was nothing in either her face or her voice to suggest anything other than honest curiosity.

"I used to live with a group of people who knew about…such things," I admitted. "But then I had to leave them because things got – uh, well, they got bad."

"I'm sorry," she said softly. "You don't have to tell me about it. But I'm here to listen if you do."

I smiled at her weakly and she smiled back. In that moment I realised that everything was going to be okay. Mrs Alcoon poured the hot water into the teapot and gestured to the table and chairs next door. I sat down and curled my feet around the legs of the chair, relaxing back into the wooden frame. This was good.

CHAPTER SEVEN

THE NEXT FEW DAYS PASSED WITH SURPRISING SWIFTNESS – AND with very little action. There were no more disturbing Voice communications from Corrigan, for which I was eternally grateful, and I had settled into a routine at Clava Books, even being fortunate enough to serve a number of customers looking for information on the local sights and sounds. I spent most of my time rearranging the shelves and properly cataloguing the inventory. Mrs Alcoon hadn't quite made it into the twenty-first century just yet, and the shop was computer-less, but I brought my battered laptop in with me every morning and planned to print out the inventory once I was finished, so that she could make use of it too. Neither of us had mentioned the Fae book again, but it sat on one of the dusty shelves in the kitchen and demanded my attention every time I entered the little room to make myself a drink. At least I'd finally managed to bring in a small cafetiere and some proper coffee so I could avoid the herbal concoctions that seemed to be getting stronger and stranger by the day.

Walking home after putting in a couple of easy hours, I stopped to look in the window of a little haberdashery store. There were balls of wool and knitting needles displayed at what seemed to be knockdown prices and I wondered whether I could teach myself to knit so I could sort out some proper winter wear. A scarf couldn't be that hard to do, surely? I turned on my heel to go inside when I felt a hand clasp my shoulder. Without thinking, I grabbed it and twisted hard, and was rewarded with a pained ooph. I looked down to see who my would-be assailant was and was faintly pleased to note that it was my one-time fuckwit of a nemesis, Derek.

"What do you want, arsehole?"

"Just thought I'd say hello, sweetheart," he gasped. "Now let me fuck go."

I twisted harder and he moaned. "You're a hard bitch. Thought you'd have had the sense to get out of Inverness by now."

I leaned in towards his ear and spoke softly. "Why? Because I should be scared of you? Does it look like I'm afraid, Derek?" I gripped his wrist harder to emphasise my point.

"Fuck you!"

Suddenly his arm was wrenched from my grasp and he went flying backwards. It happened so quickly that I barely had time to register it before a trilby hatted figure swept a bow in front of me.

"Well, now that's hardly the way to talk to a lady now, is it?"

"Piss off, Solus." I rotated away from both him and the now sprawled Derek and made to move away.

He stepped in front of me with ease, blocking my path and I looked at him in irritated exasperation.

"Leave me, alone."

"I will leave you alone when you tell me what you are."

Pushing my hair out of my eyes, I aimed a sharp kick at his shin, which he unfortunately dodged. "I told you. I don't know what I am. Besides, I am no threat to either you or yours so what's the big deal?"

"You're a conundrum, Mackenzie. Or is it Jane? Perhaps I should just call you Red?"

Solus reached out and brushed the hair away from my face. I jerked backwards, although not quite quickly enough.

Shooting Derek a quick glance, I snapped at the Fae. "Watch it, Seelie shithead."

He smiled, baring his teeth. It wasn't entirely pleasant and I could barely suppress a shudder. "Oh, I think your little friend has got more than enough to worry about right now without listening in on our little chat." His smile grew wider. "I could take care of him for you, you know. It wouldn't be hard. I could make him forget he ever knew you with a quick breath. Or perhaps punish him to make him understand the error of his ways? Give him a donkey's head to befuddle medical science?"

"Plagiarising Shakespeare now, are you?"

Solus snorted. "More like he plagiarised us. Midsummer night's dream – what a ridiculous notion. Although," he took a step towards me, "you do realise that it's almost the midwinter solstice? Strange things happen up at Clava Cairns on that particular day. But you probably know all about that having visited there already."

I scowled. "Following me? I'd have thought you'd have better things to do."

"Oh, I'm highly entertained just by being in your vicinity." He looked me up and down assessingly. "I think what I'll do is give you a nickname all of my own. That way I can be sure I won't be accused of *plagiarising* anybody else. How does 'Mule' sound?"

I glared at him and tried to sidestep around. He moved with me and I clenched my fists, trying to keep my temper in check.

"No," he continued musingly, "you might be as stubborn as a mule but I don't think being compared to a packhorse quite works. Perhaps I should keep it simple and go with 'Fire'?"

My head snapped up at that one but fortunately Solus didn't seem to notice and carried on. "But, no, that might prove difficult around the police. If people randomly call out 'Fire' when you're around, they may just get out their guns and shoot you and then where would I be?"

"The police in Scotland don't carry guns you feckless Fae. And my name is Mack."

"You must miss having people around who call you that," he stated smoothly. "Why don't I make you feel a bit better about that?"

Before I could stop him, Solus encircled my waist with his arm. I yanked away from him but his grip was tight – it didn't really matter anyway because almost as soon as he had hold of me, the air started to shimmer. It took a second or two for it to sink in and then I really started to struggle in alarm.

"Solus, what the fuck are you doing?" I spat.

But I knew. The fucking idiot had decided to transport me somewhere using that handy Fae tactic of nipping in and out of dimensional existence. God only knew where he'd decided to go, pulling me along for the unhappy ride. Wherever it was I was pretty sure it wouldn't be anywhere that I'd want to go. My whole stomach exploded in flame in a way that I'd not felt in months, not since Iabartu, and this time I let the sensation flood my body. Because I was furious. How dare he do this?

The ripples in the air turned purple and then silver. I blinked several times to try to maintain my vision but it was to no avail, everything remained blurry. Nausea rose in my stomach, combating the rising fire of ire. All of a sudden I realised that Solus' arm was no longer round my waist and I was falling forward onto a polished wooden floor, retching. My head was spinning and I felt incredibly ill. I choked and spat, trying to regain a sense of self.

After a few moments, once my poor stomach had finally settled, I looked up to see a pair of shiny stylish wingtips in front of me. My gaze travelled upwards. Well tailored black trousers, snugly fitted at the groin, an unbuttoned white shirt, with a trail of black hair peeping out leading upwards to a well sculpted chest and a rather bemused set of golden green eyes flashing a hint of surprised satisfaction down at me.

Oh fuck.

"Well I knew we'd meet again, kitten, I just didn't expect you to suddenly materialise and hock up the contents of your stomach onto my floor."

I scrambled to my feet as fast I could and backed away until I felt a solid wall and couldn't go any further, my heart thudding loudly in my ears. I looked around, panicked, desperately searching for a way out and realised that I was in a huge bedroom. Corrigan's bedroom. Oh God. Not only that, but my humanity wasn't being masked by any scented lotion this time. All Corrigan had to do was to take one small sniff and my secret would be out. The Cornish pack – my surrogate family - had never been in more danger. If I ever saw Solus again, I'd rip his throat out.

The Lord Alpha stared at me. "You look frightened. That's not the Mackenzie I remember. So why don't you tell me just how you got here and why you're so afraid."

He took a step forward and I threw up my arms in warning. "Don't come any closer! I…" Shit, I what? "I, er, might have been exposed to something when I was transported here. And, in fact, where is here?"

Please don't say Scotland, I inwardly prayed. If this was London then I would still have time to get out of Inverness and away from him. Assuming Solus ever decided to transport me back that was.

"You're in the bastion of the Brethren." He licked his lips, slowly. I swallowed. "I don't think anyone has ever managed to invade our fort before without setting off a very elaborate alarm system. So you're going to tell me how and why you're here."

My mouth was suddenly dry. Out of nowhere came a whining siren then the sound of banging. "Finally," Corrigan murmured softly, his gaze intent on me. "Well, little cat?"

I pulled my posture up straight and tried to stop cowering. "I'm not a cat, my Lord, I'm a hamster." At least that was what the smell of Julia's lotion had suggested when I'd had to slather it over myself to keep him from discovering that I wasn't actually a were-anything back when he'd come with the rest of the stupid brethren to investigate John's death in Cornwall.

"Of course, you are." His eyes gleamed with flecks of dancing gold.

"And, as to your question, I don't know how I got here. One minute I was walking down the street, minding my own business and the next thing I know I'm throwing up on your lovely floor. I apologise. I will leave and get out of your way." I looked pointedly at his half bare chest. "You're clearly in the middle of something."

He snapped forward in a blur of movement and gripped both my arms, leaning in close. "You're not going anywhere, Mackenzie."

Shit, shit, shit. He must be able to smell me now. I sent up a silent prayer to anyone who might be listening to keep the Cornish pack safe. The panic inside me melded with the heat of my bloodfire and I exploded into a twist to wrench away from him. What I hadn't counted on was just how strong Corrigan actually was as I barely managed to budge myself by more than a couple of inches. Without thinking, I started squirming and clawing, trying whatever I could to pull myself away from him. I punched into air and missed connecting with his body, lashed out with my feet trying to kick him, but he just shifted his weight against me until I was completely pinned against the wall.

He smelled clean with just a hint of spicy aftershave. I waited for the inevitable realisation to hit him that my own scent was all wrong. Maybe I could get away before I had to answer any questions about it. And then I'd go and hide in a cave for the rest of my pitiful existence. Isn't that what dragons did anyway? The silver needles were in holding my hair together at the back; if I could just reach out and grab one of them…I strained and just came up against the steel of his muscles. His face swam forward and he looked me directly in the eyes, then he started to lean in forward until our noses were almost touching. My heart was banging painfully against my ribcage and the fire inside me changed somehow. It was transforming from an angry, scared, attack mode heat to something altogether more consuming, more passionate, more…

A door to my right swung open and a voice suddenly filled the room. "My Lord Alpha! There's an intruder somewhere in the building, we need to –"

Corrigan turned and snarled at the voice, the owner of which immediately backed away with abject groveling apologies. I rolled my eyes. Not much had changed in the Brethren then.

The interruption had at least allowed me to regain some of my ragged emotions. He'd obviously not noticed that I smelled like a human yet. I had no idea why not but I had to keep my fingers crossed that it stayed that way. Maybe he had a cold. I cleared my throat. "My Lord Alpha, I believe I mentioned earlier that I may have been exposed to some kind of, um, disease, on my way here. I suggest you back away as it could very well be lethal."

Corrigan stilled for a moment, his grip on my wrists tightening until I winced in pain. "What kind of disease?"

He'd fallen for that? Clearly the Lord Alpha wasn't as intelligent as I'd once thought. I widened my eyes to convey the horror even more dramatically. "A terrible, terrible one. It makes all your hair and teeth fall out and your skin turn green. Then it starts to attack your nervous system making you throw up violently." I gestured to the remains of my earlier lunch now deposited in a sticky mess on his polished floor. "As you see. So you should stay away from me. I'm sure it's incredibly contagious."

He appeared to relax infinitesimally and growled at me. "I'll take my chances." He slid his hands from my wrists up to my arms and gripped painfully. "Now tell me where you've been, why you ran away and how you got here. In that order."

"I'm a rogue, my *Lord*," I spat. "I don't have to answer to you anymore."

"Funny," he said softly, "I don't think you ever answered to me, even when we first met." *Tell me now.*

He was using his Voice to command me. This was too easy. I looked into his emerald green eyes and stated firmly, "No."

I was pretty sure that once shifters went rogue, their alpha's Voice no longer worked on them so I could avoid having to pretend that I was compelled to answer. What it did mean as well was that Corrigan still thought I was shifter, lack of shifter scent or not. I'd worry about the why later, right now I was just relieved. For his part, however, he wasn't as impressed at my bravura as I was, and he pulled his right hand away from my arm and slammed it around my throat, choking the breath out of me.

"Mackenzie, you need to start talking before I rip it out of you."

My bloodfire flickered back into action at the violence. I sent a quick thank you to whoever was looking down on me for that small mercy. Corrigan had moved enough that I could get some purchase with my legs so I pulled my knee up as hard as I could and shoved with every ounce of strength I had into his groin. He immediately let his grip loosen from around my neck and gasped in pain. I managed to move away from him and the wall, and into the centre of the room.

Corrigan rotated round and glared at me furiously. He was obviously still in pain but trying not to show it.

"Who's the big bad Lord Alpha now?" I taunted softly.

He snarled at me in return, sparks flying from his eyes. A sharp knock came at the closed door and a muffled voice called through. "My Lord Alpha? Is everything okay?"

I blinked. Oh fuck that was –

"It's fine, Tom. Go away." Corrigan's voice was hoarse but he was obviously not going to be crippled for life. Shame. He watched me, raising his eyebrows. "Do you remember your little wolf boyfriend, kitten? It must be difficult for someone of your proclivity to keep track of everyone you sleep with. Would it hurt you to know that he barely remembers you? He won't even mention your name and when I ask him – or his fiancée – they both just clam up. You clearly have an interesting effect on those around you."

So Betsy and Tom were engaged? That was good news; in fact, I almost betrayed myself by smiling at the information that Corrigan had probably hoped would hurt my feelings. I wondered as well whether the geas was still in place and that was why they both clammed up when he interrogated them about me. Interesting...

I lifted up a shoulder and attempted to remain nonchalant. "Pass on my sincerest congratulations to them both. And now, my Lord, I must take my leave." I glanced over at the windows, which were draped in some kind of opulent golden brocade curtain. "Which floor are we on?"

"It's the penthouse." He smiled lazily at me. "Fifteenth floor."

Aah.

"I don't suppose you're well equipped for fire regulations and have a proper outdoor fire escape, do you."

His smile grew broader. "Unfortunately not."

He started to walk towards me. Fuck it. I didn't think I could pull the old knee defense trick again and he was just too strong for me to fight, even with all my blood blazing. What now?

"Well, I hate to break up this little party but it's time that we were going." Solus appeared in a wink of purple shimmer from seemingly nowhere at my left and grabbed my arm.

"You prick," I yelled, without thinking. "What did you do? Get me out of here!"

"With pleasure, my lady."

And, with that, the air started to blur again and I could feel my stomach yet again churning. I only barely had the chance to see confusion and bewilderment cross Corrigan's face – an emotion I imagined he didn't feel all that often – and then hear his snarled, "Mackenzie!" before Solus and I were slamming back onto to a cold, grey and wet Inverness pavement.

"That WAS fun!" Solus said with a grin, just as I turned around and punched him in the mouth.

CHAPTER EIGHT

Solus' hand immediately went up to his mouth where my fist had connected and he rubbed it with a look of hurt on his face. I felt a momentary gleam of satisfaction that I'd finally managed to strike the stupid Fae.

"I don't see why you're so worked up," he complained.

"Worked up?" I spat. "Do you have any idea what you just did? How many people you just put in danger because of some moronic stunt you pulled just to show off? You're lucky your head is still on, Solus."

His eyes took on an innocent sheen. "Me? All I wanted was to give you a little demonstration of what could happen if you continued to hide the truth from me. Besides, you weren't in any danger and neither was anyone else."

"You fuckwit! He thinks I'm a shifter! If Corrigan puts his brain into gear and thinks, for even a moment, he'll work out that I'm not. Humans aren't allowed to know that shifters even exist. I lived with them for years – what do you think he'll do to those people who hid me for that length of time? The Lord Alpha of all the freaking shifters on the British Isles is not exactly the soft cuddly forgiving type."

"Jeez, you're a bit stressed out, aren't you? First of all," he ticked off his fingers, "you're not human. Second of all, it seemed like you were both having quite a good time. And thirdly, did he smell you? Did he notice that you're not a shifter?" Solus glared at me demandingly. "Well?"

"No," I sputtered, "but that's probably just because he was too surprised to notice at the time. He'll be sniffing around right now and then -"

"Seriously? You don't give Lord Corrigan much respect for his abilities, do you? Whereas mine, naturally, are considerable. If the Pack Lord was going to realise that you weren't a shifter, don't you think he's smart enough to have scented it on you straight away? Or do you really think he's that dumb and vapid not to even inhale?"

I stared at him. Actually, no I didn't think Corrigan was that stupid, falling for tall tales about diseases aside. I was still baffled as to how he'd not spotted immediately what I was – or, at least, what I wasn't, anyway. I'd gotten away with it once, after Iabartu had been killed and Julia's potion had probably mostly rubbed off, but the reek of her corpse and her minion's had covered mine.

Solus continued. "While I have no idea how you managed to hide your non-shifter stink from him and the rest of the Brethren before, it was patently obvious that you had. I've been paying at least a little bit of attention." He folded his arms and looked smug. "I covered your scent up, Rambo. It is a simple thing. The Lord Alpha would not have been able to note that anything was different about you from the last time you were together."

The wave of relief that flooded over me was almost overwhelming. "My name is Mackenzie."

He shrugged. "Whatever. Anyway, Rambo doesn't suit you either. Not unless you fancy stripping to the waist and sticking a bandanna round your head, that is?"

He leered at me suggestively. Lunging forward, I aimed for his solar plexus but this time he managed to dodge me easily. Fucking Fae and their stupid magic.

"Tsk, tsk," he said, shaking his head. "You don't have much control over your powers, do you?"

"I don't have any powers, you freak."

"Other than being able to break out of an impenetrable faerie ring, of course."

I jabbed his chest with my index finger. "Stay the fuck away from me, Solus."

Turning around, I stalked off in the direction of home. Then I realised that my home security was hardly tight and that Solus might decide he wasn't finished playing yet. I spun round and passed him again, heading back towards Clava Books instead.

He called out after me. "Next time, I might not be so nice. I might not bother hiding your smell. You might want to keep me happy."

His voice trailed off behind me. I resisted the urge to look back and kept on walking. At least Derek seemed to have crawled back into whatever hole he'd come out of, I thought darkly. I had a lot of pent up fury that I needed to expel somewhere and it was probably a damn sight safer for him if he was out of the way.

I must have marched in double time back to the bookshop because I seemed to arrive there before I knew it. I flung open the door, ignoring the furious jangling of the bell, and slammed it shut behind me. Leaning against the doorframe I took a moment to calm myself down, pulling in deep measured breaths. After a moment or two, Mrs Alcoon appeared from the back office. She took one alarmed look at my face and then gently took me by the arm and led me into the kitchen where she inevitably flicked on the kettle.

"Goodness, what on earth has happened, Mackenzie?"

"I…," I looked at her calm reassuring face and dissembled quickly. I felt the urge to tell her the truth, and certainly trusted her enough by now to know that my secrets would be safe. I just couldn't trust all the other irritants in my life not to concoct nefarious schemes to squeeze the information out of her. I opted for a half-truth instead. "There's a guy. He used to hang out at the pub where I worked before here – he's the reason I had to leave. Well, the reason I was fired, actually. He came upon me in the street on the way home and…"

She patted my hand, softly. "Oh my dear. How terrible. Did he hurt you?"

"Um, not really, I managed to get away this time but I'm worried about what he might do if I see him again."

I hoped her strain of clairvoyance wouldn't detect the slight lie. I had, after all, been set upon by Derek in the street. But I'd sort of swapped my pronouns when I mentioned the guy who I was worried about seeing again. Derek I could take care of easily– Corrigan, or indeed Solus, I might have a bit more trouble with. She'd foreseen that Corrigan would never come to Inverness and that Solus meant me no harm. But that didn't mean that he wouldn't do harm 'accidentally' and that Corrigan wouldn't just send some shifter minions in his place. Besides, if her clairvoyant skills were that strong and reliable, she'd probably have been a fully fledged member of the Ministry of the Mages and I was almost completely sure that wasn't the case.

Still, concern was clearly written all over her face. While I'd managed to avoid setting off her soothsaying warning system, I felt a bit guilty about not telling her the whole truth, especially when she was so obviously anxious about my welfare.

"Oh my dear Mackenzie, that sounds just awful, just simply awful. I've not felt that anything bad like that will happen but then my feelings, as I call them, are hardly an exact science." Her face took on a pensive look. "I hope you won't think I'm intruding but I have a friend who might be able to help."

I doubted that very much, not unless they happened to be a ridiculously powerful denizen of the otherworld . Still I tried to look interested, just to play along and be polite.

Mrs Alcoon continued. "She's the one I was telling you about – the one who has been a bit sick. You collected the blisterwort

for her. She has some, um," she searched around for a word, "…
tricks, that you might be able to use in case you get in trouble
again. She's very trustworthy, I promise."

This would be a total waste of time. I dreaded to think what
these 'tricks' might be – a bit of Self-Defence 101 perhaps? The
old knee in the groin ploy had worked once with Corrigan but as
a serious long term defense tactic it was going to be completely
pointless.

"I…I'm not so sure that'll help much," I started to say, trying to
think of a way to let Mrs Alcoon down lightly. Her intentions
were well meant, after all.

"Please, Mackenzie, it will make me feel so much better. You
look so pale right now that I'll be worried every time you walk
out the door." She added a little quaver to her voice for a stronger
effect and widened her eyes at me in expressive hope.

I sighed. Manipulated by an old aged pensioner. "Okay, then. I
already know some self defence though so it might not do a huge
amount of good." Well, at least when I said I knew some self-
defence I could take down most otherworldly monsters if I
managed to focus my bloodfire and concentrate hard enough. It
was just unfortunate that Corrigan wasn't most otherworld
monsters and Solus was an uncontrollable Fae.

She beamed at me, full wattage. "This isn't just a bit of karate.
I'll ring her right this minute." With a light-footed flourish that
belied her years, she immediately walked out of the kitchen. I
could hear the sounds of her picking up the phone beside the
shop's till and the soft murmur of indistinct talk. I sat heavily
back in my chair and wiped a hand across my forehead. Oh, what
a tangled web we weave.

Moments later Mrs Alcoon wandered back into the kitchen
with an even larger smile on her face. "She's just on her way over.
She only lives round the corner so it won't take long."

"What's her name?"

"Maggie." Mrs Alcoon laughed. "Maggie May, actually."

"Like the song? Interesting."

"Oh, I think you'll find there are many interesting things about our Maggie." She pulled the other chair up and leaned towards me. "You will keep an open mind, about her, won't you Mackenzie? You've taken my funny little feelings in your stride so I hope you'll continue to be like that."

Hmm. Perhaps there was more that was interesting about Maggie May than just her name. "I can definitely promise you that I have no pre-conceived judgments to make. Though it would be good to know what sort of tricks I can expect."

"Oh, if I told you that then there wouldn't be any surprise now would there? At the very least you're looking a lot brighter and perkier than you were before. There's colour back in your cheeks."

Hopefully not from embarrassment at thinking how I'd have to pretend to take Maggie May's 'tricks' seriously.

A few moments of companionable silence later, the door jangled out the front and Mrs Alcoon leapt out of her chair. "She's here! Come out to the shop front with me, Mackenzie."

Reluctantly I followed her out. The woman who stood in front of the counter and whom I presumed was Maggie wasn't quite what I had been expecting. She was short, barely five foot tall, and incredibly round and rosy cheeked. Involuntarily I thought of a red apple before throwing the thought away as uncharitable. She hugged Mrs Alcoon warmly, thanking her for the 'wonderful herbal tea' and then cast a twinkly look at me, holding her arms out.

I stared back, nonplussed, wondering if she expected me to hug her too. Fortunately she just took hold of my hands and squeezed them tight.

"June tells me you've been having a few problems."

June? I was momentarily nonplussed before realising that she meant Mrs Alcoon.

"Err...yes, a few," I mumbled somewhat incoherently. Maggie, for her part, continued to hold my hands tight and look unsettlingly into my face.

"June, lock up the shop and turn the sign to closed."

Mrs Alcoon sounded a bit nervous. "But we might have customers, Maggie. I wouldn't want to turn anyone away."

"Pssshaw! They're not exactly queuing up are they? Besides, we won't want to be interrupted."

I was starting to warm to Maggie's no-nonsense attitude. Mrs Alcoon – June – walked over to the door and slotted the top and bottom deadbolts into place and flipped over the 'Open for business' sign. Maggie meanwhile continued to look at me disconcertingly. After a few moments she finally let go.

"Right," she stated briskly, suddenly all business-like. "There are a few things that I can show you that will help to solve any further…problems that you may have. June has told me that you don't scare easily and that you'll take my little tricks on board without questioning too much."

I stared at her, wondering what on earth Mrs Alcoon had gotten me into, before blinking in reluctant acquiescence.

"Excellent. You don't need any real power to perform these tricks; in fact most people have enough latent magic to manage quite easily."

Umm…magic? Not 'tricks'? I could feel coils of heat starting to swell in the pit of my stomach and I forced them down. Rationally, this might prove to be more useful than a few basic self-defense moves. And I had to admit that I was somewhat curious to see whether I could in fact perform any magic. The research I'd done on the Draco Wyr hadn't yielded any clues as to whether that was possible and I'd definitely been fascinated by what Alex had been capable of doing when I'd first met him down in Cornwall. As a 'human', I wasn't supposed to know anything about the existence of real magic or mages though, so I tried to keep a confused expression on my face. It wasn't too hard.

Maggie dug into the little brown leather handbag she was carrying by her side and pulled out a fine silver necklace. She placed the bag on the store counter and handed the necklace out to me. For a heartbeat I paused without taking it. Silver was poisonous to shifters and after half a lifetime living among them, sometimes old habits died hard. Then I shook it off and reached out and grasped it. The metal was cool to the touch and buzzed slightly. I realised that it wasn't actually silver at all, but instead some kind of odd alloy. Interesting. She'd clearly placed a sort of ward on the necklace so her little 'tricks' definitely did include some actual real magic.

"Place the necklace around your neck," Maggie instructed.

Again I hesitated. I hadn't been around the Otherworld for years to foolishly walk straight into some kind of mages' trap. John had often warned the pack about accepting gifts from strangers and letting "meddling mages" as he sometimes called them, gain any kind of foothold of control over us. There had been a tentative peace between the mages and the shifters for decades but that didn't mean that either side wasn't often keen to try for a little one-upmanship just to prove who was stronger.

Maggie smiled at me gently, eyes twinkling again. "It won't bite, Mackenzie. I promise it won't do anything that you don't want it to do."

I debated internally for another half second and then looped the necklace round my neck, bringing the clasp round to my front so I could do it up. I fumbled for a few moments and then managed to link it together. I looked back at Maggie and raised my eyebrows slightly. Mrs Alcoon was watching me like a hawk.

"Now, we need to key it to you so it recognizes your blood."

I felt a brief surge of heat when she mentioned blood. If she wanted me to spill some of mine to complete this ritual then she was going to be getting the little necklace right back because I'd already caused enough problems by dropping my fiery red cells all over Britain. Fortunately for both of us, however, she didn't mean blood literally.

"Hold the front of the necklace with your left hand and take hold of my right." I did as Maggie bade. "Now, repeat after me – aye lee ch boil eeth aitch."

I dutifully repeated her words, even getting the proper Scottish 'ch' sound fairly accurate.

She continued. "Reek ath boil eeth aitch."

Again I followed her sound by sound, wondering idly if a little man with a TV camera was going to suddenly pop up from behind a bookcase to tell me that I'd been fooled by some elaborate television stunt. However, my fears in that direction started to fade as the necklace started to heat up. I thought I was imagining it to begin with but soon it was becoming almost painful to keep hold of.

"Ach leith fack aitch," intoned Maggie.

"Ach leith fack…" I began. I didn't manage to finish, however, as there was a sudden crack and hiss. I yelled in pain as the heat of the silver suddenly ratcheted up and dropped the necklace from my hand; it bounced painfully against my neck, searing the skin there. Instinctively, I raised my fingers to my mouth to suck away the burning pain when all of a sudden I saw little green flames sparking from my fingertips. I gazed at them, stunned, then wiggled my fingers to see what would happen. The flames wiggled along, shimmering in a cooking with gas haze. I jerked my whole right hand in a sharp snapping motion to see if I could get rid of the flames and was horrified to see a sudden jet of green flame arc out, hit a pile of books that was haphazardly placed on the counter top awaiting their chance to be inventoried, and completely incinerate them. My mouth dropped open and I stared at the smoking pile. A sweet acrid smell of burnt paper filled the store.

"Uh, Maggie, I don't want to be put behind bars for accidentally combusting someone who tries to cop a feel." I had enough trouble controlling my actions when I was angry as it was. I didn't need the power of actual fire to tempt me.

I turned back to look at her. The small woman's face was pure white and she stared at me in horror. Her hands were up in some kind of 'ward off all evil' position. "What the hell are you?" she hissed through gritted teeth.

CHAPTER NINE

I STARED AT MAGGIE IN CONFUSION AND WITH MORE THAN A LITTLE trepidation. "Umm…what do you mean? Was that not supposed to happen?"

She backed away from me as if I was carrying some terribly contagious disease, the twinkle in her eye now all but completely absent.

"Maggie?" Now I was afraid. Fuck it, this must be some kind of Draco Wyr spin off. The only thing I could do would be to plead abject ignorance. "What is it? What went wrong?" I tried to look baffled and scared. It wasn't hard.

"You're shooting green fire from your hands and you're asking me what's wrong? You are not human."

Mrs Alcoon interrupted. "Maggie, are you sure? I mean I've not sensed anything at all about Mackenzie other than that there are some men looking for her."

"Oh for goodness sake, June!" Maggie snapped. "You're hardly clairvoyant of the year."

Mrs Alcoon looked hurt at that, something which good old Maggie May clearly realised as soon as the words were out of her mouth because she immediately apologised. "I'm sorry, that was mean. But your Mackenzie is not normal. And I want to know exactly what she is."

Join the queue, darling, I thought tiredly. "Maggie, I'm sorry. I don't know what I've done. All I did was follow your instructions."

"Instructions which should lead to little more than a harmless repellent spell, not endow the recipient with full-blown attack capabilities." She continued to glare at me as though I might start shooting flames and incinerate her at any moment.

"Well, here, then." I started to take off the necklace, wincing at the residue heat, but her eyes widened even further and she looked alarmed.

"Don't you dare take that off, young lady! Who knows what might happen as a result."

Young lady now, was it? I tried not to bridle although I could hardly call it an endearment when Maggie looked as if she might try to claw my eyes out. "Like what? Are you saying I have to keep this on forever or I might suddenly spontaneously combust or something?" I was starting to get angry. I hadn't asked her to come over and start bespelling me; I hadn't asked her to give me the freaking necklace or to make me suddenly able to possibly control fire. Heat spiraled up through my aesophagus. Since when was I responsible for every fucking thing anyway? I bunched my fists and took a step forward without thinking. Maggie raised her arms once more in either some kind of defence or attack pattern – I couldn't tell which and I wasn't sure I cared - before Mrs Alcoon suddenly stepped in front of her, blocking my path and Maggie's intentions.

"There now," she said soothingly. "I'm sure this is just all some sort of misunderstanding. Are you sure that the necklace wasn't contaminated or something?"

I couldn't see Maggie any more but I could hear her spitting out a denial.

"Mackenzie," Mrs Alcoon began, reaching out to touch my arm. She didn't get the chance to finish what she was going to say, however, because she suddenly recoiled away from me as if she had been burned. Her eyes were as round and as big as golf balls. "You're a..." her voice trailed off and something flickered in her gaze. She turned back to Maggie. "You should leave."

Maggie's reply might have been muttered but I could still make it out. "I'm not leaving you here alone with that thing – whatever it might be."

"Oh, it's quite alright, she won't hurt me."

Mrs Alcoon sounded a lot more confident of that than I was. Her intervention had dampened the flames inside me somewhat, but I was still scared and angry, and the enormity of what was going on was starting to hit me. Flames inside me were one thing – at least those I could keep hidden, after a fashion anyway, but actual flames sprouting from my skin was something else entirely. Was it going to happen every time I moved my hands? And what had I been planning to do to Maggie anyway? Something was very wrong with me. No doubt this was all some kind of fucked up genetic thing and nothing to do with her spell in the first place. And yet for a flash I'd been prepared to, I didn't know what, but prepared to do something. I couldn't go anywhere without screwing everything up. My whole body sagged in defeat.

Mrs Alcoon moved to the side and relaxed her posture, putting on a smile for Maggie that even I could tell was forced. Maggie, meanwhile, stared at me with a hard expression in her eyes. I suddenly understood where the expression 'eyeballing' someone had come from. I swallowed nervously and cleared my throat.

"No, I'll go. Being here was a mistake. This spell was a mistake. All of this," I gestured hopelessly around the air, "was a mistake."

"You're not going anywhere, Mackenzie Smith," Mrs Alcoon stated, pointing me towards the little kitchen. I noted that she was being careful not to touch me again. "There are no mistakes that have been made. We just need to talk, that's all."

"I will not..." Maggie started to bluster before she was interrupted.

"You will."

The little round woman harrumphed loudly and glared at me, then stomped over to pick up her handbag. "If you do anything, and I mean anything, to harm June I will come over here and kill you myself."

"I won't hurt her," I said, hoping it was the truth.

"Maggie, I already said...," Mrs Alcoon started.

"Fine! I'm going!"

She gave me one last hard stare and then turned, undid the locks, and left through the front door. The bell jangled loudly as she slammed it shut behind her, making me cringe. For a moment, a heavy silence hung in the air, overshadowing the entire atmosphere. Then Mrs Alcoon took a deep breath and spoke.

"You have dragon blood."

I stared at her, mute, then looked down at my hands. Thankfully they were now green flame free.

"Maggie's right," Mrs Alcoon continued, "I don't have brilliant clairvoyant powers. I don't have any brilliant powers other than perhaps those of disorganisation. That's why I haven't sensed what you are until now, I suppose. The necklace's spell must have magnified what you already naturally project."

I continued to stare at her, my tongue cleaved to the roof of my mouth.

"I caught a glimpse of the future. There were a group of robed figures and they were talking about how you were a wyrm. You were with them." At my alarmed look, she quickly continued, "You were with them, not being held by them. They seemed to, I don't know, respect you, I think."

I must have still looked worried because Mrs Alcoon continued in a reassuring tone. "You have nothing to fear from me, Mackenzie, I am not strong enough to be part of the Ministry so there's no higher power that I am beholden to tell." I started at her mention of the Mages. She nodded at me. "Yes, I know what they are. They're not interested in me, although I have no doubt they'll be interested in you. These people you lived with before - the ones you learned about the Fae from – were they dragons too?"

I shook my head and found my voice. If I was really going to trust her, then I'd have to tell her the whole truth this time. "Um, no. No, they weren't. And I don't think I'm really a dragon. I'm a Draco Wyr. Well, only an eighth of me is Draco Wyr, the rest, I guess, is bog standard human."

"Mm. I don't know what a Draco Wyr actually is, dear. Something powerful though, that's for sure."

I went back to staring at her.

She smiled. "Go and put the kettle on, why don't you? I just need to check something in the office – I'll follow you in a moment or two."

When I didn't move, she raised her eyebrows and said gently, "It's alright, Mack. Everything will be fine."

That was the first time she'd ever called me Mack. Without saying anything else, I took myself off to the kitchen and sat heavily down on the chair. I lifted my hands up to eye level and scrutinized them but I couldn't see anything different about them. No weird green fire. Gingerly, I touched the necklace with my fingertips. That was cool to the touch again also.

"What the fuck is going on?" I asked myself softly.

Concentrating a bit harder, I focused on my fingers and this time willed the fire to re-appear, just to see if I could. After a second, my hands ignited. I waved them around in front of me. Un-fucking-believable. I tried to will the fire to disappear and then, bit by bit, it did. The flames just winked out across my fingers, one after the other. I stretched out my index finger and screwed up my eyes and stared at it, trying to gain a little more control. It was a bit harder but after a few moments my one finger alone caught alight. I touched other hand with the flame and felt nothing, no burn, then tried touching the wooden table. It immediately left a dark scorch mark. Hastily, and guiltily, I covered it up with a coaster, then reverted my attention to my finger.

I moved my finger down through the air and the flame followed. Then I smiled to myself and sketched out Mack in cursive script, just as I'd done years ago with sparklers on Guy Fawkes' Night. I grinned. I stared at my finger again and tried to make the flame bigger. I'd only been intending to try for a couple of inches of fire, instead of my current centimetre. The result, however, became a green inferno that enveloped half my arm. The fabric of my black top burned completely away within an instant as I shrieked and shook my arm in a sudden frenzy, attempting first to shake away the flames, then to stamp them out with my other hand. When neither of those techniques worked, I pivoted on my heel and shoved my whole arm into the small aluminium sink, awkwardly twisting on the tap. For a heart-stopping moment I thought that water wasn't going to have any effect, then the flames hissed and were extinguished. A plume of smoke was rising up from the very pores of my skin.

I glanced at the door, expecting Mrs Alcoon to come in at any moment to see what the noise had all been about and to realise that, although I might not be hurting her directly, I was burning down her kitchen. The door remained shut, however, so I opened up the small grimy window to let in some air, and flicked on the kettle. Experimenting further in such a small space probably wasn't a good idea.

By the time the kettle boiled, I was getting impatient. There was still no sign of Mrs Alcoon. I was starting to wonder if she'd gotten cold feet and had simply disappeared, hoping I'd just leave. She'd been so calm fifteen minutes before. After a few further moments of indecision, I poured a cup of her herbal tea and straightened my shoulders. I'd take it in to her and see where the land lay. If she was nervous about my presence, then I would make things easier on everyone and just leave. But then she'd just been reassuring me so why wouldn't she have thrown me out before when Maggie was still here?

I picked up the chipped china mug filled with the noxious brew and exited the little kitchen. She wasn't in the shop front and her office door was closed so I went straight up to it, balancing the tea in one hand, and knocked gently. When there wasn't any answer I knocked again, but harder. Still, there was no answer. I steeled myself and twisted the doorknob, then pushed the door open with my free hand.

"Errr....Mrs Alcoon? Is everything alright?"

She didn't answer. I peered round the door and saw her figure in the office chair, feeling enveloped by a surge of relief that she'd not left. And then, suddenly, I became aware of a faint yet lingering acrid smell that hung in the air. What was that? It could be some more of the strange herbal tea that she'd been drinking earlier but there was something else about it that didn't seem entirely natural. I peered more closely at the figure of the old woman. She wasn't moving, in fact she didn't even seem to be breathing, although she maintained a healthy glow about her cheeks. My stance changed and my muscles tightened. What was she doing? Was this some kind of trance? Perhaps she was contacting the Fae – or something even worse - to tell them what I was. I imagined a telepathic conversation in which the old woman gleefully proclaimed that she'd found a living breathing Draco Wyr with magical green fire properties whose blood could be drained straight away because they were sitting in her kitchen drinking numbing herbal tea. I tried to shake away the residual paranoia.

Stepping forward, I gingerly stuck out my hand to prod her motionless body but, as soon as I drew close, the air cracked and snapped and an electric shock ran from the tip of my outstretched index finger right the way to my toes, pulling me off my feet and slamming me back against the door, closing it against my back. The corner of my spine caught the doorknob and I yelled out in pain at the jarring streak of agony that ran down my back. I curled my fingernails into the palms of my hands and gritted my teeth, pulling myself upright and keeping my gaze steadily on Mrs Alcoon in case she moved. She didn't.

My foot crunched against something lying on the floor so I scuffed it gently with my toe and risked a quick glance down. It was a small metal spherical object. I bent down to pick it up and realised that it was iron. Well, that ruled out any Fae then. I looked back at Mrs Alcoon.

"What have you been doing?" I asked her quietly.

She didn't answer, just stared fixedly at a point above my shoulder, unblinking. I followed her line of sight, turning around to see what was there. Behind me was the plain, unadorned office wall. When she went into this trance state she must have been looking at something though. Or, judging by the height of her gaze, at someone. But who? The owner of the little sphere? I held up the piece of iron and stared at it, hard. I'd not seen anything like this before but then I didn't know much about magical objects, if that's what this was. Suddenly, a flicker of black flashed across its dull surface and it started to grow cold, very cold. The tips of my fingers felt as if they were burning and I tried to keep hold of it but the pain became too much and I dropped it. Before it hit the floor, however, it vanished. Just winked right out of existence as if it had never been there in the first place. Rubbing my fingers against each other to rid myself of the numbing pain I stared at the spot where it had disappeared. Well fuckity fuck fuck.

I might have been acting paranoid and jumpy recently with the drunk on the bus but I was pretty damn sure that now I wasn't imagining things. Something magic was going on inside the little office of Clava Books and it wasn't magic of the fuzzy David Blaine kind. Neither was it the weak kind of clairvoyant magic that Mrs Alcoon – and Maggie on her behalf – had professed to having. I backed out of the little room, taking care to avoid touching the door with my still smarting back this time. I turned the doorknob and made sure it was firmly closed. Little flickers of flame shot up through my insides. There wasn't any immediate danger – the shop was empty, I was sure of that – but this whole situation reeked of wrongness. I didn't know if the old lady had tried casting some spell and something had gone awry but I couldn't just leave her in this situation.

I picked up the bunch of shop keys that was lying underneath the till and re-locked the glass fronted door. Not that I expected any last minute customers but it was better to be safe than sorry. And if Maggie decided to return and thought that it had been me who'd put Mrs Alcoon into this state – well, it was probably better to avoid that situation if possible. I sat down on the floor cross-legged, facing the closed office door. Rubbing the spot on my back where the doorknob had attacked me, I settled in to wait.

* * *

FOUR AND A HALF HOURS LATER, nothing had changed. The door remained shut and the shop remained silent. It was just a whole lot darker outside, that was all. This was a long time for anyone to remain in meditative stasis. Risking a quick glance, I stood up and opened the door just a crack to peer inside. Mrs Alcoon hadn't moved. I cursed. She might have brought this entirely on herself by dabbling in things she should have left well alone but that didn't mean she might not be in any danger. One or two of the pack members back in Cornwall had used meditation from time to time to calm themselves after a fight with some big bad otherworld nasties – and I'd never known any of them to spend more than an hour in an unchanging state. I'd never tried it myself – I'd always figured meditation for new age mumbo-jumbo, even if it did induce some kind of magical sensations – but even I knew that too long in a deep trance was not good for anyone. I sighed heavily and looked over at the phone that hung on the wall behind the till. This was such a bad idea but I couldn't just leave her permanently stuck in whatever state she'd gotten herself into to.

Dragging my feet, I stumbled over to the phone and picked up. The dial tone hummed loudly and I stared down at it for a further second before making up my mind. Then I jabbed the number I'd memorised months before on the keypad, knowing that I was probably going to regret this.

The phone rang several times. I started counting: six, seven, eight...if it reached ten, I'd hang up. The number was probably out of use by now. It would be a sign that I should work out a way to deal with this on my own. Nine, ten. Okay, then. My thumb moved to the disconnect button when suddenly a voice filled the line.

"G'day."

For a moment I couldn't speak. The pressure of the silence hung heavily for a heartbeat and I could hear his voice suspiciously saying, "Hello?"

Then I replied. "Hi, Alex. It's, um, good to hear your voice." And it was, it really was.

"Don't tell me that's...Mack Attack? Sheeeeit! Dude! How are you? Where have you BEEN? Oh my God, do you have any idea how crazy the pack have been trying to find you? I've had Lord Dark and Scary himself turning up at my door and demanding to know where you were. He wanted me to scry for you but the Ministry refused - you should have seen the look on his face. I swear there was a vein on his head that almost popped out and then, well, never mind. Why didn't you call me? Why did you leave Cornwall? I thought you wanted to stay there forever. Shit, Mack."

I swallowed. That was a lot to take in at one time. "Alex, I'll explain everything later but right now I need your help."

"Dude, whatever you need. WhatEVER." He paused. "Hold on, you don't need me to fight, do you?"

I laughed shakily. "No, I wouldn't make you do that. I just need a bit of...advice, that's all."

"Mack Attack, advice I can do. You should come to London, tell Lord Shifty the truth and then everything'll work itself out. The human thing isn't an issue anymore because you're not freaking human! In fact - "

I interrupted him. "It's not about that, Alex, it's something else." Before he could continue to regale me with grandiose plans for how I could risk the lives of the entire Cornish pack by exposing myself, I quickly filled him in with the details of Mrs Alcoon – how she had initially seemed slightly clairvoyant and the nameless suspicions I'd had about her that had since been confirmed, up till I found her in her weird semi-permanent stasis. I even included that she knew what I really was, although I left out the part about my newly discovered fire power. It didn't seem entirely relevant and I wasn't too sure that I wanted anyone else to know what I was suddenly now capable of just yet.

Alex was quiet for a few moments. When he finally spoke, his voice was solemn. "Describe the object to me again."

"It was small, about two inches long and shape of a sphere. And made out of iron so it couldn't have had anything to do with anyone from Faery. And I held it for a good few moments before it started to chill and freeze and then…"

"Mackenzie, you need to get out of there."

I was momentarily befuddled. "Uh, what?"

"Get out. Now. Lock the door behind you and leave. And don't go back."

"I'm not leaving. She helped me out when no-one else would. So she's meddled in a bit of bad magic and then messed up. That doesn't mean that I shouldn't try and get her out of it." I paused. "Is this because she knows what I am now? That I'm…not human? Is she contacting someone like Iabartu?"

"No."

"So what the fuck is it, Alex? Tell me! I just need to know what to do. Alex, you know what this is, don't you?"

This had to be connected in some way to the fact that she'd discovered my true nature, despite what Alex said to the contrary. Either her knowing what I was had put her in danger or she'd put herself in danger by trying to tell someone else.

"She didn't do it to herself, Mack, that would be impossible. Your Mrs Alcoon is in enforced inhibitory gnosis. You can't achieve that state on your own – someone has to put you in it. Someone from the Ministry has done this."

"The Ministry? You mean the mages? You mean, you?"

"No, not me. Well, yes me. My group, at least. That's what we do when there's report of trouble."

I had a terrible sinking feeling in the pit of my stomach. "Trouble?"

"When someone reports that there is some bad magic around, the Ministry steps in to put a stop to it. The object you've described is a moot – it nullifies any magic user in the vicinity who might be a threat until a representative can arrive and deal with it."

"I have a horrible feeling that dealing with it means acting first and asking questions later."

"That is often the case, yes. Mack Attack, if whoever arrives to sort out your little old lady shows up and finds you there, you'll be taken into custody. They'll try to find out who you are. Which will take them all of two minutes given how hard the Lord Alpha has been trying to find you. If this happened hours ago then even with you in the wilds of Scotland, they'll be there soon. Leave."

"But she's not a threat, Alex. She's barely got any power."

"She worked out what you are, didn't she?"

"Only because..." my voice trailed off as the dawning realisation hit me.

Maggie. Maggie had called in the threat. And it wasn't Mrs Alcoon who was being targeted, it was me. It should be me in that strange trance-like state, not her. Yet again I'd fucked up and yet again I was dragging others down with me.

"They'll hurt her." It was a statement this time, not a question.

"Mack, they'll just do what needs to be done. You have to

realise how dangerous rogue mages can be. There's a reason the Ministry exists."

Out-fucking-standing. First I was labeled a rogue shifter and now I was apparently being advertised as a rogue mage too. I wondered if Maggie fully realised just what she'd done. That stupid woman. My blood was already boiling when I heard the snap of the telephone's outer plastic casing cracking under the pressure of my grip. I took a deep breath. Time to stay calm, Mack, I told myself.

Alex must have sensed my seething emotions from across the line. "I'm sorry, Mack."

"Alex, I've come to you for help. To help her. There must be something."

"She's beyond help now, Mack. The only people who can remove the spell are from the Ministry's Council. You need to get out of there before they decide that you're mixed up in this somehow too."

But I was already mixed up in it. In fact, I was IT. I exploded at him, instead. "For fuck's sake, Alex! She's just a harmless old lady!"

"Who you yourself admitted to having serious suspicions about! There's no other way. You have to see how dangerous this is."

"She's not dangerous. And I like her." I was aware how stupid that sounded, and how true it was. I was going to have to do something.

Alex, for his part, was silent.

I took in a deep breath. "I have to go, Alex."

"Wait, Mack, you can't do anything stupid."

"I have no idea what you're talking about. I understand that my friend has been put into this trance by some fucking jumped up mage. Because she's dangerous. Except I know that she's no danger to anyone. And I also know that the Ministry is going to hurt her to find out just what kind of threat she actually is.

Which will also probably reveal at the same time what I am too. What stupid thing would I do?"

"You can't save her. You're strong, Mack Attack, and god alone knows what powers all that Draco Wyr blood has, but you can't fight the Ministry. It's too dangerous, and not just for you. And anyway, they'll focus on the threat of her, not some harmless employee she happened to have."

Except this harmless employee was the reason she was in this state in the first place. "I completely understand, Alex. " My voice was distant and I started to hung up.

"Mack!" His voice burst through the phone. It was too late though – I slammed it down on the counter and moved to Plan B.

CHAPTER TEN

As soon as I put the phone down, I took a deep shaky breath. Things were most definitely not hunky dory in the land of Mackenzie Smith. My mind raced, considering the options. There was absolutely no way I was going to leave Mrs Alcoon to be dealt with by the Ministry – and hurt, or worse, in the process. I briefly wondered if I could get a hold of Maggie and convince her to call off the dogs. After all, I could leave right now if I so chose. It was Mrs Alcoon – June, her friend – who was going to end up getting hurt. I quickly discarded that idea, however. Maggie must have known what implications calling the Ministry in the first place would have, which meant she felt that I posed a higher threat than the relative safety of her friend. Besides, I figured, with a quick glance down at my fingers, Maggie clearly had some power at her disposal that I would probably be wise to stay away from.

I had to get Mrs Alcoon somewhere safe, somewhere no mage hell bent on terrorising and torturing a harmless old lady could get to her. That meant that pretty much anywhere in the UK was out. From what I little I knew from my time with the Pack, the tentacles of the Ministry of Mages were far reaching. Let's face it,

I'd seen the evidence of their locator spells in action myself. They'd find her wherever I put her.

So I'd have to look further afield. Going abroad might be a possibility, but it was an international organisation. I doubted there were many places on Earth I could take a prone body to where they wouldn't be able to reach us. I didn't have to stay on this plane, however. I thought of the demesnes that I'd visited when I'd been tracking Iabartu. Somewhere like that would work perfectly. I just had to work out how to get there.

I scooted quickly round to take another peek at Mrs Alcoon. Unsurprisingly she hadn't moved so much as a muscle. Fuck it. I closed my eyes briefly, then spoke.

"Solus?"

The empty shop echoed silence back at me.

I tried again. "Solus? If you want to know what I really am and you're listening right now, then I'll tell you. Just do me one small favour first."

I knew it was madness getting a Fae to do me a favour. I'd end up owing him my first twelve children or something equally stupid. I couldn't see that I had any other choice though. I just had to hope that, wherever he was, he could hear me calling his name.

"Sol.."

The air crackled and he appeared in front of me. Disturbingly, he was wearing some kind of diaphanous white shirt and ridiculously tight leather trousers, although I still felt a wave of relief that he'd elected to appear in the first place. "Well, well, well. I didn't think that the big tough Mackenzie Smith would ever be calling little old me. Have you finally realised that you can't escape me and that it's better to just give in?" He grinned with the leer of a predator. "You could have chosen your moment better, I must admit. I was somewhat….tied up."

I didn't want to imagine what the truth behind that statement actually was. I could feel a hot white band of heat squeeze my heart, but did my best to ignore it and instead looked at him with a far steadier gaze than my inner churning emotions should have allowed. "You want to know what I am? "

Solus took a step towards me. "Oh, there are so many things that I want, my little prickly ginger one." He reached out and brushed a stray strand of hair away from my cheek. I had to fight not to flinch.

"Well, then," I said, all business-like, "I will tell you if you do me one favour."

The Fae threw back his head and laughed. "Favour? You don't demand favours from me. You're just a..."

He didn't finish his statement. I used the moment to take control of the situation and folded my arms. "Exactly. You don't know what I am. I could be a thousand times more powerful than you. I could use the strength I have to bend you to my will. Until you know what I am, you can't control me."

"You actually think that you could use your strength to make me do something?" The disbelief dripped from his voice.

"I broke your sister's cruinne, remember?" This time I was the one taking a step forward. "Who knows what I can do?" I hoped that my bravado was working. I was pretty sure that there was nothing I could do to control any Fae; even the weakest of their species could probably grind me to a dusty pulp if they so desired. I tried to remember that I had bested a demi-goddess, even though that had been with the help of Anton and Corrigan. Okay, Anton and Corrigan had bested a demi-goddess and I'd been the warm up crew.

Solus regarded me with a mixture of wariness and amusement, then airily flicked his hand through the air. "Fine. Tell me what you want and I'll consider it."

"No. Either you grant me this boon, or all deals are off. I don't have time for you to go away and consider anything."

"You demand a lot."

I stayed silent and just waited, trying not to let the desperation show on my face. It couldn't be long until the mages showed up.

He sighed expressively and ran a hand through his hair. "Okay. Tell me what you are."

"Do you really think I'm that stupid? First the favour, then I'll tell you."

"A Fae's word is his bond. You should not dare to question my integrity."

"Oh puhleeeze," I drawled sarcastically. "How many double-edged promises have your kind made? Eternal life but in a decaying body? Or how about granting perfect beauty and yet leaving no soul? Or aiding childless couples and then demanding the longed for baby as payment?"

Solus scowled. "You read too many fairy tales, shrew."

I ignored the unpleasant nickname. "The favour first, Solus."

"Fine. What is it?"

I gestured to the office door. "I need you to take her to your… wherever it is that you live, and keep her safe until I can work out how to sort all this out."

Solus stared at me silently for a moment and then stalked over to the office. He stepped inside and then almost immediately sprang back out. "The mages," he hissed.

I shrugged. "You promised. All I need you to do is keep her safe."

"Why would you do this for her? You barely know her. She has no power to speak of."

"She's in trouble because of me. This is my responsibility."

He glared at me. "I have no desire to get mixed up with the human wizards. They can be...tricky." He blinked slowly. I had no idea whether it was in exasperation or acquiescence and didn't realise that I was holding my breath to hear his answer until he spoke again. "But I did promise. I will take her to Tir-na-nog."

"And you won't harm a hair on her head."

"What do you take me for? You should learn some manners, shrew."

"Stop calling me that and take her now."

"I...," Solus began before looking up at the exit to the shop. "You're out of time, I think. The mages are here already."

Before he'd even finished speaking, the dark shape of three cars drew up outside. "Then go now, Solus."

"I cannot get my answer if you are taken by them."

"I can handle myself," I stated, more calmly than I felt. I gave the Fae a little shove. "I will keep my side of the bargain but you must get her to safety."

He gazed at me expressionlessly for a heartbeat and then walked over to Mrs Alcoon and scooped her up effortlessly into his arms. Her body sagged like a rag doll's. "I will find you and get my answer."

"I'd expect nothing less."

The doorknob of the glass entrance began to turn. Solus stared at me solemnly for a moment and then with a brief shimmer in the air suddenly both he and Mrs Alcoon were gone.

CHAPTER ELEVEN

I WASN'T QUITE SURE WHAT I'D BEEN EXPECTING. I THINK A PART OF me had had visions of a Gestapo style entrance, complete with clicking heels and straight armed salutes. There would be a commandant of some kind trailing behind the main group, black leather gloves tugging at a lit cigarette. My experiences with Alex , the 'surfer dude' magician, should probably have prepared me for the opposite.

The lead mage didn't look like a member of the Nazi secret police. He didn't even look like a mage. He was just impossibly young, with chubby cheeks and tousled hair. The waft of stale marijuana smoke clung to his clothes and assailed my nostrils, even from the other side of the room. Not far behind him, a girl tripped in wearing quite possibly the most bizarre costume I'd ever seen. It was in the shape of a saucy French maid's uniform, with a high puffed out skirt held in place by layers of frilly stiff petticoats, with colours that were, well, arresting. There was a neon green heart on the front, with further neon pink and yellow starburst shapes shooting out from behind it. Her hair was black, probably dyed, and hairsprayed into pigtails that jutted out at least half a foot from her head and of which Pippi Longstocking herself would have been proud. I wondered for a brief moment if I should be offended that the Ministry of Mages thought that sending a pair of circus clowns would do the trick, before reminding myself yet again that appearances were deceptive and that I should probably just be glad they hadn't sent more than two minions.

The pair of them were clearly in the middle of a pressing argument.

"No, no, no, no, no. Are you a mentalist, Martha? Are you mental? There is no way that Captain Kirk, Captain James Tiberius Kirk, would be beaten by anyone from the X-men. He might not have super powers, but he's clearly of superior intellect and with superior cunning and all round ability."

Seriously? Mage Trekkies? I half considered calling on Solus to tell him the deal was off. Martha, for her part, simply grunted, unimpressed at her partner's assertion. Perhaps she wasn't much of a Star Trek fan either.

He continued on. "I mean, sure Wolverine has mad skills but you have to take into account that James T. Kirk is quite simply..."

The Trekkie stopped dead in his tracks and stared at me. Mute Martha didn't quite notice me so quickly and slammed into his back. Swearing loudly, she lifted a hand to cuff him round the head, and then her eyes widened as she too saw me. Her arm dropped by her side and her mouth fell open.

Clearly this didn't happen to them very often. I pasted a wide bright smile. "Hi! Welcome to Clava Books. How may I help you?"

They both continued to stare at me. Wow. These two really did have to work on their reaction times. If I had been some big bad nasty (and maybe I actually was) then I could have probably pulverized these two into dust by now.

I tried again. "Is there any book in particular that you're looking for?"

Martha recovered first. She flicked her fingers and sent a flash of orange light hurtling towards me. I dodged out its way, skipping to the side behind a bookshelf and calling out, "Well, that wasn't very nice, was it?"

The beam of light smashed into the wall behind where I'd been standing and sizzled an old poster with curling yellow edges advertising the latest Gaelic 'blockbuster' on famous salmon spawning spots in the highlands.

Grunting again to her hash sodden partner, Martha said something. I could hear both of them moving, taking up different spots around the shop floor, trying to outflank me. I felt the heat inside me uncoil and smiled humourlessly at its return. For a moment, I gazed at my fingertips and watched them spark at the edges with flickers of green flame, before dismissing them by curling my fingers into my palms. Displaying my newly found witchy powers might not be a good idea if this went against me.

All of a sudden there was a rumble and a crash. One of them, I assumed the Trekkie, was over-turning the bookshelves. They were stacked pretty close to each other and towered high up to the ceiling. The effect created was something of a domino line, with each shelf crashing into the next one, taking away all of my cover and leaving me nowhere to hide. Well, if that was the way they wanted to play it then fine. I jumped out from behind the safety of the shelf just before it too went crashing against the hard wooden floor, and pulled out the silver needle from behind my head. My hair fell loose, swinging irritatingly against my face, but I ignored it and focused on the figure in front of me. The heat inside me directed my actions and, with one twist of my wrist, I sent the needle flashing towards it. I sprang back behind the sturdy counter that housed the till and ducked down, without waiting to see if I'd hit my mark, although the answering yelp of pain assured me that I had.

"We could just talk about this first, you know," I shouted out to the now dust-filled shop. "There's no need to be so hasty."

Silence answered me. Clearly they weren't in any mood to negotiate. I shrugged. I'd given them their chance and already made my point. It had been a while since I'd had a real fight. Punching a Fae and dealing with a drunk Derek had hardly allowed me to let loose much of my pent up energy. Neither had struggling against the steel hard grip of Corrigan for that matter. It was about time I had a little fun. The tension of the last hours swam through my veins in unrestrained heat, until prickles of fire hit my eyelids and took over. Without conscious thought, I leapt out from behind the counter and pulled up the heavy old-fashioned till, yanking it from its power socket and flinging it towards where I'd heard the needle induced shout of pain. It banged against the leg of the fallen male mage who went from clutching his cheek where the silver had pierced through to grabbing hold of his leg. Martha was standing in the opposite corner, next to the fallen stacks of shelves. Her body was tense and her fists were clenched, leaning every so slightly to the left. I jumped to my right and just managed to escape the shooting orange beam that she sent, then I ran at her headlong, barreling into her stomach and smacking her against the window.

The impact of her body against the hard glass sent me momentarily bouncing back, scuffing a fallen bookshelf with my heels. I heard sounds of Trekkie staggering slowly to his feet so I picked up one of the fallen books, flinging it hard in his direction. The buzz that registered through my hand before it left my fingers gave me the sudden grim satisfaction that it was the Fae book that had become my weapon. It must be my day to be making the Wee Ones work for me, I figured. Unfortunately, it didn't deter him too much and the air in the small shop started to hum with power. His eyes had turned glassy and he was chanting something under his breath. Blue light was starting to ripple around him, not unlike what Alex had conjured when he was using a tracing spell down in Cornwall. Before I could react further, I felt a clawing, suffocating band of pain round my throat, squeezing it tight. Panicking I gulped for air. Martha was back on her feet, also muttering something, also with blue light suffusing itself around her.

I sank to my knees, fingers scrabbling at my throat as I tried to suck in air desperately. Almost every vestige of conscious thought had fled from my mind – all I could think of was my closed airway and the screaming pain and pressure building in my lungs. I scrunched my eyes up tight and sucked up the last part of flame from inside my stomach and then, without thinking further, wrenched my hands away from my neck and flung them out in opposite directions each pointing towards a different mage. Imagining a flash of green fire behind my eyelids, I concentrated as hard as I was able, feeling the tingle of Maggie's unhappy gift shoot again from my fingertips. Air crackled around me. The chanting from both magicians abruptly stopped and the hum in the room blinked out like a light. I fell forward onto my hands and knees, choking, opening my eyes and becoming dimly aware of the green tinged glow coming from both sides of the shop. Forcing myself to move as quickly as I could, I pulled myself to my feet and flicked a glance in both directions. The green fire was completely consuming both mages, who were silently screaming from behind a wall of flame. It didn't seem to be burning them conventionally in the way that a normal fire would, although the shop and its contents around them were lighting up like dry kindling. Rather my attack seemed to be holding them in place, nullifying their own blue light and rooting them to the spot as the building around them burned.

The acrid smell of burning paper and wood had completely filled the area. Martha's eyes were wide and terror filled, while Trekkie's arms were flailing around uselessly. I paused for a heartbeat then sprang towards him, pulling his body away from the flame and yanking him towards the street. I placed my hand on the knob of the glass front door to turn it, but the metal seared into my skin, tearing off shreds of flesh as I snatched my hand back. Still holding onto Trekkie's arm with my other hand, I mustered up every atom of power I could and kicked out with my booted foot at the glass. Thankfully it shattered easily and I jumped out the jagged exit I'd created, dragging him after me. I thrust his body down onto the road, away from the kerb and the heat of the now explosively burning bookshop, then ducked my head down and went back inside.

Martha was in the spot where I'd last seen her, against the front window of the shop. The shelves that she'd so cleverly knocked down scant moments before were ablaze and fire was licking up the sides of the walls, eating up the curling faded wallpaper. The smoke was becoming thicker by the second. Pulling up my t-shirt to cover my nose and mouth I reached for her and tugged her arm sharply to get her away from whatever strange immobilising properties my shot of green light had created. She barely moved, however. Through the clouds of smoke I just made out her eyes staring down in panic at her foot. I glanced down. It was caught underneath the edge of one of the heavy wooden shelves. I could feel her pull at it to get out but it didn't seem to shift. The heat inside the shop was becoming almost completely unbearable. Martha stared at me with wide eyes. Flecks of orange light danced behind her pupils. Raising up a single index finger, I pointed at her as if I was holding an imaginary gun. Her muscles tensed and her eyes squeezed tight. I moved my finger down and then flicked it at the offending shelf. A flickering beam of green light shot its way towards the wood, which then, abruptly, exploded in cloud of splinters. Barely registering the shards of wood that had embedded themselves into my clothes and skin, I tugged at her body again. This time, her feet came free and we were moving towards the shattered door and out into the sweet clear night air of the street.

. . .

IN THE DISTANCE, the wail of sirens could faintly be heard. I turned and stared at Clava Books, sucking in the fresh air in loud gasps. The paint was peeling away from the old sign and flames and smoke were billowing out from the hole in the door. I felt a dull ache in my chest as Mrs Alcoon's pride and joy disappeared as I watched. Tears streamed from my eyes and I tried to blink them away. Feeling a yank from my hand, I turned to my left and realised I was still holding onto Martha. I let go and she backed away, tripping up over her feet and falling to the cobbled road below. Trekkie was now on the opposite side of the road, away from the searing heat emanating from the shop, looking from me to Martha to the inferno and back again. I opened my mouth to say something then thought better of it. The sirens were getting louder. I turned on my toes and just ran.

Internally, I knew the smart move was to get as far away from Inverness as possible. I was desperate to pick up my box, my laptop and my clothes from the bedsit, however. I'd had to cut and run and leave everything in Cornwall; I had no desire to do exactly the same thing again. I figured that the police and the fire brigade would have their hands full for at least the next hour putting out the blaze at Clava Books to worry about coming by to see where one of the bookshop's employees were. They'd probably try and track down Mrs Alcoon as the owner first and there was no way on earth that they'd find her any time soon. A Fae's word was their bond and, while I didn't believe I could completely trust Solus yet, I knew that as far as she was concerned he wouldn't let me down. The police would assume that she'd been killed in the fire, which would at least mean that, for the time being, they wouldn't be looking for a missing person. I stopped momentarily in my tracks. Fuck. That did mean that they might be looking for someone who might have committed arson and tried to kill her, though. The logical suspect would be me. I started running again, scenarios tripping through my mind. There was no-one who would vouch for my good character. The regulars back at Arnie's bar – and Arnie himself – would tell them that I had a nasty temper and was capable of violence. And as for Maggie, well, she'd been prepared to set the Ministry onto her best friend because of the threat she believed I posed, so clearly I couldn't expect any help from that direction. Alex had said on the phone that when Corrigan had asked the Ministry to set up a locator spell on me they'd refused. That was probably because they didn't wish to involve themselves in shifter politics. I was pretty sure they wouldn't be so reluctant now that I'd almost killed two of their members.

Outstanding. I'd gone from having to hide from the Pack, to now having the human side of the law and the magical side of enforcers on my heels. How I was going to get out of this, I had absolutely no idea. I supposed I could get Solus to help hide me with Mrs Alcoon in Tir-na-nog. But not only was there no guarantee that he'd do that – after all I'd already bargained away the only thing I had to offer – it was also only a temporary solution. I had to find some way to put things right as far as she was concerned. I owed her a lot and I wasn't about to let her languish in the land of the Fae for the rest of eternity because I'd fucked up.

I rounded the bend onto the main street. The sirens of the fire engines were now just a bare whisper on the wind. I could see the building of my bedsit up ahead and didn't think I'd ever been so glad to get back to it. I slowed to a fast walk so that I could double check that it was safe to get in, grab my stuff and skedaddle. I still had no idea where to go or what to do – my options were fairly limited, let's be fair – but if I was going to help Mrs Alcoon at all, I had to make sure that I didn't get caught by any of the various denizens of both the human and the otherworld that were after me.

The street itself was silent and still. I scanned up and down its length but couldn't make out anything. Figuring that I probably only had moments at best before either Martha and the Trekkie caught up or they contacted the Ministry, who would send someone a damn sight faster – and stronger – than they already had, I jogged across, already pulling my key out of my pocket. I caught a moving shadow out of the corner of my right eye and spun around, attack stance already prepared. I had nothing left to attack with, however. My remaining weapons were inside and I'd lost the silver needles in the shop. It was fortunate, therefore, that it was just a cat, frozen in its tracks as it had caught sight of me. It had sleek black fur and green eyes that gleamed in the glow of the streetlamps.

"Corrigan," I half-whispered to myself, watching it decide I was of no interest after all and slink off into the night.

Kitten.

I yelped aloud as the man himself entered my head.

What's the problem?

Now I was frozen in place, clutching the keys in my suddenly very sweaty palm and barely daring to breathe. I composed myself and answered him.

Problem? I have no idea what you're talking about, my Lord. Now fuck off and leave me alone. There, that told him.

There was a moment of silence then his Voice reappeared. *Except that this time you called me.*

Errr…what? It was impossible to initiate Voice contact unless you were an alpha. I wasn't even a shifter so there was just no way…

Stop playing mind games with me, My Lord. And with that I slammed him out of my head and walked up to the door, beginning to fumble with the lock. It must just be a coincidence that he'd decided to start fucking with me at this point in time. The bastard. He should just learn to leave well alone.

Once inside, I carefully and quietly closed the front door behind me. I tried to sense whether there was anything or anyone lurking around inside the entrance waiting for me but everything appeared normal. I waited for five beats and then took a deep breath and sprinted up the stairs. Fortunately the carpet was deep enough to mask the sounds of my hurried steps so I swung quickly round the corner and made for my own door.

As soon as I was inside I rapidly reached under the bed and pulled out my box. I flipped it open, double-checking that everything was there and then opened up the drawers of the rickety wooden dresser, pulling out clothes and stuffing them into my backpack. I laid the box on top, then thrust a couple of replacement silver needles in the loose knot of hair at the back of my head. Finally, I left without looking back.

CHAPTER TWELVE

I REALLY DIDN'T HAVE THE FAINTEST IDEA WHERE I WAS GOING TO go. It was just as well that I left when I did, however, as moments after I'd shut the heavy front door after me, a large black SUV screeched up alongside the kerb. I managed to duck behind the row of cars on the other side of the street, heat coursing through my veins at the nagging worry that if these were mages and they decided to cast a locator spell right now, then it'd take them all of three seconds flat to find me. Fortunately for me, whoever they were, they concentrated instead on the door of the flat. What it definitely did mean was that I had to get as far away from Inverness as possible, regardless of the fact that it was after 2.30 in the morning. I started moving away from the street, keeping low, in case one of them decided to suddenly look up - and then notice my small figure scurrying away. I didn't need to give them any more opportunity to unleash the powers of the magic otherworld upon me than they already had. Damnit, where was I going to go though?

I thought quickly. I needed to be somewhere the Ministry's spells wouldn't be able to reach me and where the police wouldn't be able to find me. That meant another plane, effectively. The last time I'd been to one it had been through a portal that Iabartu, the demi-goddess, had opened. I didn't think I was likely to bump into anyone with that kind of power who'd kindly let me into their otherworldly plane just to be friendly. A gust of wind blew sharply against my face and I shivered involuntarily. It was just my fucking luck that all this was taking place in the frozen north of Scotland in the middle of winter. It would have been nice to have been on the run in the balmy sunshine of the Bahamas, sipping a cocktail and hiding behind the odd sand dune instead of frost laced cars.

The wind blew again, picking up and causing me to turn up the collar of my inadequate jacket. I turned the corner away from the long street that my little bedsit lay on and straightened up, starting to jog away so I could put more distance between myself and all those who were behind me. Trying to keep my wits about me, and my senses alert, I strained to catch any sounds behind me. From the street parallel there was the distant hum of a car engine and, for an instant, my whole body froze to the spot. Then everything went silent again and I managed to lift up my feet and keep going.

I considered whether running was the right thing to do. I'd always been much more of a fight girl than a flight one, but the dents to my confidence lately suggested that I might struggle against the wrath of the mages who would be furious that I'd dared to tangle with their own. And, of course, this was coupled with the fact that I was now responsible for finding a way to get Mrs Alcoon out of this mess without getting caught – because getting caught would no doubt mean that Corrigan would hear of it, get involved, and find out that I was human (sort of). Then I'd have his inevitable repercussions on the Cornish pack forced on my conscience also. No, I had no choice but to run, much as it galled me.

· · ·

WITH THAT THOUGHT I picked up the pace and began to jog faster. Which was my undoing. From the shadows of one of the parked cars, came a sudden streak of blackness across the pavement. My foot caught on the edge of whatever it was, and I tipped headfirst down to the hard cold ground. Instinctively, I shot my hands out to catch myself, scuffing the skin on my palms painfully, knees knocking against the concrete with an unpleasant thud. A screeching yowl came from the shape, which then shot past me, turning to stare at me in hatred as it did so. It was the sodding cat that had decided not so long ago that I was a pathetic human not worthy of contempt. I harrumphed.

"Noticed me now, didn't you, stupid moggy."

The cat glared at me balefully again with its Corrigan green eyes and then slunk off. I shifted my weight, twisting my body to the side to get up from the ungainly position I was in on the pavement, suddenly mindful not only of my raw grazed hands, but also the other aches, pains and embedded wooden splinters from the attack at Clava Books.

"Fucking cat!" I swore, more at myself and my predicament than at the animal itself.

As I turned to stand up, slowly, I caught sight of the night sky. Stars glimmered more brightly than I thought I'd ever seen before.

"Fucking stars," I hissed at the sky.

The wind began to blow again, whisking past my cheek.

"Fucking wind. Fucking night. Fucking Scotland. Fucking freezing," I continued to curse. "Fucking longest night in the middle of the longest fucking winter, isn't it?" I wasn't sure who I'd been expecting to answer me, but just then dawning realisation providing me with the answer for myself hit me like the whack of a sledgehammer. Which was interesting because that's kind of how my body felt.

"Fucking Winter Solstice."

I stood up, wincing slightly at the pain, and grinned. The

Clava Cairns. My trip to pick up the blisterwort for Mrs Alcoon notwithstanding, I didn't know much about the Cairns themselves. However what I did know from a few of the old tomes from the bookshop was that during the Winter Solstice, they attracted a number of hippy druid types because when the sun went down, the light hit one particular spot at the back wall of one of the Cairns which gave enough of a hint to humankind that they were built with much more design than first glance might suggest. I'd had an inkling when I'd read about them after entering Mrs Alcoon's shop for the first time and pulling that first book off the shelf; I just hadn't allowed myself to really think about it in depth because I'd been trying to avoid having anything at all to do with the Otherworld, even if that only involved my own thoughts. But what I'd always really known without consciously forming the words was that they were a portal, or had been once. Not a particularly powerful one - my previous visit to the Cairns had proven that - but one that worked most effectively during that one particular moment. That moment was gone – it was far too dark and far too late now – and the knowledge of how to work the magical gate had probably also disappeared into the annals of lost history anyway. But whatever lingering otherworldly traces there were might well be just enough to cover my tracks. That would solve the immediate problem of the mages and their tracking spells. And the hippies were no doubt still there, camping out and stoned, so I could slot myself into one of their groups. That would cover the problem of the police.

"Outfuckingstanding," I said aloud. I had a plan. Not a great one, or a long term one, but one that would get me through the next hours at the very least. It was a start.

I reached inside myself and pulled up a fat tendril of heat, willing it to pump through my veins. With the fire heating me up from the inside and providing me with the energy I'd need, I knew I could get to the Cairns inside ninety minutes. And this time without a smelly bus and a smellier drunk. I ignored the aches and jabs of pain rippling through my body and began to run. Faster than before, although with more care to avoid any more feline collisions, I started to pelt my way through the streets of Inverness.

CHAPTER THIRTEEN

THE LAST TIME I'D MADE THE JOURNEY TO THE CAIRNS, I'D BEEN able to take advantage of the local transport system. Unfortunately buses don't tend to run at 3am in rural Scotland, so I was going to have to travel by foot this time. I knew that this was when I would be at my most vulnerable. The mages would no doubt be casting their locator spells right at that very moment, so it wouldn't be long before they'd be able to catch up with me.

I ran fast, wending my way through the different twists and turns that led me out of the small city. The air was still bitterly cold but the pace I kept up and the adrenaline skipping through my system was keeping me warm. The curl of heat from the blood fire inside me was also active, allowing me to fire, no pun intended, on all cylinders. I kept my eyes out for any more potential collisions with crazy midnight moggies with death wishes, but my luck was finally in and I didn't see a soul, whether it be animal, human or otherworld.

Before too long I was on the edge of Inverness, making my way onto a small worn path that ran alongside the road that the bus had taken when I'd travelled that way weeks before. Despite the frigidity of the night air, sweat was beginning to form on my forehead and I could feel my body getting sticky. Prickles of pain from the wooden shards that had embedded their way into my skin during the fight with Martha and her sci-fi friend were sending unpleasant shivers through my body, but I resolutely ignored them and kept on running. At one point, I clenched my fists as I stumbled slightly over the uneven ground and the pain level increased dramatically; when I glanced down at my hands a rippling green flame was flickering over them, barely half a centimeter high. I swallowed and looked away. I supposed about the only thing I could be thankful for right about now was that Corrigan hadn't tried to contact me again. I wondered what he'd meant when he'd said that I had initiated the Voice. He was obviously just trying to unsettle me, but I wasn't sure to what end. His little mind games were becoming irritating.

I made good time and reached the turn off where the bus had previously dropped me without any further incident. By now I was breathing hard with the exertion and feeling slightly dizzy. Not for the first time I wished that I'd paid more attention to my ever decreasing fitness levels.

There was a glow of light from what I assumed was the hippy encampment up ahead, and some kind of distant humming drone that sounded vaguely familiar. The familiar heady scent of lavender rose into the air around me and, now that my goal was in sight, I started to slow to a more manageable jog. The fact that there had been no sign of any mage-like activity was comforting and I was starting to hope that perhaps I was getting away and that they wouldn't bother coming after me.

As I got closer to the Cairns themselves, I realised that the humming sound was coming from a particularly annoying didgeridoo. I winced. Aborigines aside, it baffled me as to why anyone would choose that as an instrument to play. I could now make out some individual campfires and clusters of people sitting around chatting and drinking, occasionally taking long drawn out gulps from bottles that were being passed around. The smell of the lavender was giving way to the pungent odour of marijuana, and the low chatter of a couple of dozen voices was becoming more distinct. Trying to appear less conspicuous (after all, who goes for a jog in the middle of night in wintery Scotland?), I slowed now to a walk, thrusting my hands into pockets just in case they were still glowing with green fire.

I was a bit surprised, and definitely relieved, that there wasn't a police presence. It was possible, of course, that they were all off dealing with a sudden terrible fire in the middle of town. The people chatting all around barely registered me, although as I swung around towards the stones themselves, one slurred voice did call out lazily.

"Want a smoke, flower?"

Flower? A spasm of irritation caught me and I flicked my eyes over in the direction the voice was coming from. A lanky long haired lout wearing a yellow anorak was lying propped up on one elbow, casually holding out a joint. As if clouding my mind was going to help me now.

"No, thanks mate," I called back, struggling to keep the edge out of my voice.

"Hey, no problem," he drawled. "Come back if you change your mind."

At that point his eyes focused on some point behind me and I could just make out his pupils widening in the dark. "Far out," he whispered, and whistled softly.

A tendril of dread joined the heat in my stomach and I glanced around to see what he was looking at. My stomach lurched as my eyes fixed on a snaking blue light that was making its way inexorably through the groups of people, following the path I had just taken and heading right for me. Shit. I turned round and ran.

The stones were just up ahead, scant metres away. It would do me no good reaching them if the locator spell found me first however. I lacked the skill to open the portal, even if it had still been dusk and the Cairns were at their most powerful. I didn't know much about how these tracing spells worked, despite having seen Alex put them into action, and I didn't know if having tracked me this far it was already too late, but I had to try to avoid it and then maybe I'd still have a fighting chance somehow. Perhaps if the power of the Cairns interfered with it, it would get confused and head off in another direction. I had to hope.

I sprinted, avoiding some empty cans of lager that were scattered across the pathway, as well as managing to just stop myself colliding with a couple who were snogging next to one of the standing stones. Mustering up every last ounce of energy I had, I pelted through the corbelled passageway towards the back wall of the cairn, afraid to look behind me. Tea light candles were flickering next to the wall of rocks, creating some sort of miniature shrine. What the reason for this was, I had no idea, and I inadvertently kicked a few over as I slammed into the rock face. I turned, pressing my hands against the rough stone surface and blinked rapidly, trying to focus on where the blue snake of light was.

It was hovering back at the entrance to the cairn, flicking its almost animal like head one way and another. The kissing couple had broken off from their embrace and were poking at it with outstretched fingers, eyes widened in wonder. I spared a moment to wonder how the Ministry would prevent reports of a mysterious blue light appearing during the winter solstice from filtering across the internet, but that thought quickly vanished into a wave of desperate relief as the light abruptly blinked out of existence, leaving just the dark night behind in its wake. I sank down against the wall until I was on my haunches, closing my eyes in a mixture of disbelief and liberation. It had worked.

I allowed myself a moment's respite, resting my head against the rough cool stones and blanking my mind. Then I straightened up and prepared my mental checklist. I had to, in no particular order, avoid being either detected or found by the Ministry of Mages, the Pack or the police; I had to find some way to rescue Mrs Alcoon from the coma-like stasis the mages had put her under and convince them that she was exactly what she appeared to be – nothing more than an elderly Scottish woman with a bare smattering of magic; keep my promise to Solus and tell him that I was of the Draco Wyr and hope that he didn't attempt to drain my blood so he could use it for whatever it could be used for; and, last but not least, find out why, all of a sudden, I could call up green flames at my fingertips. Easy.

Mrs Alcoon was relatively safe for now and, besides which, there had been no sign of Solus since he'd bundled her off to Tir-na-Nog. I was somewhat surprised that he'd not taken advantage of the differences in time to show his face again and to demand his 'reward', but I decided that I couldn't worry about that right now. Notwithstanding annoying mental intrusions, the Pack were nowhere in sight and therefore would be easy to avoid. More pressing were my concerns about the mages and the police. The cloaking power of the Cairns wouldn't last long – the Winter Solstice was already over. My magical knowledge was not strong and I knew I couldn't count on the Cairns to hide me forever. Unless the mages were absolute idiots they'd work out I was here sooner or later anyway, as would the local police. Enough so-called druids and hippies, no matter how stoned they were, had seen me here. My previous idea of merging myself with one of their groups was probably a foolish one. If I involved myself with more humans, I'd probably only succeed in involving them in lots of trouble. I didn't need any more on my conscience than I already had.

I chewed my lip. The longer I hung around in indecision, the less power the Cairns' portal would hold. I looked over at the hazy figure of the long-haired man who'd called me flower and made up my mind, pushing myself away from the relative comfort and safety of the stone passage-way and walking slowly back in his direction.

Pasting a smile on my face, I called out to him. "Hey, mate, any chance you have a phone I could borrow?"

"What do you need a phone for, flower? Let's hang back, and

enjoy the moment and forget the outside world." His voice trailed off and, as I got closer to him, I realised just how unfocused his eyes were. I fought the urge to slap him around the head a few times.

"I…uh…need to call my sister. She promised she'd be here but I can't find her. I'll give you money for the call – it'll only take a minute." I gazed at him beseechingly.

He blinked at me slowly. "Well, then, sure, flower."

He reached into the side pocket of his stained yellow windbreaker and fumbled around for a few moments. I had to fight the urge to push his hand out of the way and find it for myself, despite whatever communicable disease I might pick up in the process.

"Hey, did you see that freaky blue light? This Winter Solstice is rocking, man!"

I just stared at him. He shrugged amiably and finally pulled out his phone, holding it towards me. I snatched it out of his hand before he changed his mind, and stared down at it for a moment. Alex would probably know what to do but I wasn't convinced I could trust him now that all the mages were involved. Not that I could blame him for that; his first loyalty would have to be to the Ministry and I got that. It didn't help me much though. There was someone else I could call though.

I took a deep breath and dialed, jabbing out the numbers without thinking about it any further, and hoping that the right person answered.

It took some time before someone picked up. Well, it was around five o'clock in the morning although that didn't stop my impatience from sending pinpricks of tension across my body. I was aware that the phone's owner was watching me with his head cocked, a lazy grin on his face, so I turned away and took a few steps in the other direction.

Finally a sleepy voice answered. "Hello?"

"Hi." I coughed slightly, trying to disguise my voice. "I need to speak to Johannes. It's important."

"Huh? It's the middle of the freaking night." It was a girl's voice, sounded like Ally but I wasn't completely sure. At least it wasn't Anton.

"Yeah, like I said it's important," I repeated.

Ally muttered something and put the receiver down. I turned round and looked at the stoned yellow windbreaker guy who was still watching me. I gave him a strained smile and held up two fingers.

It seemed like an age before someone picked up the phone again.

"Yeah?"

Thank fuck. It was Johannes.

"J, I don't have much time. I need your help."

"Mack? Far are ye? Whit's going on?"

The comfort of hearing a familiar voice almost overwhelmed me. "J, I need to find out if I can get an old portal opened. I don't have much time."

"Whit happened tae ye? Ye disappeared! Thae Brethren's efter ye, ye know?"

"I know, I know, J. I'll explain some other time. Please, the portal?"

"Whit kin' is it?"

"It's an old one. Centred around a cairn that's only really got power during the solstice. That's..."

"Now," he interrupted. "Hol' on."

I could hear him talking to someone in the background and felt my stomach muscles tighten. I didn't want to involve more people than I absolutely had to. I could hear the phone being passed to someone else.

"Mackenzie? Where are you? What happened to you?"

A pain rose in my throat as I fought to hold back my tears. "Julia. Are you...are you okay?" The last time I'd seen her she'd been lying unconscious and fighting for her life – and there'd been nothing I could do about it.

"I'm fine. In a wheelchair, admittedly, but I'm fine. Why did you leave?"

I struggled to explain. "Anton, he...I..."

The voice on the other end of the line was grim. "Yes, that's what we thought. You didn't have to leave, Mackenzie. We would have helped you."

"It was for the best, Julia. I had no choice. I...I miss you." The cloud of tears threatened to spill over and I had to fight hard to maintain my composure. "I don't have much time though. I need your help."

She became all business-like. "Yes, a portal? At a cairn site?"

"Yes. I need to know if it can be opened. I don't have much time before dawn hits and I don't think it'll have any power at all left then. I need to..." I took a deep breath. "I need to get through it."

"Do you know where it leads? You know how dangerous portals are, Mackenzie. It could go anywhere. It could open up in the demesnes of anything."

"I know, and, no, I don't know where it leads but I don't have any choice right now, Julia. Please, help me."

"Okay, okay. Johannes?" I could hear more muttering before she came back on the line. "Right, this is what you need to do. If the portal is still active, there will be one stone marked with a rune. You need to touch it with both hands and say the incantation."

"And what's the incantation?"

"That will depend on whoever built it, dear. Is it a human cairn?"

"I think so. Around four thousand years old. In..." I hesitated for a moment because I didn't want to give too much information away in case Julia would be compelled at some point in the future to give it up. "In Scotland."

"In that case, you'll need to try the Gaelic for open. I don't know if that will work, but it's worth a try."

I kept my voice calm. "Do you know what the Gaelic for open might be?"

"I don't speak Gaelic, dear."

"Can you find out? Does Johannes know?"

I could hear Julia asking Johannes in the background, and heard him answer in the negative. Shit.

Julia came back on. "If you hold on, we can find out. I'll just get the computer up and running. There'll be a translation website we can find. Mackenzie..." Her voice stopped abruptly as I heard someone else's voice suddenly appear in the background, demanding to know what was going on. I swallowed hard as I recognised the deep timbre.

"Lord Anton, it's an old friend," came Julia's firm voice.

Lord Anton? John had never demanded that we use the pack honorific to address him. I wondered if Anton was feeling the need to assert his authority because he wasn't naturally receiving the respect that he thought he deserved in his new position as alpha.

"And who might that be?"

Despite the distance, I could hear Anton's voice loud and clear. He'd use his Voice on the pair of them and find out who I really was. It wouldn't go well for them. I decided a pre-emptive strike was my only option.

"Put him on, Julia," I said calmly.

"Wait..."

"Just do it." I didn't like ordering Julia around. After all, she'd been my alpha, even if it had only been for a short period. But I couldn't let Anton decide to punish her for my actions.

The receiver clunked faintly as it was passed over. "Who is this?" demanded Anton.

"It's me, Anton. Mackenzie."

There was a moment of silence before he replied with a dangerously quiet voice. "Mack, I thought I had made my feelings clear."

"You didn't tell me I couldn't call up for a chat, Anton."

"I would have thought it wasn't necessary to make that explicit. And it's Lord Anton to you."

"Not any more. I'm not part of the pack, remember?" I couldn't resist taunting him.

"Of course you're not. That's why you're out there on your own without a friend in the world."

I balled my fists up. The wanker. Irritated heat flashed up through my veins. "Now you know who this is, can you put Julia back on the phone? We have some catching up to do." I was impressed at how even my voice managed to sound.

"Actually, no, Mack, I don't think I will do that. It's 5 o'clock in the morning. My pack need their sleep. Don't call here again."

"Anton, wait, I…"

He hung up the phone. I cursed loudly, causing several of the solstice hippies to glance over in my direction. The yellow windbreaker guy was staring at me. I dug into my jeans pocket and pulled out a crumpled note, passing it over to him with his phone.

"Thanks," I muttered.

"Any time, flower. Did you find your sister?"

I ignored him, aware that I was being rude but unable to muster up the energy to care, and walked back towards the back of the cairn, then paused suddenly and turned round.

"What's the Gaelic for open?"

"Huh?" He looked baffled.

"The Gaelic for…" I gave up. "Never mind," and turned back towards the stones. These so-called druids were just here for show, it would be stupid to think that they'd actually know anything about the real history and culture of the place. Let's face it, Yellow Anorak had a state of the art mobile phone and probably a job in the city. I doubted he knew anything even remotely helpful about the reality of the Cairns or the culture behind them.

"Hey!" he shouted from behind me.

I ignored him and kept walking.

"It's oscail."

I paused and turned back. He was holding his phone aloft and beaming. Of course, a state of the art mobile phone would be able to access the internet, even here in the middle of nowhere. I felt immediately guilty for dismissing him so readily and for, again, being so quick to judge. The kindness of strangers... I smiled my thanks at him and jogged back, giving him a quick peck on the cheek.

"Thank you," I said softly. "You might have just saved my life." He gave me a lazy salute back, before settling down onto his previous spot on the ground. I smiled gratefully at him again, and then headed back to the stones.

When I got back to the edge of the cairn, I began feeling around with my fingers to see if I could find the rune. Many of the stones were covered in a soft moss, and the shrouded darkness at the back of the passageway made it difficult to really see anything. I felt my way along each stone, fingertips brushing against the surfaces, trying to feel for anything that might suggest a marking. Tracing round the edges, and feeling nothing, I could feel my frustration rising yet again. I took a deep breath. I HAD to get a grip of myself. I took a step back and inadvertently knocked over yet another flickering tea candle. Bending down to pick it back up, something caught the edge of my eye. I knelt down and reached over, carefully brushing the edges of the dark green moss aside. There was a rune after all!

I closed my eyes and touched it gently with the tip of my index finger, hoping I'd be able to recognise it so I could have some clue about where the portal might lead. Having advance knowledge would be helpful. The rune was one of the more obscure ones, however, and my weak knowledge of Otherworld languages wasn't enough to help me translate it. I supposed it didn't matter. Dawn was approaching and if I didn't try something soon, then it wouldn't be long before the long arm of the law – magical or otherwise – caught up with me. I took a deep breath and pressed the palms of both my hands against the cool rock and whispered, "Oscail."

For a horrifying moment, nothing seemed to happen. Dread filled me; all this risk-taking: running around the freezing Scottish countryside, getting Julia and Johannes into trouble, all of it, had been pointless. A silent wail built up inside my chest. Maybe it was too late, the moment of the Winter Solstice was too far past, or the power of the portal was just too diminished. I sank down, defeated, my fingers falling away from the stones, and then, without warning, the air around me started to crackle and shimmer. The pit of my stomach was hit with a familiar wave of nausea and I was falling, falling through the ground.

CHAPTER FOURTEEN

I HAD ABSOLUTELY NO WAY OF KNOWING WHAT TO EXPECT WHEN I emerged on the other side of the portal. As I'd previously experienced when I'd entered Iabartu's demesne, the journey made me ill and, despite my best intentions to be prepared to meet any nasties headlong when I arrived, I instead was on my hands and knees puking up bile. It reminded me of how long it had been since I'd eaten a decent meal.

Once I'd finished eking out the last of the contents of my stomach, I staggered up and looked around, ready to pull out the few weapons I had if I needed to. But there wasn't much to see. The air was considerably warmer than it had been at the Clava Cairns, but the buzz of voices and the crackle from the fires had disappeared. The whole place was eerily silent. I tried to peer into the dark gloom, but could see little. Fortunately there seemed to be no signs of life, which meant that I was probably safe for the time being. I looked behind to check out the gateway from where I'd arrived and realised that there was just a vast empty space of darkness. Errr....what I clearly hadn't considered was an escape route. I might be safe from the police and the spells of the mages here, but I hadn't considered what on earth I was going to do to get myself back to my own plane so I could start sorting things out. That had been stupid. I had no idea where I was, no idea how to leave and no idea about how to sort out all the messes that I'd created.

I took a few steps forward and felt a wave of dizziness overcome me. The night's proclivities were starting to catch up with me. Stumbling forward in the darkness, I reached out and felt a stone wall ahead of me, not unlike the edges of the cairns that I'd just left behind. I sank against the wall and rested my head against it, briefly closing my eyes. I'd just rest for a few moments, I decided, and then I'd find somewhere safe to settle down for a few hours and catch up on some sleep before I worked out what to do next. Before I knew it, however, I was fast asleep.

I dreamt I was in a great hall, not unlike the vestibule back at the keep in Cornwall. Julia and John were both there, staring at me with unhappiness in their eyes.

"You've messed everything up, Mack."

I stared at them both mutely.

"You could have lived out your days in peace and quiet in Inverness, but instead you got that little old lady into trouble. You involved the mages and you destroyed her shop, and now you're on the run."

"What are you going to do?" Tom's face swam before my eyes. He was bouncing a ball of green flame from one hand to the other, then he threw it over my shoulder. I turned round to follow it and saw Trekkie, who was now sporting a pair of Vulcan type ears and carrying Mrs Alcoon in a fireman's lift over his shoulder. I tried to step forward, to get her away from him, but my path was blocked by Maggie.

"Don't you dare touch her!" she hissed at me. "You are evil, you're a daemon! Stay away!"

Maggie made the sign of the evil eye with her hands and I felt a bolt of pain strike me, making me stagger backwards and into something solid. Steel arms circled me until I couldn't move. Warm breath caressed against my ear.

"You're human. Do you know what we do to humans, kitten?"

I struggled to get away, but I couldn't move. Anton came up and jabbed me in the chest, laughing.

"You're going to pay now, you ape."

I lashed out with my foot, trying to kick him, but Trekkie pointed at me and a bolt of blue light hit my leg, transforming it into a dead weight. He cackled in laughter. Corrigan's arms tightened round me until I was gasping for air. He was squeezing tighter and tighter, all the while whispering into my ear about the punishment he was going to wreak on everyone I'd ever come into contact with. I couldn't breathe and little lights started to dance in front of my eyes. I tried to scream for help, but nothing came out of my mouth and I was feeling fainter and fainter. Something grabbed hold of my arm and started to shake it. It was the cat that I'd tripped over in the street. Its teeth had latched onto my flesh and were burrowing their way through. Blood starting to seep through my skin, making the cat's fur catch alight, but it kept on shaking and shaking and….

I woke up. A figure wearing a brimmed hat was standing over me, clutching my arm and shaking me awake. Solus.

"How…? What…?" I stuttered, wrenching my arm away from him.

"How did I find you?" he inquired, moving his face close to mine. "What do I want? Why that's easy, spitfire. I am Fae. Did you really think that I wouldn't be able to follow you here? And as for what I want, well I think you know the answer to that." His teeth gleamed in the darkness. "You owe me an answer."

I pushed myself up to my feet and folded my arms. "Solus, I promised you, didn't I? You'll get your answers. Just right now help me out a bit. Where exactly am I?"

He took off his hat with one swift smooth movement and flicked his blond hair to the side, snorting. "That one's easy, my little chinchilla."

"Chinchilla? Fuck off, Fae."

"Actually, I think it fits rather well." He reached out and tried to chuck me under the chin but I dodged away and glared at him.

Solus laughed. "Chinchilla are quiet, shy and highly strung creatures. Attributes that seem to fit you particularly well."

"Fuck you." I kicked out at him but this time it was his turn to dodge.

"Then tell me what you're doing here, Mackenzie." He drawled out my name with emphasis.

"What do you mean? I'm making sure the mages don't catch me so I've got time to sort out what I can do to save Mrs Alcoon and sort out this fucking mess."

"No," Solus said softly. "You're hiding. You're scared. You've decided that instead of standing up for yourself and sorting this out, you're going to run away and hide."

Anger flooded through me. "I'm being sensible! Letting the ministry get hold of me, or the police for that matter, would not help anyone. This was the only solution."

"Bullshit. Instead of fighting, you're hiding. You could have taken those mages on. Do you know that the Pack, the whole Pack, not just your little friends in Cornwall, are spinning tales of you as some kind of superhero? A shifter who despite being a mere werehamster will fight tooth and nail to save the meek." He straightened out the lapels of his shirt. "There are rumours that you left the Pack and turned rogue in order to patrol the cities at night, hunting down unwary Otherworld monsters; tracking down members of Iabartu's family to wreak your vengeance upon them. You've become the Batman of the were world. They say that even the Lord Alpha is afraid of you."

I was momentarily taken aback.

"That's right," he continued. "Surprising, isn't it? Because instead of being some dark avenger keeping the Pack safe in their beds at night, you're cowering in some long forgotten dark plane, too scared to face the music."

Flames curled at my toes and fingertips.

"Ooooh, does the truth hurt?" Solus taunted.

I shot a punch out, aiming for his solar plexus. I missed.

"You can't even land a hit on one little fairy, can you?"

I growled at him and tried again. I missed, again. "I've hit you before, Solus."

He blew air out of his lips dismissively. "You got lucky. How lucky are you going to get now by hiding away from all your problems?"

I side-stepped round him and feinted left, before swinging round a kick and catching him satisfyingly on the back of his leg. "Hah! Got you!" I spat.

Solus folded his arms. "But I'm not trying to get you. It would be a different story if I was. Then you'd be running away, trying to find the nearest hole to crawl into, afraid that I might hurt you..."

I launched myself at him, knocking him over. My legs straddled his torso and I started raining punches down onto his body. Reaching back into my ponytail I yanked out one of the silver needles, even though I knew it would do little lasting damage to the Fae, and jabbed it in his direction. He grabbed hold of my wrist and twisted till I dropped it, and laughed in my face.

Blood thundered in my ears and hot fire took over my body. Without even really being aware of it, I summoned up the green flames at my fingertips and shot them out at him. The smell of burning hair hit the atmosphere and his eyes widened infinitesimally.

"Am I hiding now, you fuck? Watch me incinerate you." I sent out another bolt of flame and then I was falling forward into nothing. He'd performed some kind of sneaky Fae transportation trick. "Oh yeah?" I shouted out into the darkness. "Who's the one who's hiding now? Who's the one who's running away? Bring it on, Solus, I'm not afraid of you."

"No, you're not," he said softly from behind me.

I spun round and prepared to attack him again, but he held up his hands in submission. I paused for a moment and glared at him with every ounce of malevolence that I could muster.

"You're afraid of yourself, aren't you, Mackenzie?"

I hissed at him and took a step forward, still on the attack.

Solus continued. "That's a neat trick with that fire, darling. And yet I have never sensed a mage's flicker in you before. I don't sense it now. Neither have I ever seen a mage manage green fire before either." His eyes gleamed in the darkness. "You could have taken on that bear in Cornwall, and you know it. I've done a little digging and I know that you could have bested him in a fight. That you already had bested him in a fight in fact. You could have been alpha right now, not him."

"One slight problem there, Einstein, I'm not a shifter."

He shrugged. "Semantics. The rest of the Cornish pack would have supported you and kept your secret. Instead you chose to run."

"I did what I had to do." I kept the flames on my fingers at a steady flicker, ready to attack him again at the slightest opportunity. The flames inside me, however, boiled with an intense ferocity.

"When I transported you to Corrigan's lair, your first instinct was to run. You could have taken him on too. You might not have been sure of the win, but it would have been close." Solus gazed at me assessingly. "That human, the annoying one?"

"I take it you mean Derek?" I inquired through gritted teeth.

He waved a dismissive hand through the air. "Whatever his nomenclature is. You could have – should have – destroyed him. And yet you didn't."

"Perhaps I just happen to have some morals, Solus. I'm not a soul-sucking Fae out for only myself."

"Morals? If you had morals you'd have done something to stop him from pestering any other girls in the future. But you didn't. Because you were afraid of what you'd actually end up doing. The same with those two wizards. I didn't see what happened but I can guess. You could have put the two of them down then and there. Solved the problem with the Ministry in one fell swoop. But you didn't. You're scared, Mackenzie. And not of shifters or of mages or even of me. You're afraid of yourself."

I stared at him, nonplussed. Solus gracefully lowered himself to the ground and crossed his legs into the lotus position. He patted a spot on the ground in front of him and gestured at me to join him.

"What?" I asked. "You want to partake in some friendly yoga?"

"No, Mackenzie. You are going to keep your promise and you're going to tell me what you really are and what you're so afraid of."

"Is Mrs Alcoon safe?"

"Tucked up safe and sound, snoozing away where no-one can touch her." The look in his eyes was serious. "I promise."

I stayed standing for another heartbeat and then joined him on the ground, crossing my legs. Taking a deep breath, I forced the heat inside me to dissipate. It would do me no good now. I looked into Solus' eyes without blinking. In for a penny, in for a pound.

"I'm one eighth Draco Wyr."

If I'd expected an immediate reaction, I didn't get one. Solus stared back at me implacably.

"My mother left me at the pack in Cornwall when I was just a kid. I don't know why. I think there had been something after us, something chasing us, and that was the only place she thought I'd be safe. Somehow she'd known John or he'd known us, I don't know. And I grew up there with them, thinking I was human. I had a bad temper, and sometimes I got...hot inside when I got angry but I thought I was just human. They all thought I was just human. When I reached eighteen, John bit me. I wanted to be turned, to be a shifter. I wanted to be one of them. It didn't work."

I was silent for a few moments, remembering that terrible time. I'd been in a fever for days, twisting and turning in sweat soaked sheets, my body fighting the shifter infection. All that pain had been nothing compared to the crushing disappointment when I'd come out the other end and realised that I hadn't changed and that I was still the same. That I'd never really be part of the pack no matter how much I wanted it.

"I stayed with the pack though. They were my family. John trained me to help them and I helped keep the perimeter safe. It turned out that even though I didn't have it in me to be a shifter I still had certain skills that proved useful. I was a good tracker, and I could hunt and kill with the best of them. When there was a problem, John called on me." I couldn't keep the pride out of my voice at that.

"And then he was murdered. Because of me. Because somehow Iabartu found out what I was and she wanted my blood." I shrugged. "Apparently it has some special qualities. It has healing power as well as being somehow addictive to anyone who tastes it. And it gives me power. I didn't find any of this out until I found some papers in John's study." I swallowed painfully. "He'd known all along what I was but hadn't told me. I don't know why. But still, I went after Iabartu to kill her for what she did and I was arrogant enough to think that I had enough power to bring her down. I didn't. Corrigan and Anton were the ones who killed her; I was just a momentary diversion."

Solus continued watching me in silence. The weight of his gaze became too much and I looked down, away from his eyes, before continuing.

"Anton made me leave the pack. He said I was dangerous to have around and he was right. Being what I was had caused John's death. If I hadn't been there, he wouldn't be dead. So I left. I couldn't tell anyone why. Corrigan still thinks I'm a shifter because if he knew differently then he'd destroy the Cornish pack. No-one is supposed to know of their existence, you see? So I ended up in Inverness, hiding. Like a chin-fucking-chilla. Much good the hiding part did though because all I've done is cause even more problems."

I looked back up at Solus. "So, there you go. That's it. Do what you want with the information."

Solus cleared his throat. "And the green flames?"

I motioned to the necklace that lay heavy round my neck. I really should just have taken the stupid thing off, consequences be damned. "That was some weird thing a witch did to me. A friend of Mrs Alcoon's. It was meant to help me with Derek and Corrigan and...you. Instead all it did was make me spout fire from my hands and get the Ministry to put Mrs Alcoon into that coma because the so-called friend told them about me. So now I need to put it right."

"Let me make sure I understand this perfectly. You're part dragon. You're not a mage but you have the power of fire. And a bad temper. And crazy blood."

"I guess that about sums it up, yes."

"How did you break through my sister's cruinne?"

"I hit it until I bled. The blood, I don't know, the blood did something to the ring and broke through it. Like I said, it does stuff. I don't really know what. I've tried to find out more about the Draco Wyr but there's not much around."

Solus ran a hand through his hair. "I don't believe it."

That stung. "I'm not lying. I told you I'd tell you the truth and I've kept my word." I got to my feet and dusted my jeans off. "Just tell me how to get out of this place, Solus. You've got what you wanted."

"I didn't mean I don't believe you, I just don't believe it. The Draco Wyr are a legend. They're not real." For the first time since I'd known him he sounded unsure of himself.

"You mean like faeries and wizards and shapeshifters?" I put my hands on my hips. "Come on, Solus, get a grip."

He stood up also and took me by the shoulders. "This is big, Mackenzie. If the High Queen – or King - knew what you were..."

I jerked away. "You don't have to tell them."

"No, I probably don't. But I also don't think you can keep this secret for much longer. Who else knows what you are?"

"Tom, a werewolf from Cornwall, and Alex, a mage. And Mrs Alcoon."

Solus' eyes widened slightly. "So effectively the mages and the Pack know what you are?"

"No. One mage and one shifter know what I am. Plus one very, I cannot stress this enough, very minor witch. And now one Seelie Fae."

"You don't think that they will give you up? If this Tom is compelled to by his alpha then he'll have no choice. It won't matter how much you trust him. The same with the mage. A bit of magic to loosen his tongue and the whole world knows." He rolled his eyes. "At least the old lady isn't going to be blabbing to anyone any time soon."

I winced at that last comment. "They've not given me up thus far. And the werewolf's alpha is Corrigan."

"Fucking hell, Mackenzie, you like sailing close to the wind." He sighed deeply.

"And you, Solus? Will you be compelled to give me up?"

"I don't know yet, Mackenzie. We could use your blood."

I must have looked faintly sickened by that because he hastily backtracked.

"Not your actual blood. We're not vampires." His lip curled in distaste. "I just meant that your powers would come in handy. Come with me to Tir-na-Nog. We'll talk to the Queen. I can guarantee your safety."

"I need to sort out Mrs Alcoon, Solus. I can't just leave her in stasis."

"She's safe. We'll work out something."

"No. I need to talk to the Ministry to get them to lift the spell. It's the only thing that will definitely work. You're right. I've been hiding and I need to face the music. I still need to stay away from Corrigan and the shifters but if I can get to the mages before they kill me then I can save Mrs Alcoon."

I eyeballed Solus. I'd known him for all of five minutes and had absolutely no reason to trust him. The only thing he'd promised me was that he'd keep Mrs Alcoon safe. Beyond that, what he decided to do was anyone's guess. But he'd been right. I'd been hiding myself away instead of confronting the issue. I needed to sort this out, for Mrs Alcoon's sake if nothing else.

"Will you help me get out of here, Solus, and get to the Ministry?"

He was silent. I prodded him. "Solus? Please?"

"You have to understand, my little dragonlette, that I can't get you right to the Ministry. They are very…security conscious and they don't like the Fae. There's a considerable amount of iron and magic surrounding their headquarters that prevent someone of my kin getting close."

"But..?" I forced the issue.

"But okay, I'll see what I can do."

"What about your High Queen?"

"I don't know yet, I've not made up my mind."

'Well at least you're being refreshingly honest, Solus."

"Rather that than be eaten alive by an angry red-headed dragon."

I scowled at him in annoyance and he grinned back. "Then let's do this."

CHAPTER FIFTEEN

"I don't know much about the interior of the Ministry' headquarters, you understand, just its whereabouts in London," Solus stated solemnly.

"Yes, yes," I dismissed him with a wave. My mojo was returning and having the absence of a workable floor plan was not going to get in my way.

"I can transport you from here to about half a mile away. That way we'll definitely avoid triggering any of their sensors. The combined magical forces of the Ministry in protecting their own can be…formidable."

"Ooooh, is the great Solus scared of a few pesky human wizards?"

"Shut it, human."

"I'm not human, I'm a dragon." I pulled back my shoulders and tried to look impressively wyrm and scary like.

Solus stared at me in baffled puzzlement. "What ARE you doing?"

I slumped ever so slightly. "Nothing. I'm just mentally preparing myself for battle."

"Well, you've changed your tune, my little Konglong."

"Konglong?"

"It means terrible dragon in Chinese. You know, they revere the dragon in Chinese culture and…"

"My name is Mackenzie," I said primly. "You may call me Mack. Nothing else."

"Whatever you say, gorgeous."

I thumped him on the shoulder. "I'm going to need some weapons. All I have are my needles and silver ain't going to do much against a mage."

Solus stared at me. "You can shoot fire from your fingertips and you want some weapons?"

I shrugged. "I would feel more comfortable with some steel to work with. Can we make a pitstop somewhere along the way?"

He harrumphed. "Fine. I might know a guy."

"Great." I looked around the gloom. "There's absolutely nothing on this plane at all, is there? We should leave."

"I beg to differ, Mack. This is a halfway house between your world and one of the underworlds. The portal was created to provide a link for the dying between what you call Earth and, well, hell."

I was alarmed. "Hell?"

"One of many," Solus stated airily. "Of course it's been out of action for centuries. I don't think anyone ever comes this way anymore. I was surprised in fact that you found your way here, although I have to admire your ingenuity."

"Hell?"

"Yes," he said impatiently. "Where you go when you die."

"If I kept walking down that way I'd be in hell?"

"Really, Mackenzie. For someone who has lived her life amongst denizens of the Otherworld, your education is sorely lacking."

"We lived quiet lives in Cornwall," I protested feebly. "We didn't go thinking about…hell. Where's heaven?"

"It's not THE hell. It's just A hell. There are many. And really heaven or hell are just words. You end up in the same place."

"But…"

"Do you want to leave this place or not?"

"Okay, okay, I want to leave." A shudder ran through me. "Now would be good in fact."

"Then let's do it."

Solus gripped my shoulder and the air around us started to shimmer. The nausea began rising in my stomach again until I was biting back the urge to vomit. I screwed my eyes shut tight and held my breath.

A few moments later, Solus' hand squeezed my shoulder painfully and then he removed it. "Okay, we're here now."

I opened one eye and then the other. It was daytime and, after the darkness of the limbo plane, it was painfully bright.

"Do you know, I think I must be getting better at this. I don't think I'm going to be sick this time," I said confidently, just before my stomach rocked greasily and I started retching.

"Yes, you're a real dimension tripper," Solus stated without a trace of humour.

I stood up, wiping the back of my mouth with my sleeve. "Oh God. I'm going to need food and a toothbrush before we do anything."

"And here was me thinking that you were a big bad scary dragon who needed nothing more than a sword to batter down the Ministry of Mages."

"Well, I could bowl them over with my breath, I suppose, but I'd rather do it on a full stomach." I eyed him seriously.

"Fine," he said, and starting pulling me across the road. Oblivious to the rules of good road safety, Solus ignored the car careering round the corner and slamming on its brakes to avoid hitting us. The owner honked his horn loudly and painfully. I gestured an apology to the driver, who gestured something far ruder back.

"How terribly ill-mannered," I murmured.

"What?" snapped Solus.

I didn't bother to give him an answer. Spotting a small café on the corner of the street, I began heading in that direction. Solus looked at me, annoyed. I gestured towards the café.

"Food."

"Please." Solus rolled his eyes. "I am not eating there."

"Why not?" I protested. A huge fry up would be just the thing to settle my stomach. I bet myself that they did vast urns of coffee as well. If I was going to take on the entire Ministry of Mages, there was no way I was going to do it uncaffeinated.

"Alcazon is round the corner. We shall eat there."

"Alcazon?"

"Yes, it's very cultured. You'll like it."

I'd heard of Alcazon. The girls back at the Cornish pack had often mentioned it in conversation. It was Otherworld friendly – and particularly over-priced and frequented by the elite at the same time.

"Solus, don't you think we should be flying under the radar rather than eating somewhere where people go to be seen?"

"I like the pickled quails' eggs with celery salt," he said simply.

"What? That's not food! I want bacon and eggs and beans and coffee. Lots and lots of coffee."

He stopped for a moment and looked at me. "Do you have any money?"

"Ummm…," I paused. I was pretty sure I'd given everything I had away to Yellow Anorak for the use of his phone.

"Well then. I'm paying, so I get to choose."

"Solus, I'm wearing clothes that reek of bonfires. I've not showered for two days. I've not cleaned my teeth for two days. I'm carrying a backpack with all of my worldly possessions in it and look as if I've slept on the streets for a week. I don't think Alcazon is the kind of place that will like having me as a patron."

"You're with me, you'll be fine."

I took that moment to glance him over. He was wearing some kind of tailored suit with a perfectly crisp white starched shirt. How did he manage that when we'd just been planted for hours in a halfway house to hell? I supposed I should be thankful that his shirt wasn't gigolo transparent this time. But really, while my appearance was the least of my worries, being clean would surely be some kind of vague prerequisite to gaining admittance to one of the swankiest restaurants in town.

"My face has been plastered all over the Pack website for months. If someone spots me…"

"MACKENZIE, people at Alcazon don't care about that. They care about their own celebrity too much to be paying attention to a grubby little girl, whereas I care too much about what I put into my mouth to want to eat anywhere else within a fifty mile radius."

"Solus…"

"Shut up."

I bristled, but kept my mouth closed. I'd save my battles for when it was really important. It would be all Solus' fault though if some Pack hero spotted me and tried to take me down. He'd be sorry if I ended up as some minced up dragon meat on the floor of the swanky restaurant, so he would. I stuck my tongue out at him behind his back. He turned and glared at me and held out his arm. I looked down at it and then back at him.

"What?"

"Mackenzie, if you are not going to look like a lady then at least pretend to act like one."

"Huh?"

"Oh for goodness' sake, take my arm."

Oh. I caught on and hooked my arm round his, beaming at him.

He sighed. "Not like we're maypole dancers, Mack." He unhooked my arm and then placed my hand on his forearm, just so. "Like that. Like you're a lady."

I rolled my eyes. "Seriously?"

Solus glared at me.

"I thought you'd have liked maypole dancers, being a faerie and all, you know."

"Just because I am in your company right now does not mean that I am not usually refined and cultured. We Fae are creatures of renaissance. We are not thugs."

"I am learning an entirely different side to you, Solus."

"And you would do well to remember it, my little dragonlette."

"My name is Mack."

"Whatever."

We rounded the corner and ended up at the base of a gleaming building, all chrome and shiny glass. The morning sun was hitting the edges of it, making it painful to look at directly. My grip on Solus' arm must have tightened somewhat because he shot me another look of irritation. I loosened my hand and smiled at him, batting my eyelashes. He sighed yet again and looked away. Maybe this would be fun after all.

A doorman wearing a bespoke red uniform and a very silly hat bowed as we walked through the door. I had gone no more than three steps inside however when an alarm started to sound. Oh dear god, was this the fashion police coming already? My cheeks started to warm as a security guard came over.

"I'm sorry madam, but it appear that you are carrying some weapons upon your person. You need to check those in at the desk before you proceed."

I stared at him blankly. I didn't have any weapons on me, other than the silver needles in my hair, and they could hardly be counted as real weapons. Not in the human world at least.

"Uh…"

"I believe your hair ornaments, madam?"

Really? I reached up and pulled the needles out and gazed at the guard askance. He smiled without showing his teeth.

"Thank you madam. You may pick them back up again when you leave."

He turned on his well polished heel, holding the needles out in front of them as if he was worried he might catch some terribly contagious disease from them. I looked at Solus with a question in my eyes.

"You'd obviously already heard of this place, dragonlette."

"Yeah, so?"

"Well, its patrons are hardly going to be comfortable coming here if anyone can just walk in with silver or iron or the weapon du jour and take them out with a quick swish. Alcazon prides itself on being a sanctuary, free from inter-species violence. This is why we shall visit the weapon shop after breakfast, not before."

"And here was me thinking it was because you had some regard for my stomach."

Before Solus could retort, we were greeted by the maître'd who clearly recognised my Fae companion and inclined his head before leading us through the restaurant to a quiet corner. He pulled a chair out for me and, after I was seated, proceeded to unfold a crisply starched white napkin onto my lap, all without saying a word. I had to admit that I was impressed at his lack of reaction to my unkempt appearance. Perhaps I would like it here after all.

We were seated towards the back of the restaurant, next to a vast smear free window that briefly reminded me of my efforts at cleaning the shop windows of Clava Books. I contemplated asking the silent maître d' for tips on window cleaning, but decided it would probably be unwise. I have to admit that I did take a surreptitious sniff to see what products I could detect, but Solus sent me such a terrible glower that I backed quickly away. Fortunately, an impeccably dressed waitress deposited a menu in front of me before he had the chance to make further comments about my lack of ladylike qualities.

After ordering a sumptuous sounding plate of eggs benedict with apple wood smoked bacon and grilled asparagus, and lots and lots of coffee, I took a moment to drink in my surroundings. I had never been anywhere as ostentatiously posh as this before. The greasy spoon at the corner it definitely wasn't. I smiled to myself at the thought of my old pack mates seeing me here, and then soberly remembered just why I was here in the first place. To distract myself, I sneaked a few peeks at the other diners, trying to see if I could work out what manner of otherworldly creatures they were. There was a gentleman wearing an old-fashioned suit that looked like it included a jacket with tails, a la Bing Crosby. With old-fashioned dress sense like that, he had to be one of the longer living otherworlders. Vamp, perhaps, although I couldn't sense much power emanating from him. His companion, however, took that moment to lick her lips, displaying a set of scary white fangs. She must have sensed my stare because she looked up in my direction. I hastily switched my gaze to another table before I caused myself any more problems.

"Dragonlette?" purred Solus.

I ignored him, taking a sip of the carefully negotiated room temperature water that sat on the table.

"Mack?"

That I would answer.

"Yes, Solus?"

"If you continue to stare so unabashedly at every patron who comes in here, you do realise that sooner or later you will stare at the wrong person and get yourself into trouble?"

"Well, I wouldn't be staring at anyone if we'd gone to that café, Solus. You're the one who wanted to come here. It's hardly my fault if I am unused to these kinds of surroundings."

"It's fortunate that I am here to solve these little issues," he said softly, looking at me with a stern expression on his face.

"What issues?"

He jerked his head over in the direction of the female vampire who I noticed, to my alarm, was heading in our direction. Oh, shit.

"I didn't...I mean...er...I'll deal with this, Solus." After all, as he'd said earlier, I didn't really need weapons to fight my battles when I had sparky green fire to call upon. I was a dragon!

"Don't you dare," he murmured in warning, standing up to greet the walking undead.

The vampire, who'd looked quite pretty from a distance, was terrifying up close. Although I'd certainly heard plenty about vamps from some of the more well travelled pack members in Cornwall, I'd never had the opportunity to meet one myself. I wanted to ask her how she was going to leave the restaurant when it was daylight outside but figured that might be a bit rude. Her skin was not white, exactly, more a sort of ashen grey colour. The whites of her eyes were more yellow than white and there was the faintest whiff of rotting meat that she'd barely disguised with some sickly sweet perfume. I struggled not to recoil away.

Solus inclined his head. "Good day," he intoned.

She ignored him and fixed her gaze onto me. For my part I remained seated and just looked back at her.

"Is there a problem, little human?" Her voice was icy and filled with the suggestion of threat.

"I don't believe so," I replied as pleasantly as possible, although I could feel my bloodfire awakening in the pit of my belly.

"Then why were you staring at me so rudely?"

I opened my mouth to speak but Solus interrupted. "My dear, my partner is but a novice to this side of the world. You will forgive her rude naivety."

His voice had deepened but I shot daggers at him with my eyes for his words and was about to speak back at him about my so-called 'rude naivety' when I noticed the gold flecks of light dancing across his eyes. I flicked a glance at the vamp and realised that she was staring at him, lips slightly parted.

"Of course," she said in an abruptly breathy voice. "She is forgiven." She widened her eyes ever so slightly and leaned in towards Solus. "If there is anything I can do to help you both, explaining any nuances of our behavior or showing you around town, then please do let me help you."

I noticed that she didn't once look in my direction. The wait staff, who had suddenly been poised for any potential action, had relaxed back into their serving jobs and gone back to pretending to ignore us. For my part, I was fascinated by the look of concentration on Solus' face and the puppy dog look on the vamp's.

He took her hands and murmured, "You should rejoin your partner, he looks lonely."

"Yes, I shall." She held onto his hands for a moment longer than was necessary, and then departed back to her table.

I stared at Solus. "Well I guess these aren't the droids we're looking for."

The pop culture reference went right over his head. "What?"

"You glamoured her. You got her to say and do and act exactly the way you wanted her to." I thought for a moment. "And you tried to do that to me too! When you came into the bookshop that first time." My eyes narrowed at him in disgust. "You wanker!"

The heat that had been slowly building with the vamp was quickly exploding into life. Solus held up his hands. "Okay, okay, Mack. Yes, I tried to glamour you. Is it really so bad?"

"It's brainwashing! I can't believe you would take advantage of me that way. I cannot believe that you thought that would be acceptable!" My voice was rising but I didn't care.

Solus tried to calm me down, which just annoyed me even more. "It didn't work though, did it? You resisted the glamour so you proved that you're mentally strong. It was a pretty large clue, dragonlette, that you were definitely more than you appeared to be."

"But you tried to do it in the first place, Solus." I stood up, flinging my napkin to the floor. I was aware that I was making a scene but I didn't really care. How dare he do that to me? "Do you know what? I don't actually think I need your help after all. How do I know the glamour didn't work? How do I know that you're not glamouring me right now?"

Solus' face suddenly looked alarmed. "Mack, sit down."

"I will not sit down. I'm leaving and you can sit here alone in your posh restaurant eating your posh food while I go kick some ass. And if I see you again, Solus, I swear to God I will…"

"Mackenzie! Sit the fuck down!"

"No! You're not the boss of me!"

"If you don't sit down, Mackenzie Smith, then we are both screwed because between transporting you here and doing that glamour to stop that vampire from snacking on you between courses, I don't have enough energy left to mask your scent."

"Why the fuck would you need to mask my scent? The only time you need to do that is when…" my voice trailed off. Oh. I looked over at the group of people just entering the restaurant and sat down very quickly.

Corrigan had what appeared to be a huge entourage. I counted at least eight different heads and, despite the lurching sensation of fear induced nausea that was flooding my system, wondered if it helped him to feel important to surround himself with many different shifters. Recognising his de facto chief of staff, Staines, I sank further down in my seat and suddenly became re-fascinated by the window.

"I'd like to remind you that this was your bright idea," I hissed at Solus, who was looking vaguely apologetic and also alarmingly entertained. I hoped that his Fae nature for causing mischief wasn't about to suddenly kick in at my expense.

He shrugged an elegant shoulder. "What can I say? To be honest, I didn't think he was in town."

"Some help you are. And what happened to 'I am a Fae therefore I have more power than you can possibly imagine'? That's not much good if you run out of juice before the day has even started."

"Hey, dragonlette, if you hadn't insisted on trying to go head to head with a vampire, then we wouldn't have a problem."

"We wouldn't have a problem? Are you kidding me?" My voice rose to high-pitched whisper. "Were you listening when I said that he would destroy every shifter who I consider to be family if he finds out that I don't have a were?"

"You could try telling him that you don't have a were because you're actually a dragon."

"Yes, because that's working out amazingly well for me so far."

I ripped my eyes away from the window to glare at Solus and then sneaked a peek back over at Corrigan. I had to admit that he was looking good, albeit rather tired, wearing an elegant grey suit that was tight over his muscled arms and snugly fitting in all the right places. His dark hair didn't have a strand out of place and I caught myself wondering if his eyes were really as green as I'd remembered. I tried hard not to stare so that he wouldn't feel my gaze, but couldn't resist checking out the rest of his group to see if he'd brought a love interest. Only because I was curious, that was all, not for any other reason. Lucy was there, along with a few other female shifters, but I didn't see anyone who looked as if they might fit the title of main squeeze. My eyes travelled over them all until I reached one set of blue eyes staring right back at me. My stomach lurched. I gave a weak smile but Tom didn't smile back. He just stared. I hoped that I could still count on him as an ally and that he wouldn't immediately give me to his lord and master.

"One of them has spotted you," said Solus calmly.

"I know."

"He's staring at you."

"I know."

"He knows who you are."

"I know."

"Mack…"

"It's Tom."

"Tom? The one who knows that you are a Draco Wyr? You'd better be right that you can trust him, dragonlette."

"Solus, I swear, if you call me that again I'm going to punch you in the face."

I pulled my eyes away from Tom and looked back at the Fae. He was leaning back in his chair, arms folded and a relaxed smile on his face.

"Don't push me," I warned.

Corrigan and his followers, Tom included, started to move towards a table that was fortunately out of view of our own seats and the waitress came over with two steaming plates of food. Almost as soon as she'd placed the plate in front of me, I started shoveling the food into my mouth. Solus watched me, slightly agape.

"What? I'm hungry. And the faster I eat, the faster I can get out of here and away from him." I jerked my head back to where Corrigan was seated. "And you, of course. Don't think that just because you've been temporarily saved by the presence of the Lord Alpha that I've forgotten what you tried to do to me." I took a large gulp of coffee and swallowed, then gestured toward Solus' plate. "Eat, Fae."

Fortunately for him, he did as I suggested and picked up his knife and fork, taking small delicate bites of his quail eggs. It was just as well that the eggs he'd ordered were so small because if he ate like that all the time, he'd never finish any meals. I continued eating my own breakfast, occasionally punctuating mouthfuls with swallows of hot coffee. The burning caffeine almost helped me forget exactly who was scant feet away from where I was sitting.

Before too long, I was putting my knife and fork down on the table and pushing my plate back. Solus barely seemed to have made a dent in the food on his plate. I stared at him and started drumming my fingers on the table, resisting the urge to crane my neck back around to see what was happening with Corrigan and Tom.

"You know, looking at me like that is more likely to make me feel nervous rather than encourage me to eat up quickly," Solus stated.

I continued to just stare at him. He sighed and picked up his napkin, dabbing delicately at the corner of his mouth and signalling the waitress for the bill.

"Just so you know," I said flatly, "I am not trying to run away and hide from the Lord Alpha. I am just recognising when it is prudent to avoid some confrontations."

"It wouldn't have occurred to me to suggest otherwise," Solus said, signing the bill with a flourish.

"But if he spots me, and spots that I'm not a shifter, then…"

"Then he'll maim and kill all your little shifter friends. Yes, I believe you've mentioned that before."

"I'm not making it up, Solus."

The Fae stood up and looked down at me with a glint in his eye. "Don't think I didn't notice the lascivious look you were giving him, dragonlette."

I spluttered. "Lascivious? As if! And I told you not to call me that."

He just grinned and offered me his arm. I scooted round however to his other side so that if Corrigan did suddenly decide to look up, I would be shielded from his gaze. I was still trying very hard not to start sprinting out of the restaurant.

I was picking up my silver needles from the security guard, with Solus looking impatiently on, when I abruptly felt someone at my shoulder. Without thinking I put my hand onto their arm and twisted, flipping them onto their back with a dull thud. I instinctively knew it wasn't Corrigan – there wasn't much chance that a simple flip would be enough to floor him – but it didn't mean that it wasn't someone else I had to watch out for. The security guard raised his eyebrows but, when I glared at him, he started to pretend to look busy, shuffling bits of paper around. I looked down at my would be assailant and groaned as Solus studiously examined his fingernails.

"Jesus, Tom, you should be more careful!" I reached down and offered him a hand. He ignored it and staggered to his feet.

"What the hell is going on, Red?"

"I might ask you the same thing," I said, cuffing him round the head. "You're looking pretty cosy with the Lord Alpha there."

"He's a good guy, you know," Tom said softly.

"Yeah, up until he rips you from limb to limb for daring to disobey him."

"He's not really like that. And besides, Red, I think I asked you first." He pointed at Solus. "Who is that?"

Solus bowed ostentatiously. "I am Solus. Miss Mackenzie's companion." He put an odd emphasis on the word companion.

"Are you shagging a Fae now, Red?"

I bridled. "First of all, it's none of your business. Second of all, it's none of your business." I paused and looked him in the eye. "So is it everything you wished for?"

"What do you mean?"

"Being part of the Brethren. Are you fulfilled now, Tom?"

"It's not like that. It's not as sleazy as you suggest."

"I wasn't suggesting anything."

Tom ran an irritated hand through his hair. "You know things got pretty messy after you ran off. The Lord Alpha was…upset that you had gone."

"I didn't run off. Anton made me leave."

Solus raised his eyebrows at that comment but stayed silent. I pointedly ignored him.

Tom took a step towards me. "Are you in trouble? Is that why you're in London?"

"No." I shook my head to emphasise the point then glanced back into the restaurant. "I should go."

"Red…"

"I need to go, Tom. I'm sorry, okay? I'm sorry if I messed things up. And I'm glad you're happy now with the Brethren. Corrigan told me you're engaged to Betsy. Congratulations on your new life."

Tom started for a moment. "When did he tell you that? Red…,"

"I have to go," I repeated and turned to walk away. Solus followed me.

"Wait! Red! Mack!"

I stopped for a moment and turned. Tom jogged up and threw

his arms around me, squeezing me to him. I clung on for a moment, breathing his familiar scent.

"If you need anything, Mack, anything at all, just call me." He pulled away and reached into his coat pocket, passing over a small white business card.

I didn't bother looking at it; I just stuffed it into the back pocket of my jeans and smiled sadly at him. "Sure I will, Tom."

He reached out and touched me gently on the arm, then I turned again for the revolving door with Solus by my side and left.

"I've got to say," murmured Solus once we were out on the pavement, "the Brethren's recruitment policy seems to have become rather lax in the last year."

"Fuck off, Solus."

"I mean, really, I get that he's a wolf but…"

"Solus, I swear to God…" I turned and faced the Fae, tears threatening to spill over. "Don't say another word."

For once, he seemed to understand, and cocked his head slightly for a moment at me, before offering me his arm again. "Okay," he said softly. "Let's go get us some weapons."

CHAPTER SIXTEEN

THE STREETS WERE CONSIDERABLY BUSIER NOW THAN THEY HAD been earlier but Solus moved along at a fast gait, weaving in and out of pedestrians. I struggled to keep up with his long legged lope and spent the first five minutes biting down hard on my lip to compose myself. We veered right at the first intersection onto a much quieter road that looked as if it was entirely residential. Leafy trees lined the edges of the pavement and, despite the claustrophobia I felt at being locked inside a city, I had to admit that it was rather pretty. Solus began to move even faster, with my hand still clutching his arm, and I had to almost start jogging to keep up. Therefore it wasn't my fault when I missed the uneven paving stone and tripped right over, heading face first down to the ground before he caught me. He grimaced at me in annoyed exasperation and yanked me back upright. Not trusting my voice to be quaver free just yet, I simply shrugged and carried on. At least Solus slowed down a bit after that though.

Eventually he turned right again, into a dark little alleyway that I would have missed if I'd been on my own. Of course, it was a dark alleyway, I figured to myself. 'Stereotypes are us' when it comes to the Otherworld. I dodged a few garbage bins lying out on the street until Solus pointed up some uneven stone steps to a door set back into a grimy grey building. At some point the door had been painted a shiny red colour, but now the paint was peeling off and cracking. Solus reached up to the old-fashioned knocker and rapped it a few times.

We waited for what seemed like an age. I opened my mouth to say something but Solus shushed me before I could begin. Annoyed at being treated like a schoolchild, I folded my arms and looked away. Eventually the door opened. At first, I didn't think anyone was actually there, then I registered movement below my eye line. Standing in the threshold was a short stumpy character with extraordinarily large ears and small dark beady eyes. A troll. I quickly looked at Solus but he seemed unperturbed.

"We need to procure some weapons," he said solemnly.

"Certainly, my lord. If you'll follow me." The troll opened the door wider and motioned for us to enter.

My eyes narrowed at the Fae as I followed him inside. My lord? I frowned at Solus' back and hoped that the shopkeeper was just being polite.

We were led through a dark passageway to a room at the back. There was a rickety old wooden table and two dirty plastic chairs that might once have been white. I sat myself down on one and crossed my legs, trying to appear relaxed and as if I regularly went shopping for deadly weapons in dodgy back street stores run by trolls. I hoped there weren't any bridges nearby.

Solus murmured something to the shopkeeper who went scurrying off.

As soon as he left, I opened my mouth to speak. "A troll? You've taken me to a shop run by a troll?"

"What's your point, dragonlette?"

"They can't be trusted! John always said…"

Solus put his finger to my mouth, again telling me to be quiet. "Are there any other nearby Otherworld weapons shops you'd rather visit? Perhaps we could go back to Alcazon and ask the Lord Alpha for a recommendation." I scowled at him. Solus continued. "And stop your prattling and complaining. Trolls have excellent hearing. Offend this one and you are out of options."

I sighed deeply to illustrate my mistrust but kept my mouth shut. I tried to remind myself that I should be grateful to the Fae for all his help; after all, he'd only promised to keep Mrs Alcoon safe in return for knowing my secret about being a Draco Wyr. He had no reason to continue helping me out. Before I could wonder too hard about the real reasons for Solus' charity, the little troll came bustling back in holding a tray. He set it down on top of the table, glaring malevolently at me as he did so. Okay, I guess he had heard my comments about trolls then.

Solus looked over at me and raised his eyebrows. Shrugging, I reached over to the tray. There were several different dirks and daggers. I picked one up and was immediately impressed at its balance and weight. I offered it over to Solus who recoiled from me.

"Mackenzie…" His voice was strained. I looked back down at the dagger and realised that it was made of iron. Oops.

"Sorry," I murmured, placing it gently back onto the tray.

I reminded myself that I was going to see some mages. Whether my weapons were made of iron or steel or something else wouldn't really make a whole lot of difference. The memory of seeing Corrigan and his cronies in the restaurant was still very fresh in my mind, however, so I picked up the nearest silver dirk instead and rolled it around in my hands. It felt good. There was a matching one so I grabbed hold of that also and stood up, feeling the weight of both in my hands. I tried a few thrusts into the air, being careful to avoid aiming anywhere near the shopkeeper who was leaning against the wall and watching me with narrowed eyes. I touched the edge of one of them with my fingertip and was pleased to note a bead of blood appear on my skin. Remembering what trouble I'd invited the last time I'd let my blood fall, I sucked it away and nodded to Solus who was watching the proceedings impassively. He nodded to the troll.

I cleared my throat. "I'll…uh…need sheaths as well, if you have them."

The troll blinked in acknowledgement and scurried away, tray in hand. He returned a few moments later with some leather straps. I selected two at random and began to try to attach them to my forearms, fumbling with the straps. Solus watched me for a moment then hissed in irritation, reached over and did them up for me, slotting the dirks into place at the same time. I murmured my thanks and practised sheathing and unsheathing the dirks a few times. They were different to what I was used to, but they would work. I rolled down my sleeves to cover them and looked over at Solus who permitted himself a small smile and nodded again to the troll. Then we left.

Once we were back outside I sucked in fresh air. It was a relief to be away from the shop, even if the air was heavy with city smells instead of the country atmosphere I was used to.

I waited until we were back on the main thoroughfare before I spoke. "Solus, you didn't pay the troll."

"Mmm," he answered noncommittally.

"And he called you 'my lord'."

"Mmm."

"Solus, is there something I should know?"

He paused for a moment and looked at me, then continued walking. "No, dragonlette, there isn't."

"I will pay you back when I get some money."

He laughed sharply. "At the rate you're going, if you live long enough to make even a fraction of the money those knives cost, I'll be impressed."

"I do appreciate your help, you know. You don't have to be this nice."

"I don't want to be responsible for a sleeping pensioner for the rest of eternity, Mack. I'm a Fae, remember? This is entirely self-serving."

I didn't believe that anymore, not really, but I chose not to challenge him. "Thank you, Solus," I said quietly.

He remained silent for a few heartbeats and then answered back gruffly. "You're welcome, dragonlette. Just don't do anything to get yourself killed before all this is resolved."

I punched him in the arm and he drew back with a pained hiss. "What the fuck was that for?"

"My name is Mack."

He snorted with laughter. "Yeah, okay."

We walked for several minutes in a companionable silence. I'd never really spent any time in a big city like London before, at least not that I could remember anyway, and I was struck by how much more space and greenery there was than I'd expected. Yes, the air wasn't as fresh as in Inverness or Cornwall, but considering the millions of people crammed into the area, neither was it as chokingly bad as I'd imagined. It didn't mean that I would be in a rush to move here, mind, but I could cope with it. There were people of every shape and every colour and, I had to admit, the diversity was refreshing. There were also more 'people' associated with the Otherworld than I'd expected. At one point, my attention taken by a colourful hoarding proclaiming that 'There is no God so get on with your life and enjoy it', I banged straight into a cloaked woman from whom I got such a buzz of power that I almost leapt right off the pavement. She growled at me in a language that I vaguely registered as some kind of Old French before heading back off in the opposite direction. Solus wisely managed to keep his tongue to himself but I could sense him trying very hard not to pass comment.

He finally stopped at the side of a road that was decorated with some very fancy graffiti. I was admiring the artwork, and wondering just how much skill was needed to produce such intricate designs, when he pointed out the cleverly hidden runes behind the various tags. I suddenly felt a bit queasy. Up until this point, since leaving the troll's shop anyway at least, I'd allowed myself to be distracted by the sights and sounds of the big city. Now it was clear that my real business was about to begin.

"I can't go any further, Mack."

I appreciated that he'd bothered to use my real name. I nodded.

He pointed down the street ahead of us. "You need to walk about half a mile down that way. The Ministry will be on your left. It's a big ugly grey building with a sign outside saying Charters College."

"I understand. And," I hesitated for a moment, "I really do want to thank you for all you've done. If I don't make it back, will you look after Mrs Alcoon for me? I know it's a lot to ask, but she's really a lovely person. Maybe some of your faerie friends will be able to sort her out, you know? Bring her out of stasis?"

"I'll do whatever I can. It's good you're not hiding any more but I need you to promise me that you'll be careful."

"Sure," I said, winking at him. "Those big scary witches and wizards won't know what's hit them though."

He took both my hands. "I mean it, Mackenzie. Their wards are too strong. If you get into trouble once you're inside the Ministry, I can't help you out. And I've grown to like you. Well, tolerate you, anyway."

"Gee, you certainly know how to make a girl feel good about herself, don't ya?"

"Promise me."

I was a bit taken aback by the serious tone in his voice. "I promise, Solus."

He leaned forward until our foreheads were touching and closed his eyes, then turned round and walked back the way we'd come, not looking back. I watched him disappear into the crowds.

"Well, that was weird," I muttered to myself.

I ran my tongue around the inside of my mouth, realising that I hadn't managed to get hold of a toothbrush and toothpaste before he'd left. I didn't have any money to buy them either. Using the corner of my sleeve, I rubbed my teeth, but it did little good. At least I could try breathing on the mages and knocking them out that way, I figured, giving up and continuing forward. I shifted my backpack on my shoulders as I walked, double-checking the shiny new silver daggers strapped to my forearms at the same time. I took in a big gulp of air and pictured Mrs Alcoon lying motionless in her chair in the now burnt out shell of Clava Books. No matter what happened, I was going to make sure that they freed her. I was not going to have yet another body on my conscience.

Barely five minutes later, I was standing in front of the Ministry. The sign reading Charter College that hid the Ministry in plain sight was dull and unassuming. The building itself, while imposing, would hardly encourage visitors to drop by. There was an iron fence circling the property, which didn't look particularly difficult to scale. That was probably to avoid appearing too challenging to any local youths looking for a dare I guessed though. I had no doubt that if I went straight up and climbed over it there would be all sorts of magical alarms suddenly being set off. I decided also that I couldn't very well just stroll up to the front door and knock. They'd probably fry me first and ask questions later. I'd have to get myself inside and find someone important to speak to. A pre-emptive strike. I could always phone Alex again and ask him for tips but his involvement would probably only complicate matters. Keep it simple stupid, I told myself.

Looking around, I noted an old abandoned house in a row of terraced properties behind me. It offered a clear and unhampered view of the 'College'. I decided that my best possible move would be to keep the place under surveillance for a time so I could work out how best to enter. Very Cagney and Lacey. I frowned for a moment, realising that there was only one of me now that Solus had vamoosed back into whichever Faerie plane he'd come from. Cagney and Lacey wouldn't work. Inspector Morse? No, he had Lewis by his side. Horatio Caine? Nope, no hard-working CSI team to back me up. Ummm, I thought hard. Every sodding police detective I could think of had at least one side-kick with them. Eventually I shrugged and gave up. I was a lone wolf. Or at least a lone dragon anyway. We liked to work alone. Others would merely cramp our style. Or steal our treasure. I nodded to myself sagely and wandered round to the back of the house, yanking off some of the nailed on wooden boards that were barring the downstairs window.

I hopped up and crawled through the space I'd made, snagging my t-shirt and ripping it slightly. I swore out loud and pulled myself through. The interior of the house was better kept than I'd expected. There was no furniture and everything was covered in a layer of thick dust, but the place appeared untouched by squatters or druggies looking for their own holes to crawl into. Satisfied, I strode through to the front and peered out through a crack. I had a perfect view of the Ministry's front door.

"Phase 1 complete," I said aloud, my voice echoing in the quiet house. I was prepared to stake out the mages.

CHAPTER SEVENTEEN

HALF AN HOUR LATER I WAS DESPERATELY WISHING THAT I WERE somewhere else. The lack of any furniture in the house meant that I was unable to sit down, and yet the positioning of the window meant that I had to stoop to see through it. I tried kneeling but I was too short then to peer through the crack. The upshot was that my lower back was now absolutely killing me and I wasn't convinced that I'd in fact ever be able to stand up straight again. I rubbed my spine with both hands but it was a pointless effort. I sighed deeply and wiped my hand across my forehead. It might be winter but the little house was entirely airless and I was starting to sweat profusely. Stakeouts looked a lot more fun on television.

I reached down and touched my toes, attempting to stretch out my back. When I moved back up and looked through the crack again, absolutely nothing had changed. No-one had come in and no-one had come out. I straightened up for a few moments, wincing at the creaking pain. Fucking hell. I walked around the room a few times and then resumed my stance at the window. There had to be an easier way to do this. I stared out at the railings surrounding the Ministry. Maybe they weren't warded at all. I could just climb over them and drop into the garden, then…get zapped.

I took a deep breath. I could do this.

Why are you in London?

I shrieked aloud at the sudden mental intrusion, jerking my head upwards and banging it off one of the wooden boards barring the window frame that was jutting out ever so slightly.

"Goddamnit!" I swore aloud.

Kitten? I know you can hear me.

Perhaps if I just stayed very, very silent he'd think I wasn't really there. If I ever saw Tom again, he and I would be having some serious words together.

Don't be upset at your little wolf friend. He had a bruise on his neck. I compelled him to tell me who had given it to him.

Don't respond, Mack, I said to myself. Just don't say or think anything.

I'm disappointed that you didn't come over and say hello. Or introduce me to your new… friend.

I snapped. *Really, my Lord? Are you really going to continue to imply that I spend all my spare time shagging every male I can get my hands on?*

Hello kitten.

His Voice that time was virtually a purr.

Get lost, Corrigan.

You don't need to stay out there in the cold, you know. Tell me where you are and I can help you out. It's not too late to still be one of us.

The metal gates that formed part of the fence to the Ministry were starting to open. They must be remote controlled. I concentrated my attention on them.

You should stop this stalker like behaviour. It's most unbecoming for the Lord Alpha. Surely you've got better things to do.

There. I could be calm and reasonable. A garage door that I'd not noticed before because it was camouflaged by some trees began to wrench upwards.

I concern myself with every member of the Pack.

Well, I'm not part of the Pack, my Lord. Get over it.

Mackenzie, it's not safe here. You need to...

Corrigan's Voice was cut off abruptly. Whatever. And he was damn right it wasn't safe here, but if he thought that I was going to slink off with my proverbial tail between my legs then he had something else coming.

A shiny black Mercedes van bounced out of the garage and headed towards the now fully open gates. My heart was thudding. I told myself that I was just excited because there was finally some action. At the Ministry, not with Corrigan. Nooooo, definitely not with Corrigan.

The van's windows were darkened so I couldn't actually see who or what was inside. It didn't matter though. Now I knew that part of the Ministry's security relied on technology – and technology often failed. They might have magic on their side but I was fairly certain that if I could cut the power to their security system, they'd go into panic mode for long enough to allow me to slip in. If they relied on remote control to operate their doors and gates, then they weren't relying on magic to stop people from entering. Sure, I'd trip the wards and set off their warning systems, but they'd work out I was there soon enough anyway. All I actually needed to was to get inside and find someone powerful enough to plead my case to before I got caught. And now at least I had an idea about how to get inside.

I sank back on my heels and allowed myself a moment to wonder about Corrigan. I didn't know why he felt the need to keep on bothering me. Surely it couldn't be because he was that troubled about one little rogue? He'd certainly never given a damn about any of the shifters in Cornwall before John had died so what was different now?

I tightened my ponytail and forced him out of my thoughts. I couldn't make him a concern of mine, not right now with everything else going on. If I managed to sort out the mages and get them to release Mrs Alcoon then maybe I'd try to talk to him and get him to leave me alone. If he was going to keep chasing, then maybe I really couldn't keep hiding, as Solus so charmingly put it. But right now I had other things to worry about.

I glanced around the room and looked for the least dusty spot. I couldn't move any further now until it was dark, so I may as well make the most of my time and sleep. Scuffing away some of dustballs from one corner, I lay down and curled up in a ball, closing my eyes. Initially my thoughts kept tripping over one another, ticking away till I felt more awake than I really would have thought possible. Remembering an old breathing trick that John had taught me back when he was first training me in martial arts, however, I managed to calm myself down and empty my mind. Eventually I drifted asleep.

When I awoke, I was briefly disorientated and unsure where I was. It was so dark that for a moment I thought I was back in the halfway plane after entering the Clava Cairns portal. Then I remembered that I was in the middle of London and about to storm the Ministry of Mages to save a little old lady from being stuck in a coma for the rest of her life. I stood up slowly, still feeling a nagging ache in the small of my back from my minor attempt at a stake out earlier on in the day. I stretched out, pushing first against the wall and lengthening out my hamstrings, then performing a few yoga poses on the floor.

I dusted off my clothes, then sniffed them unhappily. There was still the remaining odour of eau de bonfire, whether from the Winter Solstice campfires or the blaze at Clava Books, I wasn't completely sure. Now there was the added reek of stale dust. I cupped my hand round my mouth and breathed into it and then tried to sniff my breath. Nope, that wasn't very pleasant either. Oh well, there was little I could do about either right now.

I headed to the back of the house and eyed the window I'd clambered through earlier. Somehow the gap seemed smaller than it had previously. I pushed my head through the hole and wiggled myself out, managing to catch myself on exactly the same nail that I had on the way in. This time, instead of just ripping my clothes though, it scratched its way across my skin. I tried to remember if I'd had a tetanus booster recently. In fact I tried to remember if I'd ever had a tetanus shot in the past. Lockjaw wasn't a disease that shifters had ever tended to worry about. Perhaps I'd go see a doctor if I ever got myself out of the Ministry alive.

I made my way through the garden of the abandoned house. It wasn't quite so dark outside; in fact despite the lateness of the hour it actually seemed quite light. One of the drawbacks of living in the city, I decided. I hopped over the wooden fence and wandered back to the front of the house – and the front of the so-called Charters College.

I crossed the road and began searching. I was trying to appear nonchalant, as if I was just out for a stroll, should any mage suddenly decide to look out of the window. There were several lights on, on several different floors. I attempted to take a snapshot in my head of them all so that when – if – I got inside, I'd be able to find my way around, avoiding any unnecessary encounters. I pictured the potential room layout in my head, committing it to memory. Of course I had no way of knowing what the rooms that weren't south facing were like, but I had to do what I could. I trailed my fingers along the iron railings, walking slowly in the direction of the gates when I finally saw what I was looking for. In a corner, where the railings stopped and the low brick wall started, was a small black box. It was on the opposite side to the railings, so in theory any potential intruder wouldn't be able to reach it without first climbing over the railings and tripping the very alarm they were trying to stop. But of course most intruders didn't have groovy green fire that they could shoot from their fingers.

I took a quick look around to make sure the street was quiet. There were a few lights on in the houses on the terraced row where the abandoned house was, but their curtains were closed and there was no-one out in the street. I briefly closed my eyes and pointed my left hand towards the box, concentrating. I felt, rather than saw, the flame reaching out. There was a crackle and a hiss. Opening my eyes, I noted the small plume of smoke rising from the box and held my breath, waiting for the alarm to be sounded. The street remained quiet. No new lights appeared in the windows of the mansion and slowly, inexorably, the huge metal gates began to open. I realised that I'd been holding my breath and exhaled slowly.

As soon as the gates had opened enough, I darted inside and hugged the exterior of the Ministry's grounds, holding myself against the railings and the wall and running towards the cluster of trees behind which the garages lay. I knew that if there were any warning wards to be tripped, I'd already have set them off by setting foot inside the grounds, so I had to make sure that I got into the building quickly, before anyone could stop me.

Picking up speed but staying in the dark shadows, I pelted my way forward. There were actually six different garage doors, none of which had been completely visible from the street. I frowned for a moment, but I didn't have time for eeny meeny miny mo, so I just aimed for the nearest one. I tried tugging at the handle first, but it wouldn't budge so I felt around the edges instead. The electricity box controlling the garage doors would be inside, but the wires weren't. As soon as I found one with my fingers, I shot another blast of flame towards it, incinerating the rubber and the wiring within, and short-circuiting the system. Or so I hoped anyway.

The smell of burnt rubber began to fill the air and it seemed as if, for a moment, nothing was going to happen. Then, with a great trundling creak, the garage door started to jerk upright and open. I flattened myself against the wall, just in case there was anyone waiting right inside. Other than the sounds of the door, I could make out little else, however. I craned my neck around, and could see the shapes of a few cars shrouded in the darkness, but little else. Holding my breath again, I ran inside.

I moved stealthily towards the back of the garage and where I presumed the door to the main house would be. There were a few stone steps up to my left and then a simple looking wooden door with a stainless steel handle. I jogged up the steps and turned the handle, praying to whatever gods might be out there that it would turn.

My luck was in. It was just possible that the mages were so secure in their own omnipotence that it didn't occur to them that anyone would actually try to break into their own fortress. Regardless, when I opened the door and light flooded the garage from the carpeted hallway within, I knew that I'd made it inside.

I gingerly stepped out onto the plush carpet. Clearly the mages spared no expense on their interior. This was definitely not like the threadbare floor covering I was used to from the keep. My feet actually sank down into this carpet. I was in more danger of lying down and rolling around to luxuriate in it than trip on an old hole and embarrass myself. At least it would help me stay quiet, if nothing else. Keeping in mind that I would only have a limited amount of time before I'd get caught by whatever defence systems the mages had in place, I quickly tried to get my bearings. I knew that I was on the ground floor. It made sense that this would be where I'd find the kitchens, dining room, assuming there was one, and the offices.

I would need to get myself to the office of someone high up in the Ministerial hierarchy if I had any chance of pleading my case. Logically, anyone who fit that description would have an office positioned in the most desirable position. That would mean on a corner, probably far away from the kitchens and the garages, and looking out onto the front gardens. There had been several lights dotted around at this end of the Ministry but only a few towards the other end, opposite side to where I'd entered. It stood to reason that it was at that other end where I'd find the kind of person I needed to talk to.

Treading lightly, I jogged along the soft carpet and down the hallway. I passed several doors, all carved out of some ornate tropical wood, and all shut. I didn't waste time opening them to peer inside, however, and instead headed straight. There was a wall at the far end with corridors peeling off both right and left.

A painting of some stern looking gentleman with grey hair and a pinched nose gazed down at me. I raised my eyebrows up at him, almost hoping that it was some kind of magical painting that would suddenly come to life and direct me to some magical senior manager. I must have read too many children's stories in my past, however, because the paint stayed motionless. Feeling somewhat disappointed, I elected to turn left. The right hand side would keep close to the front of the house where I'd surely want to be, but it was also where there had definitely been lights indicating signs of life. I reckoned that I'd be able to flip right again at some point once I'd passed the danger zones.

Rolling up my jacket sleeves, I unsheathed my daggers, clutching one in each hand. My palms were sweaty and I could feel the adrenalin coursing through my system. I allowed the bloodfire to take over, feeling the welcome surge of heat swirl around my innards.

There were more old paintings dotting the walls of this corridor, mainly portraits of what I assumed to be mages from the past. In another life I'd have paused to admire the workmanship and wonder about the subjects, but this was not the time to let my attention drift. From inside another room I heard a clatter of dishes and froze for a brief moment, waiting to see if someone would emerge into the corridor with me. Everything stayed quiet, however, so I continued on my way. I was surprised that there had been no sign that the mages knew an intruder on their premises. I hoped I wasn't walking into a trap. The thing was, I had very little choice in the matter. I couldn't leave Mrs Alcoon to rot away in Tir-na-Nog and I didn't know anyone other than the mages who'd put her in that position in the first place who could de-spell her, so to speak. If it was a trap then they would at least know why I was here. I reckoned that my daggers could be persuasive enough to make them remove the stasis spell from her before they took me down.

Up ahead, where the corridor stretched out into the distance, a door abruptly opened. Panicking, I scooted backwards and threw open one of the wooden doors I'd already passed, from under which a dark shadow had indicated the absence of light or indeed anyone within, and flung my whole body inside. I carefully pushed the door behind me, trying to be quiet, but left it ajar just a crack so I could see who emerged and what they were doing. Muffled voices drew closer.

"He has to listen to me, Argo, this girl is dangerous."

I frowned. That voice was suddenly dreadfully familiar.

"I think given that she managed to neutralise both Martha and Miles is an indication of that," the other mage stated in a much more measured tone of voice.

"When I gave her the necklace, her body glowed. And it glowed green! She's some kind of Otherworld creature that needs to be taken out."

My hand went involuntarily up to the necklace that remained hanging around my neck. So Maggie, Mrs Alcoon's so-called friend, had decided to travel to the heart of the Ministry to make sure they were completely aware of how dangerous I was. I almost harrumphed out loud. I would think that the fact that I'd almost killed two of their own would be indication enough of that. My eyes narrowed as she passed by the door with her companion. I was very tempted to take her down – and in fact my bloodfire was roaring in approval at that idea. If she hadn't involved the Ministry in the first place, then Mrs Alcoon wouldn't be in the mess she was in right now.

Maggie's voice continued away from me. "She's probably killed June by now! You need to do something about this."

"Your friend is still alive. We can't work out where she is but the spell is still holding."

"She's not the one who needs the stasis spell, you idiot! It's that bloody girl you should have targeted."

Her voice, high-pitched now and whiny, continuing to bemoan the state of affairs that she'd caused in the first place, drifted further away. I rested my head briefly against the cool wood of the doorframe. Either she was a very good actor or she didn't know that I was here. It was good to know that I wasn't heading straight into a dastardly mage trap. I thought for a moment about what she'd said. The 'he' whom she'd been demanding pay attention to her was probably the very person I needed to speak to. I chewed on my bottom lip and concentrated on damping down the flames inside me somewhat. Whoever this person was, odds were good that he was present in the building. That was some good news at least.

When I was sure that Maggie May and her mage mate had left my immediate vicinity, I gently pulled open the door again and continued pushing forward down the corridor. Occasionally voices drifted in and out from other rooms, but the hallway stayed wizard-free. Before too long, there was another turn, this time twisting back to the right. I took a deep breath. By my calculations, I had to now be towards the end of the large mansion. This was where I was putting all my hopes into there being someone with some say into how things around here were run.

I followed the hallway round and stopped at the corner, peering round. In front of me was a large vestibule area. It looked like something Donald Trump might have commissioned, all shiny marble floors and gleaming sparkly chandeliers. At the far end there were two doors, one on the left and one on the right. The right hand door, the one that would face out onto the ideal garden view, had a uniformed guard outside it. Bingo.

I spun the handles of the daggers that I was still grasping, re-testing their grip and weight for the hundredth time. I didn't want to hurt anyone but, in order to help Mrs Alcoon, I would if I needed to. I straightened my shoulders and stepped out onto the marbled floor, at which point a shrieking alarm suddenly sounded. I guess their security system had finally decided to start working.

Sprinting forward to the guard who was only just halfway out of his chair, I threw my first dagger, catching him in the hand. He howled in pain and then yanked it out, eyes fixing on me. I noted with a tiny tremor that his eyeballs were completely white. The effect of no irises and no pupils was more than terrifying. From behind me, the distant sounds of doors slamming and voices shouting rose up. I had only a few moments to do this.

Dripping blood from one hand, the guard pointed his other hand at me. I just had time to roll out of the way and avoid being zapped by a stream of icy blue light. Clearly these mages were remarkably unimaginative when it came to fighting techniques because they all did exactly the same thing. I watched his body, registering the faint tensing of his muscles that indicated which way he'd go next, and ducked, then barreled straight towards him, knocking his whole body back into the chair. I snapped out a sharp kick into his stomach, causing him to double over, and then jumped behind him, thumping him hard on his bent head. He collapsed to the floor and lay there unmoving. He wasn't a shifter and wouldn't heal with as much ease as they would, so I hadn't wanted to entirely incapacitate him as I would one of them. Under the circumstances, I was rather proud of my restraint.

Scooping up the fallen dagger, I threw my shoulder against the door forcing it open. I had to reach whoever was inside before any irate mages arrived to join the fray. Inside was a large room surrounded by shelves of books and carpeted with a fine Persian rug. There was a desk towards the large bay window that was scattered with some papers and more books. What really caught my attention, however, was the floating man hovering in the centre of the room. His eyes were closed and he was murmuring something. Little lights flickered around him, and I realised that each one was forming a rune in the air. I had to do something fast. I sheathed one dagger and held onto the other, and then started to flick green flame towards each of the runes. I had absolutely no idea if it would do anything but I was rewarded with a spit and hiss as each time my fire hit a rune, it disappeared with an angry spark. More and more runes were appearing and the centre mage was murmuring faster. I shot out more and more light. Hefting the dagger in my right hand, I considered throwing it, but hurting the one person who I needed to really help me probably wouldn't aid my cause.

Hearing the clatter of shoes on the marble floor out in the vestibule, I spun round and sprayed fire across the entrance of the office, creating a curtain of flame and effectively blocking it from anyone entering. Faces started to appear, shouting into the room, but I ignored them and focused my attention back onto the hovering mage instead. His voice was getting louder and the air in the room was starting to feel heavy and suffocating.

The air runes were increasing in number and getting brighter. Several started to spin on their axis, getting faster and faster. I fought back, throwing out flames at every one I could see. Each time I did so, another took its place. Out of the corner of my eye I could see the hovering mage's face getting redder and redder. I kept on firing, trying desperately to hit each one but avoid setting the mage himself alight.

I shouted out, "I just want to talk to you! Please stop this and let's sit down together and discuss..."

My voice trailed away as the mage himself started to spin in the air. I felt pressure building in my head. I fought to call up my bloodfire, to make it even stronger and even greater. It couldn't fail me now, not at this point. I waved my dagger in the air and shouted again, "Please!"

A bass sound started to thump in my ears and I could feel myself falling to my knees. It wasn't going to work, he wasn't going to listen to me. I pulled my hand away from directing fire at the runes and instead focused on the mage. Just one shot wouldn't really hurt him, but it might stop him in his tracks, if I concentrated and didn't overshoot. I flung my hand forward to direct the flame, but nothing happened. I tried again, flicking my fingers forward, willing the fire to appear but there was nothing there. It was as if I'd run completely out of gas. I was starting to choke and bright little dots were dancing across my eyes. I shut them tight and summoned up all the energy I had, trying to muster it into one ball of power and push it through my body.

The thumping in my head was getting worse. I could feel my whole body starting to shake with each thud. I pushed open my eyelids only to see one of the runes floating right in front of my face. My eyes widened, mesmerised by its spinning shapes. Then, suddenly, it exploded and everything went dark.

CHAPTER EIGHTEEN

When I came to, I was lying prone on a cool hard surface. I struggled to get up but found that I could barely move my limbs. I cracked open my eyes. The hovering mage from before stood in front of me, although now his feet were planted firmly on the ground. I tried to reach round to my arms to pull out my daggers, but even with my weakened fumbles I realised that it was pointless and they had already been taken.

The mage bent down and cocked his head at me. "Do you have any idea how long it has been since someone dared to enter our citadel?"

I coughed and replied weakly, "This is a nice house for sure, and definitely bigger than anywhere else I've been to, but isn't citadel taking things a little far?"

"Who are you?" His eyes were cold, sending imaginary bolts of ice through my veins.

I tried to summon my bloodfire back into action, but the mage just laughed humourlessly.

"Take a look around you. We've locked you in a nullifying cage. No magic you try to use against us will work. No magic you try to use for anything, in fact, will work. Now tell me, who are you?"

I looked around. He was right. There was some kind of dull metal encasing me inside a small space. I reached out and touched the bars, receiving a nasty electric shock in return. It occurred to me that I didn't even have enough space to stand up in. Well, this was going to be fun.

He spoke again. "I am growing tired of this and will say it one more time – who are you?"

"I think the more pertinent question would be why am I here," I said, licking my lips to try to draw in some moisture.

"You are here because I put you in here," the mage said disdainfully.

"No, I mean, why did I bother to storm your citadel? I knew I'd get caught. I knew that someone would stop me. But I still came."

The mage got closer until his nose was almost touching the cage. "I would assume you are looking for some ridiculous revenge for the fact that we came after you in Scotland."

I laughed. Well, I almost laughed anyway, it came out as more of a creaking wheeze than a girlish giggle. "Revenge? Really? If I was after revenge then I'd do more than this. I wanted – no, make that WANT – to talk to you."

He rocked back on his heels and folded his arms. "So talk."

I opened my mouth to speak when a door behind the wizard opened and a figure entered. I realised that it was the guard who I'd put out earlier. He shot me a look of simmering hatred, which managed to extinguish the flicker of guilt that I was feeling. Hey, he was walking, wasn't he? I noticed that his hand where I'd embedded my silver dagger earlier in was all bandaged up.

"Hey," I called out, "How are you feeling there, skipper?"

I immediately regretted that remark when the lead mage casually flicked out a stream of light that shot into the cage and pierced my body causing ripples of agonising pain. I moaned aloud, my fists clenching and fingernails curling into my skin at the searing agony. Clearly the cage didn't nullify magic that was entering it from outside. Note to self: don't piss off the people who are holding you captive and can do whatever they want to you. I reminded myself that what I needed was for them to pay attention to me so I could get them to release Mrs Alcoon.

The guard turned to the mage. "You have a visitor, sir."

"Not now," he said, dismissing the guard with an irritated wave.

"It's the Lord Alpha, sir."

My body froze. What the fuck was Corrigan doing here? Damnit that guy was like a bad smell. The mage's eyes narrowed infinitesimally.

"Fine," he snapped, "I'm on my way. Watch her," he instructed the guard, who smiled immediately with malicious glee. Oh, excellent.

The mage turned round and glided towards the door, not giving me another look. Shit, looking at the guard he was leaving me with, I might not get another shot at this.

"Wait!" I called out weakly. "There's an old woman. In Scotland. Well, she was in Scotland, anyway. Now she's... somewhere else. You put her in a coma. She didn't do anything, you need to release..."

The mage left, slamming the door shut behind him.

The guard looked down at me and smiled again. "Oh, we're going to have some fun, girlie."

I sighed deeply. "Please don't call me that."

"I don't think you're in a position to be asking for anything now, are you?"

He sent out a stream of blue that hit me in the cheek. I yowled in agony and tried to turn away.

"Now tell me," he said, sending out another shooting beam of pain, "what kind of weird bitch has green magic?"

I didn't answer. He flicked his fingers and hit me in the same spot, just below my eye. Involuntary tears sprang to my eyes, and started rolling slowly down my cheek. They just made my cheekbone sting even more.

"Answer me!" he demanded, raising his hand up again to show just what I could expect if I remained silent.

I gave in momentarily. "I don't know, it was one of your lot that caused it. What's the big deal anyway? So it's green, so what?"

He flicked his fingers again but this time thankfully up towards the ceiling. "What are you, colour blind? That's blue. My friends are all blue. The Arch-Mage who you thought you could attack, is blue. You, bitch, are green."

Huh. I'd achieved even higher than I'd expected. The Arch-Mage was about as senior a wizard as you could possibly get. At least I'd achieved some modicum of success then by targeting the most in-charge person I possibly could have. It hadn't even occurred to me that I might get far enough within the Ministry to manage that. I permitted myself a small smile.

The guard growled and sent yet another arrow of blue flame towards me. But this time I'd had an idea. Instead of twisting my head away, I met it face on, allowing the shot to take me in the cheekbone in exactly the same spot where the prick of a guard had hit me before. The pain was white hot, and it felt as if it was eating away at my actual bone. A wave of dizziness overcame me. Once I'd recovered some of my equilibrium, however, I raised my hand to my cheek. As I'd hoped it came away wet. I reached forward and smeared my blood across the edge of the cage, doing my best to ignore the painful electrical shocks.

I wasn't entirely sure if this would work, but if I could use my blood to break through a faerie ring, then it had to be worth a try. The guard watched me.

"Jesus, you're pathetic. Are you trying to knock yourself out?"

I pulled myself up to a crouch and leaned back on my hands to rest my body weight against them. Taking a few deep breaths and feeling just the smallest satisfying flicker of bloodfire deep inside me, I lashed out at the cage with my feet, striking the exact points that I'd smeared with my blood. It worked. The metal fell away as whatever magic that had been holding it in place was dissolved by my blood. The guard's eyes widened dramatically. He started pelting me with streams of blue light, over and over. I bit my tongue, feeling even more blood fill my mouth with its hot iron rich taste. Drawing up from the well of fire inside me, I threw out green flame towards him. It met his blue light, forcing it backwards and causing ripples of sparks to shoot out in every direction.

"Fucking bitch!" the guard hissed, then ran out of the door, slamming it firmly shut behind him.

I crawled out of the cage, dragging myself by my hands. I didn't think it was possible to hurt quite this much. When I finally managed to pull my body clear, I collapsed onto the floor, panting and curling up into the foetal position. I was pretty sure that once all this was over I wouldn't be messing with any mages ever, ever again.

Now that I was out of the cage, however, I felt as if I had more control over my own body. I reached into myself, pulling out threads of fire along my veins, allowing the tendrils of heat to trickle down each leg and each arm, each artery and muscle. Eventually I was able to stir myself into a sitting position against a wall. I rested my head against it and waited for the Arch-Mage to return.

I didn't have long to wait. The door to the little room was thrown open and the Arch-Mage himself was stood there, balls of blue flame in the palms of his hands and golden runes starting to form again around his head. Behind him stood several others, all in action stances, ready to take on little old me. I sighed deeply, tucking a stray strand of hair behind my ear.

"Please, Mr Arch-Mage. All I want to do is talk."

He started to murmur to himself chanting whatever it was he had been saying when he'd knocked me out previously.

"Uh…sir? Really, I just want to talk to you." I held my palms up towards him in submission. "If it helps I'll crawl back into the cage."

He stopped talking to himself and looked at me. I widened my eyes slightly and tried to look sincere.

One of the mages clustered behind the Arch-Mage began to protest. "Your Magnificence, you can't…."

He held up a hand and the mage fell into a silence. As impressed as I was by this display of blind obedience, I was finding it difficult not to snort in disbelief at the Arch-Mage's title. What was it with Otherworld megalomaniacs? That reminded me though.

"Uh, Sir?" I was damned if I was going to call him 'Your Magnificence'. "Can I ask why the Lord Alpha is visiting?"

"I believe you just did," the Arch-Mage said softly, raising an eyebrow at me and waggling it in a manner that reminded me of some stage magician plying fake tricks to an awestruck audience. "It turns out that he was here for you. Still is here, in fact."

Uh oh.

He continued. "It appears that he is demanding to know why one of his pack members is being held here. The Lord Alpha wanted to remind me of the Aberstrong treaty."

I must have looked confused, because he elaborated. "It's an old piece of Otherworld legislation. It came about after the Crimean War."

"Half a league half a league half a league onwards?" I asked.

"That's the one. Some of the conflict and the, well, the unfortunate deaths, were caused by dissension between shifters and mages who were present at the Battle of Balaclava. It was believed that had we worked together with clear lines of cooperation and communication, then things would have gone better. Once the war was over, a contract was drawn up to ensure such issues did not occur again. One of those includes the clause that neither mages nor shifters will interfere in each other's business without first brokering a meeting with the other head of state. The Lord Alpha wanted to know why you were here and why he hadn't been contacted."

A wave of nervous nausea rippled through me. I was fairly

certain that my skin had suddenly paled dramatically also. The Arch-Mage didn't miss a beat though. "Naturally, I was going to point out that you are not a shifter and therefore not covered by the treaty. However before I could do so I was informed that you had broken free of the cage and were rampaging through the College yet again. He's still waiting upstairs."

Oh fuck, oh fuck, oh fuck.

"Sir, I would really appreciate it if you didn't do that. Tell him I'm not a shifter, I mean." I licked my lips, nervously.

"Yes, I can imagine that you would. I would appreciate it myself, however if over a hundred years of relative peace between our two groups was not shattered by some nonentity little girl who is trying to pass herself off as a shifter and yet is actually a mage."

"I'm not a mage, I can promise you that."

"You can do magic. Not what we are used to, but I can guarantee that it was magic. And you broke free from the cage." He glanced over at it for a moment and looked almost sad. "That's never happened before. So before we do anything, you are going to tell me what you are, who you are and what in damnation you are doing in my College!"

I looked down at the floor. I couldn't tell him what I was. My mother had hidden me with the pack for a reason; John had kept the truth from me for my entire life for a reason. In fact, since I'd discovered that I was Draco Wyr, I'd already told four people and I was damn lucky that they hadn't done anything else with that information. I was quite sure there were others like Iabartu out there somewhere who would be willing to wreak all manner of devastation to get hold of some of my blood. The Arch-Mage might even be one of those others.

I moved my gaze back up to the mage. "I can tell you that I am no threat to you or any of your mages."

Several of the followers in the background began to splutter. One of them shouted out, "What about Trevor? You maimed him! And Martha almost died."

I was proud of myself for staying calm and answering a level voice. "You brought the fight to me. Nobody is dead; nobody is in danger. If you had just left me alone, then I would never have come near you."

"We can't just let rogue magicians roam about the streets of Britain! Imagine the consequences!"

Heat started to rise in my stomach. I did my best to dampen it down. "I've told you, I'm not a mage." I enunciated each word. "In fact, I can promise you that I will never, ever knowingly go near any mage ever again for the rest of my life, however long that may be, if you just sort out the stasis spell that you put on my friend."

The mage who'd shouted out opened his mouth to speak again, but the Arch-Mage held up both his hands this time to silence the mutterings and exclamations. He had a puzzled frown on his face. "What do you mean?"

I struggled to remember what Alex had called it. "Uh, the 'enforced inhibitory gnosis' thingy."

The mage at the back interrupted yet again. "She knows what it's called! She just proved she's a mage! She's a rogue, we need to..."

His voice was cut off as the Arch-Mage closed the door behind him. I smiled, despite the gravity of the situation. "Thank you."

He arched an eyebrow at me again. "How do you know what enforced inhibitory gnosis is?"

"I...uh...," I swallowed. I didn't think that Alex would like it if I gave him away. "I read a lot of books. I looked it up."

"Really." The Arch-Mage's voice was dry.

"Look," I said, trying to get the conversation back on track, "I am only here to get you to free Mrs Alcoon. She's not really a witch." I briefly remembered that the word 'witch' was considered insulting to mages and re-phrased. " I mean, mage, she's not really a mage. She has a few powers passed down to her from her ancestors but really they're very minor. She's of no consequence or danger to anyone. She just runs a little bookshop and drinks a lot of herbal tea and doesn't get in anyone's way. She got caught up in all this and it's my fault. Put me into a coma instead, but please, let her go. She's not done anything."

"Believe me, if we could place you in enforced inhibitory gnosis, then we would have done so already. In fact that really was the original plan. There are very few mages who could resist such a spell. I think I know all of them. So before I even begin to consider releasing your friend, you are going to tell me what you are."

I really hate being told what to do. "I can't do that, sir."

The Arch-Mage stared at me hard. Then he turned and opened the door behind him. "Brandt? Will you go to the Lord Alpha and request his presence down here?"

For fuck's sake. "Wait!" I protested. "You don't understand what will happen if you do that. He'll hurt people."

"Then tell me what you are." He gazed at me with an implacable expression of his face.

I could feel my carefully constructed secret unraveling around me. But Brandt was hovering by the door, watching us closely. "And how do I know I can trust you?"

He shrugged. "You don't. But if you want to avoid the Lord Alpha and have any chance of me even considering freeing your friend, then you need to take a leap of faith."

I thought for a moment. "How about a compromise?"

"What do you have in mind?"

"One of your own knows what I am. That's how I knew what the spell was called – I asked him for help. He can testify to you that what I am is of no consequence to the mages. That I won't hurt you or any of you. I just want you to help Mrs Alcoon. You don't need to know what I am." I really hadn't wanted to involve Alex, but I would if I had to.

The Arch-Mage remained stoically impassive. Then he sighed deeply. "Very well. Who is it?"

"Uh, Alex, Alex Florides."

He turned back to the group of mages at the door. "Brandt, instead of the Lord Alpha, can you fetch Mage Florides here please? And while you're at it, ask the Lord Alpha for his forbearance in waiting in a little longer."

Brandt bobbed his head and began to turn.

"Brandt?"

"Yes, Your Magnificence?"

"Do be polite when you speak to the Pack Lord."

"Yes, sir." He turned and ran off.

I shifted uncomfortably. "Is Alex here?"

"No, he's in Yorkshire dealing with a small problem there. He can transport here via a portal however. It won't take long."

"Neat trick," I murmured.

The Arch-Mage smiled. "Yes, it rather is." He raised his eyebrows at me. "Is that how you gained admittance here?"

"No, I told you, I'm not a mage. You just rely too much on weak technology as a security system." I explained to him how I'd zapped the electricity boxes to the gates and the garage, figuring that they'd find out sooner or later or anyway. Besides, it wasn't as if I would be trying to sneak back in again any time soon. There were some mutterings outside the door with my explanation, but I ignored them. It wasn't my fault if the mages were stupid.

By the time I'd finished, Brandt had reappeared. "Mage Florides is on his way, Your Magnificence. And, uh," he cleared his throat, "the Lord Alpha is getting impatient."

The Arch-Mage made a moue of dismissal. "I'll deal with him in due course."

I didn't think that Corrigan would appreciate being 'dealt with' by a mage, but I wisely kept silent. Scant moments later, a friendly face finally joined the group of hovering and uptight mages.

"Your Magnificence, you requested my presence."

I stared at Alex. His surfer dude persona had all but disappeared in the presence of his 'Magnificence'.

"Yes, Mage Florides. Please enter and close the door behind you."

Alex nodded and started to make his way inside. When he caught sight of me, he started visibly and for a moment seemed to struggle to gain his composure. Then he swallowed and continued in.

When the door was shut, he raised his eyes towards the Arch-Mage.

"Alex, I am led to believe that you know this young…woman."

"Yes, sir."

"And that, in fact, you have spoken with her very recently, giving away information about one of our spells."

Alex swallowed and looked down. "Yes, sir."

"Tell me how you met."

"Uh, it was earlier in the year when I went to Cornwall. Y'know, when the alpha dude, sorry, when the alpha there, was murdered."

"Aah, yes, I remember now." The Arch-Mage rubbed the palms of his hands together. "So she was passing herself off as a shifter?"

'She' was getting rather annoyed at being referred to as if 'she' wasn't in the room. I opened my mouth to speak, then thought better of it and closed it again.

"Uh, yes, sir. It was clear that she seemed human."

"Is she human?"

Alex looked at me guiltily, then cast his eyes downward again. "No, Your Magnificence."

"Is she a mage?"

He looked surprised at this, before answering again, "No, Your Magnificence."

"Do you know what she is?"

"Yeah, I mean, yes, sir."

"Does she pose a threat to the Ministry or to any mages?"

"I don't believe so, sir."

"How about to the shifters?"

"No, sir, although she is convinced that if the Brethren discover that she is not a shifter, there will be consequences."

I glared at Alex. I *knew* there would be consequences. There were always consequences when humans found out about shifters. History was littered with examples.

The Arch-Mage picked up the thread again. "Is there anyone to whom this young lady presents a threat?"

Alex shot me another quick look. "Only those dudes who try to hurt the people she cares about, sir."

I was getting impatient. "See? I'm not going to hurt you or anyone else. Just let my friend go."

The Arch-Mage silenced me with a look. "One more thing before you go, Mage Florides. Could she perform magic when you met her in Cornwall?"

"Uh, no, sir. I don't think she knew much about magic, actually. She'd never seen a trace spell in action before, although she could recognise wards. The Cornish alpha had warded a drawer and she knew it was there but not how to break it."

"Fine, you may go now."

Alex stayed where he was. "Uh, Your Magnificence?"

"What?"

"Mack is a good person. She wouldn't hurt anyone unless it was necessary. I know that she attacked Martha and…"

I interrupted. "They attacked me! I didn't do anything other than defend myself!"

"Mack Attack, dude, I'm trying to help you out here. Shut up," Alex said kindly. He looked back at the Arch-Mage. "My allegiance is always to the Ministry, sir, and I promise you that she is not a threat. At least not consciously."

I spluttered. "Not consciously! How could I…?

"Mack Attack, you don't know that much about yourself. Who knows what you're really capable of?"

The Arch-Mage's eyes narrowed at that. "Very well. Leave us now."

Alex sent me a small smile. I folded my arms and looked away as he turned and left the little room.

Once he'd gone, closing the door behind him, the Arch-Mage raised an eyebrow at me. "So it appears you may be telling the truth."

"Of course I'm telling the truth," I nearly shouted. "Why would I want to take on the entire Ministry? I'm not a complete idiot!"

He waited until I'd calmed down. "That's as may be. However I'm starting to get the impression that, whatever you are, you yourself don't really know much about what you're capable of."

I bit my lip. The Arch-Mage continued. "And that concerns me. Mage May told me that you had appeared surprised by what occurred when she placed the necklace on you. " He jerked his head towards the thing around my neck. "And despite his efforts to stand up for you, Mage Florides has intimated that you do not understand your own limits."

"But I have no interest in having anything to do with any mages," I stated firmly. "I am not a threat. Just release the enforced inhibitory gnosis and I promise you will never see me again."

He wrinkled his nose. "Mack Attack? Is that what you go by?"

"No, it's just Mack. Well, Mackenzie, Mackenzie Smith. But please call me Mack."

He ignored my last comment. "Well, Mackenzie, have you ever heard of Helen Duncan?"

I shook my head in the negative.

"She was the last person to ever be convicted of witchcraft in this country. She went to prison in 1944 for almost releasing information that would have had devastating consequences for the war effort. She came by this information through the illegal practice of magic." He paused for a moment. "It was a very bad time in our history, Mackenzie. The damage she could have caused might have changed the course of history. There is a good reason why your Lord Alpha is so concerned about rogue shifters. Especially now."

"He's not my Lord Alpha," I protested, although I was struck by the Arch-Mage's last comment. What did he mean 'especially now?'

"There is also a good reason as to why we are concerned about rogue mages and why your Mrs Alcoon has been placed under enforced inhibitory gnosis." He leaned forward. "We do not exist in a vacuum. Every decision we make, every action we take, affects the human world. We need to live side by side with the humans; we need to support them."

I was slightly puzzled. "Aren't mages human though?"

"Yes, yes, in a manner of speaking. However we do not refer to ourselves as such. My point, Miss Mackenzie, is that we cannot allow unfettered magical beings, whether they are actual mages or not, to roam around the countryside. We have a duty to keep the peace and maintain the equilibrium."

"I'm not going to upset the equilibrium! Mrs Alcoon is not going to upset the equilibrium!"

"You say that now, but who knows what may happen in the future? I don't think even you know what you are capable of."

I held out both my wrists. "So take me prisoner. I promise I'll be good and I won't escape. " I shrugged. "Or execute me if that's what you'd prefer. But Mrs Alcoon is innocent. Please let her go."

The Arch-Mage barked out a laugh. "We don't want or need to go around imprisoning people. We certainly have no desire to suddenly become executioners." He wrinkled his nose again. "How distasteful. Besides, Mage Florides has vouched for you and we trust our own. In the interests of safety, however, I will require that you submit to training."

I was taken aback. "Err, training? What, in magic?"

"Yes," he said impatiently, "in magic. You will travel to our academy – the location of which is kept secret – and live there full-time until such time as your learning is completed. This will enable you to realise your full potential, whatever that may be, and means that we can impress upon you the consequences of you misusing your potential. You may even learn to trust us and to reveal your true self." He permitted himself a smile. "You never know, I may be able to help you with it."

I was pretty sure that as Draco Wyr had supposedly been extinct for centuries, that wasn't going to happen. "And Mrs Alcoon? What about her?"

"Complete the training to my satisfaction and, once you are done, sign a binding agreement that proves you will not use your powers to harm others, and I will free your Mrs Alcoon. Incidentally, where is she?"

"Tir-na-Nog," I muttered.

The Arch-Mage looked surprised for the first time. "You are friendly with the Fae?"

I shifted uncomfortably. "Just one of them. But I knew she'd be safe there and you won't be able to harm her. Alex said that it doesn't end well for people in her situation." There was a hint of challenge to my voice.

"And that's because we concern ourselves with the whole of society, not just the needs and desires of individuals, Miss Mackenzie. I thought I had already explained that."

"Yes, well, maybe you should ask questions first then act later." I stopped there, realising that telling off the leader of the Ministry of the Mages probably wouldn't help. "Can't you free Mrs Alcoon first? I promise I'll do this training."

He snorted. "We need something to make sure you toe the line. You don't strike me as the type who takes orders easily."

I opened my mouth to protest but he held up his hand. "This is non-negotiable. Offering you this olive branch will already cause me enough trouble as it is."

I was somewhat surprised at this statement. I'd seen nothing so far to indicate that the Ministry was run as anything other than an absolute dictatorship. The idea that there were mages who would disagree with their 'Magnificence' did not quite gibe with what I'd seen. Still, as I'd been more successful than I could have hoped, I decided that I'd just have to grin and bear it. I did, however have a horrible feeling that it would be Mrs Alcoon who would suffer the most from this.

I looked challengingly at the Arch-Mage. "And the Lord Alpha?"

"I will ask him to leave. Although it might be better if you spoke to him yourself so that he is aware you are not being coerced."

"I can't meet him face to face," I said, "I might be able to use the Voice, though. That should be enough."

For the second time, the Arch-Mage appeared startled. "You can use the Voice? Not just to answer an alpha but to initiate contact?"

I nodded.

"Are you sure you're not a shifter?"

I just stared at him.

He looked puzzled, but shrugged. "Very well, I shall lift the nullifying spell that prevents such contact from taking place. Only for five minutes you understand though?"

Ah, I'd been wondering why Corrigan had not tried to use his Voice on me just yet. In fact that probably explained how he'd known where I was in the first place – his previous communication after I'd left the restaurant had been abruptly cut off, probably because of my proximity to the College. It must work in a similar fashion for Solus. I nodded my acquiescence at the mage who moved towards the door.

"Wait," I said suddenly.

He turned and looked at me questioningly. I guessed that not many people demanded that the Arch-Mage wait but things were kind of going my way. "How long will the training take?"

He smirked. "It usually lasts for five years. It depends on the trainee, really."

"Five years?" I screeched.

"It's possible we can fast-track you. It will depend on your progress and abilities. Do you have a choice? Or somewhere else to be?"

I stared at him mutely. Five years seemed an incredibly long time. Admittedly, life wasn't exactly offering me a vast amount of exciting options at the moment, and I spent my time living in crappy bedsits and doing menial jobs, but signing away that long was ridiculous. The Arch-Mage smirked again, as if he knew exactly what I was thinking. Right now it was either agree to this or damn Mrs. Alcoon to spending the remainder of her life in a coma.

Then I thought about Solus; I equally couldn't disappear for five whole years and expect him to continue to look after Mrs Alcoon. Sure, time moved differently in Fae-land and five years for him would pass by in the blink of an eye, but the Fae were fickle. I'd have to talk to him first and solidify our agreement. As for Mrs Alcoon, I'd just have to do my best to complete the training as quickly as possible so that she could be freed. What the local police in Inverness would make of her suddenly reappearing after five years' mysterious disappearance, and after an even more mysterious fire, I had no idea. I'd have to think of something to solve that problem. Perhaps if I played the willing student for a month or two, the mages would have more faith in me and release her early. I could only hope.

"I will need to make some arrangements first," I said cautiously.

"Arrangements?"

"If I am going away for up to five years, then there are things that I will need to sort out first. I will do what you want, but you need to give me a day to clear my affairs." Such as they were. "You have my word that I will return here in twenty-four hours."

The Arch-mage was silent for a moment, clearly mulling it over. Then, to my relief, he nodded. "Fair enough. You've got five minutes now to make your Voice contact with the Lord Alpha then, after he has left, someone will come and fetch you to escort you from the building. I will expect you to return here by this time tomorrow. Goodbye, Miss Mackenzie. But, one other thing before I go."

"Yeah?"

His eyes grew dark and cloudy. "Don't fuck up. Or I will kill you." Then he turned and left.

CHAPTER NINETEEN

AFTER THE ARCH-MAGE LEFT, I PULLED MYSELF UP TO MY FEET. My hand instinctively went to my cheek. The blood had dried but I had no doubt that the over-eager guard had left a considerably visible bruise. The flesh under my eye was tender and swollen. I sighed and dropped my hand to my side.

Mackenzie?

Here we go. *I'm here.*

Would you mind explaining to me what the fuck is going on?

I wondered if I was imagining the worry in his Voice. *As I believe I've mentioned before, I'm no longer part of the Pack. This is not your concern.*

It's my damn concern when the Ministry takes a shifter off the street and holds them against their will.

I tugged at my ponytail, irritably. *I came here of my own free will. I'm not a prisoner.*

There was a momentary silence before his Voice filled my head again. *So tell me why you are here.*

The imperious tone was starting to get annoying. *No. It's got nothing to do with you and nothing to do with the Pack. It's time you left me alone.*

I will not allow a rogue shifter to wander around the streets of

London making unauthorised deals with the mages! There are rules, Mackenzie.

Screw your rules, Corrigan, and get with the programme. I left so get over it. Go play with the shifters who want you.

Well it's funny you say that, kitten, because I could swear that when you materialized in my bedroom you wanted me too.

I stiffened. *You've been Lord Alpha for too long, Corrigan. Your ego is letting your mind play tricks on you.*

I don't think so, sweetheart. But why don't you come and prove that to me in person. We are in the same building after all.

I'm busy.

He exploded in frustration. *Goddamnit, Mack! I need to see you to make sure that you're alright.*

I didn't quite know how to answer that. I tried very hard to ignore the surge of warmth that his words had caused, quite different to the angry heat of my bloodfire that I was used to. I licked my lips and took a deep breath. *And I've told you that it's not your concern.*

You're not feeling ill in any way?

I assure you that I am perfectly fine and I thank you for the thought. But it's not necessary. Now, with all due respect, fuck off.

I broke off the link. The Arch-Mage would be re-instigating the block any moment now anyway. Sinking back down to the floor, I couldn't help but feel a twinge of utter dejection at Corrigan's words. He cared for me. He wouldn't have interrupted whatever he was doing to come over and threaten the leader of the freaking mages if he didn't care for me. I wondered if it was just because he was enjoying the chase. He was effectively a cat after all – the feline shifters back in Cornwall had often spent more time and effort chasing the objects of their lust than they had in actually fulfilling the relationships that were created afterwards. I wasn't just playing hard to get though: there was still no doubt in my mind that if he found out I wasn't what he thought I was, he would rip me from limb to limb and then do the same to everyone else who knew I didn't have a were. The memory of him sitting in the pub back in Cornwall and dismissing Nick as 'just a human' was still remarkably fresh in my mind. For a moment I considered what would happen if things were different. Would I be some piece of eye candy on his arm right now if I really was a were-hamster? It seemed faintly ridiculous. No, I just got under his skin because I'd walked away, that was all. I leaned my head against the wall, suddenly feeling a wash of fatigue flood through me.

There was a noise at the door and the knob turned. It was Alex, looking rather sheepish.

"Hey, Mack Attack," he said weakly.

"Hey Alex." I didn't think I had the strength to say much more to him.

He came and crouched down beside me. "Mack Attack, dude, I hope you're not pissed at me."

I raised my eyes to his. "No, Alex. You stood up for me, that was enough."

"I feel like I shoulda done more, y'know?"

"I get that feeling a lot. I'm sorry I gave you up to your boss."

He reached out and gently brushed the wound on my cheek. "We can take care of that for you."

"No, it's okay. It's only superficial – I'll live."

He nodded. "So, turns out you can do magic as well, huh?"

"So it seems, Alex."

"Dude, that's pretty freaky. Can you show me? What else can you do?"

"I'm not a performing seal," I said irritably, then regretted it. If it hadn't been for Alex then I wasn't sure that the Arch-Mage would have given me the time of day. "I'm sorry. I'm just tired, that's all. It's not a really big deal anyway, I can't do that much."

"You've not had any training. Maybe the academy will uncover even more. You'll become some major kick-ass super-hero." He deepened his voice dramatically. "Mack Attack, the protector of the people."

I just looked at him. He shrugged and grinned. I couldn't help smiling back, despite the energy it seemed to take. Leaning over he grabbed me in a bear hug and squeezed tight, whispering in my ear. "I'm glad you're okay, Mackenzie."

I whispered back, "I'm glad too."

He pulled me up to my feet. "Lord Shifty has vamoosed back to his lair. His Magnificence has said you have twenty-four hours and then you need to get back here."

"Why do you call him that?"

"Huh?"

"'His Magnificence', 'Your Magnificence', whatever you say. Why do you call him that?"

Alex looked puzzled. "He's the dude in charge. That's what we call him."

I thought about what the Arch-Mage had said about having trouble with dissension in the ranks. "Does everyone, I mean, all the mages, do they all do what he says? Without questioning it?"

"Dude, I can't…" Alex's voice trailed off.

I felt sorry for him and changed the subject. "Never mind. Are you going to escort me off the property so I don't beat anyone else up?"

He reverted back to cheerful mode. "That's the plan, Mack Attack, that's the plan."

"Can I get my daggers back before we go?"

"Mack Attack?"

"Yes, Alex?"

"Don't push your luck."

I raised my chin slightly in acknowledgement, sending a silent apology to Solus for my incredibly brief possession of the weapons, then placed my hand on Alex's forearm. I wasn't entirely sure I would make it all the way to the exit of the College without collapsing but I was damned if I was going to let any of those mages see that they might have managed to beat me into a state of physical weakness.

Once we left the little room, and the cage behind, we emerged onto another corridor that was identical to the one that I'd entered from the garage. This time, however, rather than being impressed by the soft, sinking carpet, I was worried that I'd just trip over it. My whole body was aching now. There was a particularly painful surge in my right leg every time I placed it down on the floor. One day I'd get that guard back, I vowed. He'd thought that he was being a hero by attacking someone who was in no position to defend herself, let alone fight back. Well, he'd pay.

We turned right at one point and a small staircase was in front of us. I gritted my teeth, clinging on to Alex and made my way slowly up. At the top we came out into a lobby area. There were several mages hanging around there, silently watching our slow progress. None of the faces were friendly and for once I was glad to have some protection by my side. In my current state I probably couldn't defend myself against a kitten. That thought immediately flooded my mind with a floating image of Corrigan but I quickly pushed it away.

We were almost at the front door that led outside when a voice called out from behind me. "Wait!"

Both Alex and I turned. I stiffened to see Martha, the mage who'd attacked me at Clava Books, jogging up to us. The other mages clustered round watched us carefully. I realised that her hair was now shorn short, a side effect, no doubt, of the fire.

"Let's go," I muttered to Alex.

"No, wait," Martha said. "I want to…." Her voice trailed off for a moment then she jerked her chin up and looked me in the eye. "I want to thank you for what you did."

I must have looked confused because she quickly elaborated. "In Inverness. You could have left me there to burn, but you didn't. You don't have many friends here, but if you ever need anything…well, I've got your back."

"Uh, okay," I said, somewhat pleasantly surprised.

Martha wrinkled her forehead slightly. "Understand that this doesn't mean that I like you. But I owe you and I won't forget what you did." She held out her hand. "I'm Martha, by the way."

I carefully took my hand off of Alex's arm, and shook hers, concentrating hard on not falling over. "I know. I'm Mack."

She smiled crookedly. "I know."

We both stared at each other for a moment, acknowledging what had passed between us, before Alex said softly, "We need to go."

I blinked in acknowledgement, moving my hand back to his body for support. Then we turned and headed out of the door.

When we reached the outside, I realised that we were at the front of the building. I could just make out the row of terraced houses and the abandoned wreck where I had attempted my weak version of a stakeout. Alex walked me down the driveway then waved a hand at the large iron gates which slowly opened with a creak.

"You're using magic to open these now?"

"Mmm, yes. It appears that using technology might have been a weakness in our security system. The trouble is that it takes energy to maintain the gates and the perimeter. The electrical system was more convenient."

"But not exactly secure," I commented, unable to keep the slight note of satisfaction out of my voice.

"Don't get cocky, Mack Attack. You've been incredibly fortunate that you're getting out of here alive. You didn't even have to tell His Magnificence that you're really a…"

I interrupted. "Don't say it, Alex. I need as few people as possible to know. You know what Iabartu did." I didn't mention Solus' own warnings, but I figured that my point would be clear.

"Yeah, dude, I know." He turned to me. "Mack Attack, you'd better not have any more cunning plans in place. If you're not back here in twenty four hours' time, then things will not go well."

I looked him in the eye. "I will be here. I don't break my promises, Alex."

"Okay, okay, just saying is all. Are you sure you're going to be alright? You look a bit pale and you've been clutching onto me for dear life. I think I might have lost blood flow to my hand. In fact you look a bit like you did that time back in the woods near the keep. Y'know, when we found the wichtlein and you passed out?"

"I'm fine, really." I didn't need any reminders of Cornwall. And I was damned if I was going to appear weak, even to Alex. "I'll be back here in a day."

He fumbled in his pocket and pulled out some crumpled notes. "You'll need some money."

I might not have wanted to accept his charity but I wasn't completely stupid. I took the money from him and stuck it in my back pocket. "Thanks," I said, not quite meeting his eyes.

"Take it easy, Mack Attack," Alex said softly.

I managed a slight smile and then walked slowly out of the gates. I'd barely cleared them when they began to creak their way shut again. I didn't bother turning, however, instead I just stuck my hand out to hail a taxi. I needed to put some distance between myself and the College before I tried to get back in touch with Solus. Fortunately it wasn't long before one drew up. I yanked open the door and clambered inside.

"Where to, love?"

I really tried not to let the driver's pointless endearment irritate me and thought about where to go. I didn't know London well but I'd probably need to be somewhere quiet so that Solus could find me without drawing much attention to himself. I vaguely remembered hearing that the Pack used Clapham Common during the full moon, when they had to shift and needed a large area where they wouldn't draw attention to themselves. That would do. I told the driver and he nodded agreement, managing to avoid calling me his 'love' as he did so, and we drove off.

CHAPTER TWENTY

The driver let me off next to the Clapham Common station. I paid him with the money that Alex had given me, noting that thankfully there was still some left to pick up some food and pay for a cheap B&B to rest my head before I had to head back to the College. There were several people, families and groups of friends, milling around the entrance to the park area, so I headed deeper inside to find somewhere quiet.

It was a beautiful day. Judging by the sun in the sky, it was already around midday. The cold brush of winter remained in the air, but it was a crisp and clear day. Perhaps the sun's rays would have some magical healing properties that would allow me to regain some of my energy and strength, I thought hopefully.

Before too long, I found myself next to a nook of trees, shaded from prying eyes. In theory, I'd call Solus as I had done back in Inverness, and he'd materialise himself somewhere in my vicinity. I briefly wondered how he managed to avoid transporting himself into a tree or a building. It would definitely be handy being a Fae though.

I settled myself down against a small hollow and tried. It was different to using the Voice but it had worked last time. I spoke aloud. "Uh, Solus?"

Nothing happened so I tried again. "Solus?"

A few birds twittered but again nothing happened. I wasn't so egomaniacal to assume that the Fae was at my beck and call, but I was on a clock. I hoped he wasn't going to be long. I closed my eyes and tried to summon up some bloodfire to reduce the pain from my cheek and leg. Some weak flames flickered inside me and began to get to work, taking away the edge if nothing else. In the distance, there were some shouts and drifting laughter. I opened one lid to check that they weren't heading in my direction and then scrambled to my feet in alarm. Oh shit. Stood scant feet away were five figures. It didn't take a genius to work out from their clothes and their stances that they were shifters. I didn't recognise any of them but it didn't really matter. They clearly recognised me.

"Hey," I said weakly. "Can I help you?"

"Mackenzie Smith?"

"No, that's not me. My name's Jane." Like that would work. "You must have mistaken me for someone else."

One of the shifters bared his teeth in what some cultures, but not many, might call a smile. I swallowed.

"Look, guys, I don't know what you're doing here, but I'm busy."

"You don't look very busy."

As a group they moved towards me. My hands involuntarily dug under my jacket to my forearms but, of course, my daggers weren't there. Fucking mages, I thought. Would it have killed them to let me leave with some protection? I concentrated on my hands, willing the green flames to ignite. I flicked out a stream at the nearest shifter, but it was sluggish and he dodged it easily. I felt a small glimmer of satisfaction at his surprise at my attack, even if it hadn't worked. My bloodfire was clutching itself round my heart now, not just a small flicker but instead a raging blaze. I let the flames flood my body and race through my pumping veins then smiled back at the group.

"The boss wants to see you."

"I told you, I think you have me mistaken for someone else." I watched them carefully, seeking out their weaknesses.

"No, I don't think we do."

Two of them separated from the group, flanking me. I knew I wasn't at my best but there was little I could do about it now. Abandoning the green fire for now, I tensed my muscles and waited for them to make the first move. It didn't take long.

The shifter on my right, who was wearing some ridiculous Matrix inspired full length leather coat, made a small gesture of acknowledgement to his partner and they both rushed me. That gesture was their undoing, however. I leapt up in the air and scissor kicked out, first left and then right, connecting with both of their heads. They snarled, and I heard the ripping of material.

My eyes widened slightly. The three in the middle were in the middle of a shift. Denim and cloth was scattering the ground as their bodies and muscles bulged out, and fur began to form over their skin. Fuck, they were taking a few chances, transforming out here in the open. It occurred to me that finding a quiet spot to wait for Solus hadn't been such a good idea in the first place. I very much hoped that the Fae would show himself very soon.

The two shifters who I'd kicked were moving backwards. Ah, I thought, the lookouts. No doubt, since their initial rush had failed so abjectly, they'd stay human and make sure that no passersby happened by, while the others took advantage of their were strength to best me. The shifter in mid-transformation nearest me started to slather and drool, his skull creaking as it elongated into a grey muzzle. I took advantage of the moment to rush him, lashing out with a punch to his head. I knew that this would be their most vulnerable moment. I connected, feeling a shattering pain in my fist. For his part, however, he howled in agony, as his shift continued involuntarily. He was clearly a wolf. I grinned without humour. Even in my current state, I had no problem besting a wolf. Patches of fur were appearing on his hands. I grabbed both his wrists and twisted hard, snapping each one. He howled again.

Yeah, whatever, he'd have healed himself by the time I was back with the mages.

I jumped back and focused my attention on the other two who were now fully transformed. One was a were-tiger and the other some kind of strange were-wolf/lion hybrid. Huh, that was a new one on me. Each took a step towards me. I tensed, waiting to see what they were going to do next.

The tiger raised its head, baleful yellow eyes staring at me. It sniffed the air cautiously. Panic flooded me. Oh, fuck, it would easily be able to scent the fact that I was human. I had to get out of here - and right now. I quickly turned on my heel, ready to dart through the trees and try to make my escape. I'd never be able to outrun two transformed shifters, but all I had to do was to get in sight of some humans and I'd be safe. They'd never dare to let themselves be seen by the public. Standing in front of me, however, leaning casually against a tree, was Corrigan. He was examining his fingernails, as if mildly bored. He started to open his mouth to speak, and then jerked his head up, eyes widening. He was smelling the same as the were-tiger.

The bloodfire inside me was starting to choke my system. Involuntary tears were springing to my eyes and I could feel myself losing control in a way I never had before. I tried to turn back towards the other shifters, but I stumbled and lost my footing. Fire was roaring in my ears. I worked on summoning the green flames to my hands again; this time it was less of slow sluggish stream of light and more of an explosion. From a distance away I heard Corrigan calling my name, but the heat was so over-powering and all-encompassing that it barely registered. The dry grass around my feet was on fire, keeping the shifters at bay. I wasn't going anywhere though. Through the haze of green flames and smoke, I could see them circling me, waiting for a moment to douse the flames and grab me. My blood felt as if it was boiling. I let out an agonised scream and then, for the second time in less than twenty-four hours, the world went dark.

* * *

WHEN I CAME TO, everything was completely black. I began to panic, feeling claustrophobic and stifled, realising that there was a blindfold over my eyes and my hands were tied securely behind my back. I concentrated on my fingers, attempting to ignite a small spark to loosen my restraints, but there was just an unpleasantly familiar numbing sensation. I tugged hard, trying to see if there was any give, but whatever had been used to secure my wrists wasn't going to budge. I wanted to dig inside myself, to find my bloodfire and use it to my advantage, but a large part of me was too afraid. The all-encompassing fire that had lit inside of me had been so strong and had smothered me so completely that I had no idea what would happen if I tried to summon it again now.

Realising from the vibrations underneath me and the sounds outside that I was in some kind of moving vehicle, I pushed myself up against the side of whatever I was in so that I was at least in a sitting position. My ankles had been bound together too and I found a faint glimmer of humour in the situation. The thought that Corrigan was so intimidated by my suggested powers that he'd send five shifters, not including himself, to grab me, and that he'd then make sure that I was trussed up like a chicken and virtually unable to move an inch, was vaguely satisfying. Of course, I comforted myself, if I hadn't been feeling already so weak after my round with the Ministry, then I could have made my escape.

Then I remembered that he and his cronies had scented me. The cat was well and truly out of the bag now. I wondered if it had always been inevitable that he would find out that I wasn't a shifter. Probably. That didn't make me feel any better though, and I had to warn Cornwall. After apparently being able to initiate Voice contact with Corrigan himself, in theory I should be able to do the same with other shifters. Hey, if the Lord Alpha could do it, then why couldn't I?

I clenched my teeth and concentrated, focusing on Julia first.
Julia? Julia? Can you hear me?

Deep silence hung in my head as an answer. That was okay, I thought, taking a deep breath. Perhaps the physical injuries that she'd sustained when Iabartu's minions had attacked the keep had affected her mental powers too. I aimed for Johannes next.

J?

Nothing. I tried again, screaming with all my might this time.
Johannes!

The only thing that answered me was my own panic. Fuck. I'd have to get Anton instead. As alpha of the Cornish pack, his Voice would be stronger so it would stand to reason that he would be more likely to hear me. I tried to calm myself. All I needed to do was warn him that Corrigan knew that I was human, not that I really was human but it's what he'd think, and that he'd have to prepare the pack for the Brethren. Maybe he could concoct some sort of story? He wouldn't be able to lie to the Brethren though, they'd scent that out in heartbeat. The thought of the shifters' watchdogs storming down to Cornwall and taking their vengeance out on my adopted family was almost too painful to even consider. Anton would have to listen to me and would have to do something. I curled my nails into the palms of my hands.

I was tentative at first, not wanting to anger or surprise Anton so much that he'd push my Voice straight out and erect mental barriers that would stop me from communicating with him.
Uh, Anton?

Okay, that was too quiet. I tried again, a bit louder this time.
Anton?

Fuck it.
ANTON!

The answering silence was devastating.

I could feel my heart thudding hard against my ribcage. There had to be something I could do. I thought of Tom and Betsy. Okay, that might work. I wasn't Lord Alpha, there was no reason why I'd be able to communicate over long distances. In fact, as far as I knew, Corrigan was the only Lord Alpha who'd ever been able to manage that feat. But Tom and Betsy were in London. And whatever vehicle I was in right at the moment was probably taking me closer to them, rather than further away. I acknowledged to myself that Tom had given up my presence in London to Corrigan, but you wouldn't be able to fake the shock that had registered on the Lord Alpha's face when he worked out that I was human. Tom hadn't completely deserted me. It might have been the geas but I would choose for now to believe otherwise. He was no doubt aware that Corrigan had been coming to capture me; perhaps he'd thought I'd be able to get away before that happened. There was no way that he'd have been able to contact me to warn me of course. But if I could contact him then he could telephone the Cornish pack and…I straightened my shoulders. I could do this.

I focused on Tom's face, imagining it in my mind. In my head, he winked warmly at me. Then I threw out my Voice.

Corrigan caught me, Tom.

There was a big fat nothing.

Tom? Tom? Tom? TOM!

Why the fuck wasn't it working? I tried Betsy but got exactly the same response. Nadda. Nyet. Zip. I was getting more and more worked up.

There was only one other person I could think of, and that hadn't exactly worked for me back at the park.

"Solus? I really need you. Please?"

My voice echoed against the metal walls of the vehicle.

"Solus?"

Something thumped against the wall next to me and a muffled voice shouted out. It wasn't Corrigan. "Shut up back there!"

Damnit. I was completely out of options. Perhaps the shifters had gotten hold of some kind of nullifying spell from the mages?

The numbing around my hands would certainly suggest that. To be sure, I gingerly tried Corrigan.

Hello?

For a moment there was silence and I thought my suspicions had been confirmed about the spell. But then he answered, flatly.

You're awake.

I cursed. Why could I use the Voice on him but not on the people I actually wanted to talk to?

We have a lot to discuss, kitten.

I didn't bother answering. He sighed in my head and I felt the mild pressure of his Voice vanish. I realised that my fingers were still digging into my hands. I uncurled them slowly, stretching them out as I did so. Think, Mack, I thought. There had to be something I could do that would keep the Cornish pack safe. Corrigan just had to ask any of them directly whether they'd known I wasn't a shifter and they'd be compelled to answer in the affirmative. Hell, he didn't even have to use his Voice or travel to Cornwall to do so. He'd just have to walk to the next room and speak to Tom and Betsy. No, pretending that they didn't know wasn't an option.

I thought hard. I could go down the geas route. And that was actually true – the entire Cornish pack had been physically forbidden from revealing my true nature. If I could appeal to Corrigan's better side then he might just be lenient. It wasn't their fault that they hadn't informed the Brethren of my presence. Leniency was not something that I'd ever heard of the shifter overlords practising, however. I tried to formulate arguments in my head. It occurred to me briefly that I wouldn't have much time to persuade Corrigan and the whole of the Brethren not to maim or kill the Cornish pack and to release me. I was pretty sure that because we were still travelling that I'd not been knocked out for long, but I still didn't have much time before I was bound to return to the mages. I had absolutely no doubt that they'd leave Mrs Alcoon to rot without a second thought if I didn't get back to them before the twenty four hour period was up.

The vehicle lurched over a bump in the road and I went flying onto my face, scraping the very same cheek that the stupid mage guard had earlier attempted to torture. I yelled involuntarily out in pain. I rolled onto my back and struggled to lift myself back up. I was damned if I was going to let them open the door and find me flailing around on the floor like a bloody fish out of water. The uneven floor gave me an idea, however, and I tried to scrape my face against it to pull the blindfold off of my eyes. If I could see at the very least, then I'd have something to start with. It was unfortunate that opening up the wound on my cheek and allowing it to bleed would have no effect on my prisoner status this time, however. All my experience thus far had proven that whatever strange powers my blood had, they had little effect on the real world. The shifters rarely had to use magic to get their point across – they had sharp teeth and claws to manage that.

I kept trying to snag the blindfold on something and get it off. My cheek scraped painfully against something sharp and I winced in pain as I felt the warm trickle of blood against my face. I did my best to ignore it, however, and tried again. Eventually I managed to pull it halfway up my forehead, revealing one eye.

"Probably look like fucking Captain Hook," I muttered to myself.

At least I could see now though. I took in my surroundings, realising that I was in the back of what was some kind of small van. In the corner were some pots of paint and boxes but other than that it was empty. I wondered if I should take some small hope from the fact that the Brethren didn't seem to have a regular prisoner transport vehicle.

Kicking out with my legs, I managed to manoeuvre myself back to a sitting position. I could feel the van braking slightly and slowing, and then the crunch of gravel under the wheels. We came to a complete stop. My stomach flip-flopped but I kept the flames away. It was showtime.

CHAPTER 21

THE BACK DOORS TO THE VAN WERE FLUNG OPEN, BANGING AGAINST the metal sides. I had half hoped – and half dreaded – that it would be Corrigan, but it was the were-tiger instead, newly returned to human and wearing a fresh set of clothes. Did the Brethren keep spare wardrobes with them everywhere they travelled, I wondered? It hadn't really been much of a problem in Cornwall; generally if someone was going to shift then they knew in advance and came prepared. It wouldn't do if some local yokel came across a bunch of naked people in the middle of the woods. Soberly, it occurred to me that it had probably been the same today with these guys though. They'd been expecting to shift because they'd been expecting to capture me. Unfortunately it had worked.

As he was climbing into the van, with one of the shifters who'd remained human, I called out. "I want to talk to Corrigan."

They both completely ignored me.

"Hey! Where's the boss? I need to speak to him."

I didn't even get a flicker of a response. Damn, he'd trained them fucking well.

"If you're going to get me out of this van, you're going to have to untie my legs at the very least."

The weretiger simply moved towards me and began pulling at the hem of my jeans, dragging me until I was almost at the exit of the van. A stray lock of hair was irritatingly falling across my one uncovered eye and I blew at it to try to move it out of the way so that what little vision I had was unimpeded. The tiger grinned at me, displaying a set of very white even teeth, and then yanked the blindfold back down again so that I was plunged back into darkness.

"What?" I sputtered, injecting as much disbelief into my voice as I could. "You think I don't know where we are? How stupid do you think I am?"

The only place that I could possibly be being transported to was the Brethren's headquarters, the keep. I'd seen it in pictures – and of course – been in Corrigan's bedroom – and knew something of the layout from growing up with the Cornish pack. We may not have had much to do with the Brethren directly, but we still knew where to go when there was a problem so of course I was perfectly aware of where the keep was.

I felt my torso being yanked forward, and the waft of cold air against my face as I was pulled outside. Then I was unceremoniously dumped over a shoulder – the were-tiger's I presumed, and carried in perhaps the most undignified fashion that I could possibly imagine. My trussed up hands dangled down towards the ground banging against the back of my captor's legs, while one of his arms was tightly gripping round my thighs. Jeez, it was not as if I was going to be able to run away.

"Kind of overkill, don't you think?"

The only answer I got was the sound of gravel as several people moved in the same direction. At one point, a loose stone ricocheted up and smacked me against the wound in my cheek. I swore, loudly, but again elicited absolutely no reaction from anyone.

"Corrigan? Are you there? Look, you just need to let me explain…"

Finally, there was an answering voice that growled at me. "You will address him as the Lord Alpha."

Oh for fuck's sake. These bloody megalomaniacs and their sodding titles. I wasn't exactly in much of a position to argue however.

"Okay," I said soothingly, "I'm sorry. Lord Alpha, please give me five minutes and you'll understand. This was all my doing. Nobody else had anything to do with it. Nobody else had a choice – they were under a geas not to reveal that I wasn't a shifter." I aimed for logic. "And as I'm not a shifter you really have no right to take me prisoner."

I waited for a moment for a response. The shifters had clearly reverted back to ignoring me. The were-tiger walked up some steps, causing my head now to thump repeatedly against the back of his legs. I tried to twist it to the side to avoid causing any more friction or damage to my cheek but I didn't have a lot of wiggle room with which to move myself. I probably should have taken up yoga or something, I thought miserably. Maybe if I was just a little bit more flexible then I'd be able to do some amazing twisting trick that would free myself from this ignominious situation. Some big scary badass dragon I was turning out to be.

The temperature around me changed abruptly as we suddenly moved inside. The chill of winter had given way to a very cosy interior. No expense spared on central heating here, I thought sourly. Not like the Brethren's minions freezing their arses off out in the depths of rural England. There was the murmur of voices ahead of us that suddenly hushed as they no doubt caught glimpse of my fabulously rounded bottom on display to the world. I hear a whisper to the left of me and, although I couldn't make out what was said, I managed to swing my hanging arms up for just a second to give the owner of the voice the finger. There, that'd teach them. Things might be looking incredibly bad right now but I was damned if I was going to let them think that they'd cowed me into submission.

Before too long, the were-tiger was changing his gait again as we started travelling downstairs. Excellent. I was being taken to the actual dungeon. Images flooded my head of a dark slimy place filled with rusty manacles and nibbling rats. At this point in time it wouldn't surprise me. I bet myself that the dungeon didn't have central heating.

We turned round, moving down some kind of spiral staircase. From behind a closed door I heard the murmur of voices and I strained to listen. I might not be able to use the Voice on either Tom or Betsy but I could use my normal voice if I could get hold of them. We were past the sound too quickly however for me to make any kind of distinction. My hands and feet were both starting to feel numb. I began to worry that I'd suddenly be plonked upright on the floor and would just slide humiliatingly down, unable even to make myself stand up. I needed to show the Brethren that I had strength and power. If I could garner their respect, then maybe they'd feel some qualms about killing me. And if they couldn't bring themselves to kill me, then they could hardly hurt the Cornish pack either. I'd lived with shifters for most of my life; I knew that vulnerability was considered a weakness and was looked down upon. Hell, half the reason that I'd been tolerated by the human haters in Cornwall had been because they knew that I could take any one of them in a fight. They might not have liked me but, because of what I could do, they respected me.

From my ungainly position, I tried to wiggle my fingers and toes and will some life back into them. There was a brief tingling sensation but little else. I considered trying to spark back some of my green fire again, but then decided against it. Even if I could muster a few flames up, the odds of being able to get myself out of the Pack's headquarters alive were pretty much zilch. Besides which, the big secret that I'd been trying to hide from the shifters had already been revealed to the world; I'd have to find some way to get on their good side if I had any hope of everyone I knew not being ripped apart. Setting my captors on fire would not help.

My head was banging painfully against the shifter's back,

despite my best efforts to keep it up, and I was starting to feel a little dizzy at being upside down for so long. Every step down that the tiger took seemed to send a new shot of pain to some previously undiscovered part of my body. My breath hissed out through my teeth when the edge of my hip caught what I assumed was the edge of a banister. At least that meant that we were back on flat ground. A strong woody, almost floral, scent reached my nostrils that belied my expectations of a slimy dank dungeon. That alone would have made me certain that we still had a ways to go before we reached our destination, but I heard the distinct rattle of a doorknob being turned in front of me and the were-tiger began to slow slightly, before stopping altogether. I tensed up, trying to tighten my calf muscles to avoid collapsing to the ground as soon as I was let down, and clenched my teeth in preparation for the inevitable burst of pain as I hit the ground. The tiger's muscles equally shifted and I felt an arm moving round my waist and pulling me off his shoulder and onto the floor.

My knees buckled slightly and I felt myself swaying towards the ground, teetering on the brink between managing to stay upright and ending up sprawled on the ground. A hissed sigh of exasperation came from somewhere to my right and a steely hand gripped my forearm and jerked me upwards. I scowled in annoyance.

"I don't need your fucking help," I spat, and then instantly regretted the outburst as clearly I was going to need some help to get myself out of this situation.

Naturally, however, silence rebounded back at me. I sensed the were-tiger leaving, without saying a single word. That meant that I was alone with Corrigan. Okay, I could work with that. I'd remind him of how I helped defeat Iabartu and bring peace back to shifter world, without mentioning of course that it had been me she'd been after in the first place. I briefly thought of the knee weakening closeness we'd shared in his bedroom and wondered if I could also use that to my advantage.

A pair of hands reached around the back of my head and tugged at my blindfold, eventually yanking it painfully off from around my head. The sudden blast of unnatural light hurt my eyes and blinked hard a few times, beginning to speak.

"Corrigan, look, I…."

"What makes you think the Lord Alpha wants to waste his time being here in person?"

I jerked, my eyes eventually adjusting to make out the features of the figure in front of me. Fucking hell, it was Staines. A wave of hurt anger swept through me. After all that, the big man himself couldn't be arsed to come and interrogate me? That prick. And he'd left me with Staines who'd never liked me.

I eyed him warily, managing to respond with a calm voice. "I apologise for the confusion. Given that the Lord Alpha," the title stuck in my craw but I swallowed it down and continued on, "came to bring me in himself, I had expected that he would be the one here to question me. But of course I am delighted to see you again." I managed a half smile in the direction of burly were-bear.

He growled at me and leaned forward. "Let's cut to the chase. Did you murder the alpha of the Cornwall pack?"

I blinked in shock. Err… what? "What are you on? That was Iabartu. You were there, remember? At least for part of it, anyway, I'm sure you heard about the rest. She was this demi-goddess? Floated above the ground? I tried to kill her and would have if your Lord Alpha hadn't gotten involved."

"It appears that the official version of events may not be as straight forward as we had once believed. After all, you're not even a shifter." His voice remained even and steady but there was a definite underlying tone that promised menace and pain. "Were you in cahoots with the demi-god?"

Cahoots? Dear god, what century was this guy from? "No."

"Then why does it appear that there was some sort of link between the two of you?"

I swallowed. Link? I'd thought all tracks leading in that direction had been covered. "Look, you've got Tom and Betsy from the Cornish pack here. They were there, they know what happened. Just ask them. You'll know when they are telling the truth."

"Oh don't worry, Miss Smith, we are talking to them."

The glint in his eyes sent an involuntary tremor of fear for them through my body. The tone of his voice didn't make it sound as if they'd be sitting for a little old chinwag over afternoon tea. Fuck it, I'd been an idiot to bring them up.

I sighed heavily and looked him in the eye. "They don't have anything to do with this. They were just there by dint of fate. If there is any fault to be had, any blame to be placed, then it needs to go on my shoulders."

Staines stayed silent and just stared at me.

"I was not working with Iabartu. I did not murder John. Yes, I'm not a shifter, I'm sorry, but that's no-one else's fault but mine. The others, the Cornish pack, they didn't have a choice. It was a geas and they couldn't say anything if they wanted to. And I left them anyway. They made me leave. Anton made me leave because I'm not a shifter. So they did the right thing – it's just me who messed up."

I was aware that I was starting to babble.

Staines opened his mouth. "Why was a mage trying to pass herself off as a shifter? What did you hope to gain?"

Disbelievingly, I shook my head at him. "I'm not a mage! The mages don't even fucking like me. I have to go back there in less than twenty four hours and become their effective prisoner because they don't like what I did to them." The familiar swirl of heat was starting to rise up. At least that meant my body was starting to recover somewhat.

"You can shoot fire from your fingertips and you expect me to believe that you're not a mage?"

"I don't know why that happens!" I touched the necklace at my throat. "This weird Scottish lady put this on me and then all of a sudden the green fire happened. It doesn't mean I'm a mage!"

"You can transport yourself at will into highly guarded buildings."

"That was a – friend of mine who was messing around!" I was going to fucking kill Solus if I ever saw him again.

"You can go into a fight against otherworlders, including at one point, I might add, the future alpha of a local pack, and win."

"I work out! I've trained for years! That doesn't make me a fucking mage!"

A deep voice suddenly smoothly spoke from behind me. "So, kitten, if you're not a mage, then what are you?"

My stomach dropped with a horrifying lurch and I turned to face Corrigan. It irked me that I was very much aware that I was covered in dried blood, wearing smelly old clothes, and looking like I'd been squatting in an abandoned house and then unsuccessfully trying to attack the might of the magic otherworld before being set upon by a group of shifters in broad daylight. But, oh wait, that's what I had been doing. I peered at Corrigan and noted heavy dark shadows under his eyes and a pallor to his normally tanned skin. At least I wasn't the only one who was looking a bit worse for wear then at least. I forced myself to stay calm and keep my recovering bloodfire to a minimum. I needed him on my side.

"I'm nothing, my Lord. Just…nothing," I answered, hoping that the tremor stayed out of my voice.

Staines spoke again, with the first hint of clear emotion that I think I'd heard in him up till now. "He's not your Lord. You don't have the privilege to call him that."

Well, I was hardly going to lose sleep over not having that 'privilege' any more.

"Oh no," I muttered sarcastically, unable to help myself, then immediately inwardly cursing at my stupidity. Five seconds into the 'conversation' and I was already letting my emotions get the better of me.

I turned back towards Staines and the glowering malevolence that he was shooting at me, and raised my eyebrows. His body tensed, about to launch out a hit. Fuck it. I prepared myself to block with my shoulder. Even with my hands tied behind my back, I could take him.

"You can go now, Staines." Corrigan's voice was so quiet that I barely heard him.

Staines blinked and immediately relaxed, bowing his head and moving past me towards the door. My mouth hung open slightly in shock. Jesus, Staines had been ready to murder me a scant moment ago. That was some serious self-control. My eyes followed his departure, opening the wooden door behind Corrigan and stepping out, shooting me just one quick look of undisguised hatred, before he closed it and disappeared from sight. Corrigan for his part didn't move a muscle.

"That's what loyalty is, Mack," he said softly. "Something that seems to be in short supply as far as you're concerned."

I stared at him, my tongue suddenly clawed to the roof of my mouth. Despite his calm voice, the tension seeping from every muscle of his body coupled with the hard glint in his eye belied his anger. He took a step towards me. I took a step back.

Running an irritated hand through his black as night hair he spoke again. "You do realise that I almost caused an interagency war on your behalf?"

I regained my voice. "Er…I'm not quite sure what you mean."

"The mages. I thought they'd captured you." He smiled mirthlessly. "I was coming to rescue you. But of course I didn't know that you actually were one of them."

I almost howled. "Corrigan, I'm not fucking one of them! They've done something to a friend of mine and I'm trying to make it right."

He folded his arms across his chest. I tried not to notice the way his muscles bulged and rippled. "So explain to me, Mackenzie, how you suddenly happen to have magical powers."

"I don't have magical powers! How many times do I need to say that I'm not a fucking mage? As I said to your bitch slapped minion there, some witch up in Scotland put this necklace on me.

Now I have freaky green flames that shoot from my fingertips. Up until last week, the most magic I could perform was pissing off everyone I came into contact with."

A ghost of smile flickered across his face but was gone so quickly I thought I'd imagined it. "Well, I'll give you the part about pissing people off, sweetheart. And yet," he paused, his green gold eyes flashing sparks of ire, "you also appear to inspire the most bizarre acts of loyalty."

"I thought you said that loyalty was in short supply as far as I was concerned."

"Oh, on your part certainly. But tell me, if you are not a mage then why do your little Cornish friends refuse to open their mouths to state one single truth about you, even when I compel them to do so?"

I took a deep breath and raised my eyes to meet his. It was now or never. "It's a geas, Corrigan. My mother dumped me with the Cornish pack when I was a kid and some kind of geas was placed on everyone to prevent them from revealing that I was human. It's not their fault. It's not the fault of anyone in Cornwall – they had no choice. You can't invoke Brethren law against them when they couldn't have done anything about my being there even if they'd wanted to."

A muscle ticked in his cheek. "You expect me to believe that you're human? You can take down otherworld creatures that send the best of my shifters running for the hills, and you're human?"

I shrugged and tried to smile. Corrigan circled the room with visibly coiled feline grace, before stopping right in front of me.

"I suppose on one level it makes sense. You never did smell quite right. You refused to shift for so long as well. And the alpha - Anton? That's one of the reasons why he hates you so much."

I jumped on the opportunity to put the Cornish pack in the clear. "Yes! He wanted me gone for years. We know it's forbidden for humans to have knowing contact with the pack. He wanted to protect them. So, you see, Corrigan, it's not their fault, you can't hurt them."

He looked momentarily puzzled. "Why would I hurt them?"

I stared at him as if he was stupid. "Because they harboured a human."

The cloudy expression on his face abruptly cleared and Corrigan's tired eyes suddenly gleamed. "Ah, yes, I see. And you think it's against the law for shifters to consort with humans. There's an easy way to solve that, you know." He smiled predatorily. "I'll just transform you. I don't know why no-one did that before. Did your previous alpha not consider it?"

I let out a small squeak. Yes, he'd fucking considered it. He'd even tried it, but the bloody dragon part of me had rejected the change.

Corrigan's eyes raked over my body. "I'm quite sure that you'll end up being something slightly different to the were-hamster you were passing yourself off as. Problem solved." He made to move towards me and I panicked and scuttled backwards until my back was against the wall.

"What's the matter, kitten? Do you have something against shifters?"

"Fuck off, Corrigan. No, I don't have anything against shifters. I consider my family to be shifters."

"Nobody else has dared to tell me to fuck off for years," he mused quietly, moving towards me until he was bare inches away from me. I prepared to move to my right to get away from him, but he placed both hands on the wall around me, effectively creating a cage. I could smell his deep musky scent and felt the bloodfire inside me respond with instinctual feeling. Oh god.

Corrigan tilted his head and seemed to see the state of my face for the first time. A strange expression flitted across his features. "You're hurt," he said softly, brushing his fingers against my wounded cheek.

I flinched and he scowled.

"Well, that's what happens when you get shoved into a cage

and tortured by a crazed mage with nothing but blood vengeance on his mind," I said lightly.

The steely arms on either side of me tensed and I saw, not just sensed his shoulders jerk back with anger. Why the fuck was he angry? I was the one who kept being taken bloody prisoner by every single faction of the sodding otherworld.

"The Arch-Mage assured me that you were alright," he growled.

"And I am." I'd have stretched out my arms at that point to prove just how alright I was, apart from the fact that they were still bound tightly behind my back – Corrigan's arms were still caging me against the wall.

"I will have words with him."

"Jesus, Corrigan, I'm not a shifter. You don't need to get all worked up on my behalf. I'm just a human. Now, please, tell me that you will leave my friends alone."

I stared into his face, praying that he'd give me – and them – some leeway. He leaned in even closer, until I could feel his hot breath against my neck.

"As I said, kitten, I will transform you and then there will be no debt to be satisfied. You will become a shifter and stay here in London." He paused and then licked his lips. "At my beck and call."

Oh dear god. "You can't do that, Corrigan."

"I'm the Lord Alpha. I can do whatever I want. Besides, your transgressions mean that you owe me. You owe the Pack."

"Yes, but…" I started to stutter.

He interrupted. "But I can't transform you. Not because you don't want to be a shifter, but because you physically can't be transformed." He looked straight at me, confirming the truth of his words before continuing. "And the only reason that couldn't work would be because you're already not human. Your scent already tells me that. And I assume that this is your real scent that is assailing the air not some faked aroma that you have cooked up somehow. Not only that but you can hear and initiate the Voice.

No human could do that. Do you think I'm a total idiot? You might have played me for a fool thus far but the buck stops here. With me."

The look in his eyes was suddenly absolutely terrifying. I swallowed.

"So, Mack, if you are not a mage, and you are not a shifter, then what the fuck are you?"

"I said it before, Corrigan," I obfuscated. "I'm nothing, no-one. I'm not trying to cause you or the Pack problems. In fact I've been doing my best to keep the hell away from the lot of you. Now, please, tell me you are going to leave Cornwall alone."

He snarled at me. "Tell me what you are and then I will leave them alone."

Goddamnit. The bloodfire rose in my stomach in nervous panic. I tried to think. It didn't really matter if Corrigan knew that I was a Draco Wyr if it meant that Julia, Tom, Betsy and the rest would be safe. But Iabartu had thought I was important enough for her to come to this plane to fight for. And Solus thought that my blood could be of use to the Fae. What if the Lord Alpha thought that he could use me to for some kind of nefarious Brethren means? It wasn't as if I knew him all that well and now that he knew I wasn't a shifter he'd have no reason to care whether I was dead or alive. I had no idea what the extent of my dragon blood actually meant, only that some people – some demi-goddesses at least- would kill for it. And my mother had abandoned me with the Pack apparently because of it, too. What if I told Corrigan and then he still destroyed the Cornish pack anyway and then took his newfound knowledge and did something terrible with it?

"You don't trust me." He said it matter of factly but the tic in his cheek was back again.

"I hardly know you," I answered.

"You'll have plenty of opportunity to get to know me, kitten."

I was confused. "What do you mean?"

He gave a short sharp laugh. "You cause trouble wherever you go. It seems far more prudent to keep you here where I can keep an eye on you."

"You can't do that!" I was suddenly alarmed.

"Why not?" He asked smoothly. "You tell me what you really are. I don't hurt your little country friends. You stay here."

My eyes widened. "Oh no no no no no, my Lord," I protested, forgetting for a moment that I wasn't 'good' enough to call him that. "I need to go back to the mages."

He suddenly stilled. "And why is that?"

"My friend, Corrigan. The one I told you they'd done something to? They'll only release her if I go back to them."

"Go back to them and do what?"

"Some weird mage training programme. Not that I'm a mage, as I keep telling you," I said hastily, "but they seem to think that it means I won't misuse my potential for power, such as it is. All I can really do is the green fire stuff and that clearly runs out of juice before I manage to do much." I gazed beseechingly up at his tanned face, trying to avoid losing myself in his liquid gold eyes. "I gave them my word. And they won't help my friend unless I keep my promise."

He lifted a shoulder in an elegant shrug. "It's of no matter. I'll talk to them."

I exploded in a fury of heat. "Fucking hell, Corrigan! It is of matter. I promised them I'd go back. And I am not going to let my friend down."

His eyes narrowed. "Is this a special friend?"

"Of course, she's a fucking special friend, you prat!"

He smiled oddly at that and relaxed. "Well, you have a choice to make then, kitten. Either you save your Cornish friends and stay here, or you save your *special* friend and go to the mages." He moved back and grinned wolfishly. "Your choice."

"What is with you and your megalomania? Why do you need me to stay here? After all, Corrigan, all I seem to do is piss you off. Just do the right thing for once and let the Cornish pack off and let me go."

"Well, no, I don't think I'll do that, kitten. If the Ministry and the Arch-Mage think that you're so bloody important that they're going to send you to their academy and train you even though you insist that you are not a witch, then you must be something special." The green sheen in his eyes became more pronounced. "And that means that I want you too."

I shook my head in exasperation. I didn't really understand what was going on at all. I'd assumed that Corrigan would immediately go running off to fulfill the Brethren's need to keep their existence a secret and punish Cornwall. But he seemed far more interested in me, than in any of them. I thought back over everything that he'd said. I realised that he'd initially seemed puzzled that I thought that he was going to hurt the Cornish pack. Either that meant that they were of so little consequence to him that he really didn't care what happened to them or he'd never had any intention of meting out the famed Brethren purge. Everything I'd always been told – and certainly everything that the Cornish pack, John included, had always believed was that if the Brethren knew that a human had been let into the shifter secret, then everyone in that pack would be destroyed as a result. But maybe that was wrong. If only my brain and my bloodfire were both a little less cloudy then I might be able to think my way out of this. The toll of the mages' inquisition and the fight with the shifters was becoming apparent.

I looked at Corrigan who was staring at me with an unfathomable expression on his face. My eyes flicked down towards his wrist. Just visible under the impeccably tailored and brilliantly white linen shirt he was wearing was a gold watch. It was typically expensive looking. No expense spared for the magnificent Lord Alpha, I thought sardonically. I craned my neck ever so slightly. It was just after 6. It had be 6 in the evening because it had been light outside when the tiger brought me in. That meant I'd only been out for an hour at the most. And that meant that I still had just under fifteen hours to make good on my promise to the mages.

"I need a break," I announced.

Corrigan arched one perfectly plucked eyebrow. Jesus, was everything about this guy perfect?

"In the last twenty-four hours, I have stormed the Ministry, been interrogated, been attacked and been kept against my will. I am tired. I need a break to think over what you have said." I pasted a fake smile on my face. "Pretty please?"

He hesitated for the briefest moment and then snapped off a short grunt of agreement and turned to the door.

"Uh, Corrigan?"

He twisted his neck back towards me. "What?"

I jerked my head down and back in the vague direction of my bound hands. "Can you...?"

"No. Don't push your luck, Mackenzie," he growled. "I'll send someone to tend to your wounds."

"I don't need anyone to look after me," I started to call after him, but he was out the door too quickly and my complaint was swallowed up into the small room. I gave myself a brief nod, however. I had a bit of breathing space and a bit of time.

CHAPTER 22

After Corrigan's departure, the silence in the room was almost deafening. My wrists chafed under the bindings and I cursed him out loud for not loosening them even slightly. What exactly did he think I was going to do? I was surrounded by hundreds of shifters; I was hardly a danger.

Sighing loudly, I leaned against the wall and let my legs relax till I slid down and hit the floor. It seemed to be my lot to keep being trapped in little rooms. I supposed that at least this one didn't have a magical cage stuck inside it. Without any idea about when Corrigan would return, and aware that my time was limited anyway because I had to get back to the mages, I closed my eyes. I was in desperate need of some rest, even if just for an hour, if I was going to have any chance of doing verbal battle with the Lord Alpha. Almost immediately I felt myself drifting off into sleep.

Usually, when I'm tired enough to fall asleep within heartbeats, I don't dream. Something about the setting perhaps and the stress of the last twenty-four hours changed all that. I dreamt that I was standing in a ring of fire. Mrs Alcoon was with me, holding a cup of herbal tea and flicking hot droplets of it at me with her finger.

"You let me down!" she screeched. "I gave you a job! I took you in! Now look at me!"

I tried to speak but no words came out. From the other side of the fire circle, Alex and Arch-Mage grinned at me. "You can't trust a dragon, Your Magnificent Sublime Most Fantastical Highness," said Alex.

"You're right, Mage Florides," commented the Arch-Mage. "We have no choice but to exterminate the old lady."

He flicked a finger and I stared in horror as Mrs Alcoon let out a blood-curdling scream and vanished in a puff of blue smoke. The cup of tea that she had been holding smashed on the floor but, instead of the remnants of tea spilling from it, thick oozing blood trickled towards me.

"It's no good, my Lord," stated Anton solemnly. "We knew she wasn't a shifter. You'll have to kill us all."

From the other side of the circle, Corrigan looked at me and winked, blowing me a kiss from his chiseled lips, then with one swipe of a massive furry black paw, cuffed Anton so hard on the side of his head that it came clean off his shoulders and rolled to the edge of the flames.

The bodyless Anton continued talking. "It's all your fault, Mackenzie Smith. All your fault. All your fault."

The repetitive phrase banged inside my skull. I felt heat inside me, and smelled burning. Looking down, I realised that where the blood from the teacup had touched me I was burning, my clothes and skin blackening into charcoal. I tried to run away but the flames were pinning me on all sides and smoke was rising and getting into my eyes and my throat.

I could hear Julia's voice although by this point I could no longer see her. "It's all your fault, Mack."

John joined me in the circle and looked at me sadly, shaking his head. "I had such high hopes for you. You've just let me down."

I started to scream; heat and terror and anguish all mixing up inside me. I couldn't breathe, it was all too much, I couldn't do anything…

"Red? Wake up!" A hand was shaking my shoulder.

I blinked myself out of the dream and managed to sit up. "Tom?"

"You were having a nightmare. Jesus, Red what the hell have you been doing?"

Although it had only been a scant day or two since I'd seen him at the restaurant, I was so happy to see a friendly face that I almost cried. I tried to fling my arms around him, forgetting that they were still tied behind my back, and just succeeded in sprawling myself across the floor by his feet. Tom bent down and gently brought me back up to a sitting position.

"Thanks," I muttered.

He leaned over and brushed a loose strand of hair away from my face, then tucked it behind my ear. It was a particularly brotherly gesture, which surprised me.

"No problem. What happened to the fairy?"

I'd forgotten about Solus in the midst of the barrage from Corrigan. "I have no idea," I growled. "But he'd better have a good explanation when he finally decides to show up." I stared at Tom, suddenly worried. "Did Corrigan say anything to you about what he was going to do? You know, now he knows that I'm not a shifter?"

"Well, he's got you tied up here for one, Red."

I shook my head in irritation. "No, I mean to you. And Betsy. And everyone else."

Tom looked uncomfortable. "I don't think he's going to do anything. That stuff about no humans ever supposed to know about us, well…," His voice drifted off.

"Tom?" I prompted.

He cast his eyes down to the ground. "Red, I'm not sure I can do this. This conversation, I mean. I'm them. I'm the Brethren now. They're my family just like John and you and everyone else was. I don't think that I can discuss these kinds of things with an outsider now. Even you."

That stung. Especially the part about being called an outsider. I tried not to let Tom see that it got to me and forced myself not to jump down his throat at his absurd tailcoat attitude but instead focused on his words. "But," I said softly, "you don't think he'll hurt you. Or them."

He looked up and held my eyes for a moment. "No, I don't."

That kind of gibed with what I'd registered from Corrigan's initial reaction. Of course, I couldn't be completely complacent but it was just remotely possibly that it was true. I wanted it to be true. Not just because I wanted him to leave my friends alone but also because there was a part of me that didn't want to believe that he would be capable of ordering cold-blooded murder like that. It didn't seem to make sense that everyone in Cornwall had believed the opposite and I knew for a fact that he was one hell of a scary bugger but still... I leaned my head against the back of the wall thoughtfully. Had all of my running and hiding been for nothing? Could I have stayed in Cornwall after all? I thought of Anton and the bloodfire and of being a Draco Wyr. No, I had to have left regardless of the Brethren's anti-human policy.

But...I looked back at Tom. "Why did he come after me?"

He rubbed his neck. "Well, rogue shifters are kind of a problem."

Huh. A bit like rogue mages perhaps? These otherworlders really didn't like anyone who tried to break ranks.

"And, you know," Tom continued, "you can do stuff."

I raised my eyebrows. "Do stuff?"

"Yeah. You can fight harder than almost anyone else. Almost more than Corrigan."

I snorted at that. *Almost* more than Corrigan? Hell, on a good day – when I'd not been beaten up already by half the world - he'd better watch his back.

"There have been some whispers too," Tom said. "Like that

you can use the Voice. Like an alpha. Is that because…?" He didn't finish the sentence.

"Maybe," I answered.

"And that green fire shit?"

"Yeah, I'm really not too sure about that and how it works to be honest, Tom."

He opened his mouth to speak again but was interrupted by a knock at the door. A huge grin spread over his face and he reminded me for just a moment of his carefree puppy dog like attitude back in Cornwall, when life had been simpler.

"You're going to love this, Red!" he said, bounding up to pull open the door.

"Mack!" Betsy rushed in, a wreath of smiles on her face.

I tried to pull myself up to my feet but failed dismally. She barely noticed, however, and bent down to give me a huge hug.

"It is so amazing to see you!" she sang out. "What the hell happened to your face? Would you believe that you've got the whole of the Brethren convinced that you're some kind of weird badass superhero?"

"Bets," Tom warned.

"Oh, pshaw, you." She hugged me again and then pulled back. "I've really missed you, you know." She held out her left hand in front of me and displayed an ostentatiously large diamond ring. "And look! We're engaged!"

"Betsy, stop smothering the girl," came a very familiar voice from the doorway.

I stopped breathing for a moment and craned my neck round Betsy's body to see if it could really be true. "Julia?" I couldn't keep the tremor out of my voice.

"Hello, love." She wheeled herself in in some kind of black metal wheelchair and beamed down at me.

Despite Tom's implications to the contrary, I was suddenly worried. "Why are you here? Is it because of me?"

Her expression flickered for a second then she smiled kindly.

"No, it's not. I rather think that the Lord Alpha doesn't actually hold with all of that archaic nonsense about humans."

I immediately felt awful. Julia still thought I was human because she'd virtually been in a coma the last time I saw her. And she ended up in that state, and now in a wheelchair because of me. "Julia, I…I'm so sorry. All this is my fault…" A big fat tear rolled down my face.

"Don't you dare, Mackenzie Smith! Don't you dare suggest that this had anything to do with you at all. You could not have done anything, do you hear me?" She maneouvred her wheelchair to my side and reached down to me with one hand. "You need to forget all that nonsense. None of this was your fault. Now where is that oaf of a Lord Alpha, anyway? How dare he tie you up as if you were some kind of criminal?"

I began to cry harder.

Julia ignored my hiccuping sobs and addressed Betsy. "I need some of the tallow ointment. The orange cream. It's on my dresser. Will you go fetch it for me, dear?"

Betsy nodded and ran off.

"Tom? I will need some hot water and clean bandages."

He looked at her for a moment before shaking himself and nodding. "Er, yes right, okay." He disappeared out the door also.

"Now, Mack, pull yourself together. I need to sort out that mess on your face and can't do it if you are weeping so unnecessarily. How did it happen? I need to know so I can help the healing process properly."

I sniffed and tried to calm myself down. "Most of it was some kind of magic attack, but some of it was me trying to get some blood."

Julia looked remarkably startled at that but managed to prevent herself from commenting. "Okay, that's good. It means that there's no chance of infection from some nasty shifter's unwashed claws. Honestly, dear, you wouldn't believe how unhygienic some of this Brethren lot can be. It's really rather disgusting."

I smiled through my tears.

"There now," she patted my shoulder again. "I'm going to have some serious words with those wizards if I ever see them though." She sniffed. "Thinking they can mess up my Mackenzie."

That almost set me off again but I managed to bite my lip and stay composed. Tom returned, carrying a bowl of steaming water and a pile of soft fluffy towels and bandages. Betsy arrived almost immediately after with some strong smelling tubs of ointment.

"Déjà vu," I murmured.

They all smiled at me.

"Now then," Julia said briskly, "let's get you sorted out."

I managed to hold it together while Julia tended to my cheek, carefully washing it first and then applying the ointment. She was determined to attach some kind of bandage as well, but I managed to persuade her to let it be. It would heal quicker in the open air and make me look less like a fragile little girl to the Brethren members. She was just about done when there was a tentative knock on the door and a nervous face peered round.

"Uh, Miss Julia?"

She didn't turn around to look straight away but I watched in open curiosity as the owner of the face gestured panickedly to Betsy, whose eyes widened in what could only be described as shock and horror. She clutched onto Julia's arm.

"Julia, you have to go."

"Mmm, what?" Julia finally looked up at the intruder. When she took in the expression of the nervous shifter, she sighed deeply and rubbed her forehead.

"I need to go, Mackenzie dear. Betsy, will you finish up here?"

She nodded and Julia swung her wheelchair round adeptly, before leaving the little room with such momentum that I was incredibly impressed at how quickly she'd adapted to having to use wheels instead of legs.

Tom started to tidy up the debris from her ministrations. There was no doubt about it; the tension level in both him and

Betsy had been raised several notches. They were both pointedly not looking at each other but something was definitely up.

"What is it?"

Neither of them answered my query.

"Come on, guys, clearly there's something quite serious going on. Is this why Julia's really here? What's up?"

For a moment they both continued to stay silent. Then eventually Tom spoke up. "There's some kind of disease going round the Pack. It's virtually decimated the Somerset group. One of the Brethren docs, a wererat called Higgins, went to try and help. Half of them were already bedridden by the time he got there and he couldn't seem to do anything to stop it. He came back here to make a report before anyone realised how contagious it was."

"There have been three deaths already, Mack. It's just awful," Betsy added in a grim voice.

"Julia's here because they think she might be able to help," I said, suddenly realising.

Tom shrugged expansively. "We've tried everything else and nothing's working. It's a long shot but her knowledge of medicinal herbs might do something."

Dawning comprehension was hitting me. It was incredibly unusual for anyone other than the local alphas to meet with the Brethren face to face in their own headquarters. I was pretty sure that in the whole time I'd lived in Cornwall it had only ever been John who'd been here before. It had been bothering me as to why Julia had been there and I felt like an idiot for being egotistical enough to think that the reason was me. Other bits and pieces from what Corrigan had let drop and the tired look on his face started to slot into place.

"Has she had any luck yet?" I asked, in a hopeful voice.

The look on both their faces was answer enough.

"This is why we need to make sure that you are kept out of the way of the rest of the Pack," Tom said, seriously. "This disease, whatever it is, only seems to affect shifters. Now that everyone knows that you're not a shifter after all, they're a bit pissed off that they've expended all this energy trying to get hold of you when their own are at death's door."

"And a bit jealous that you're going to be immune," Betsy added.

That annoyed me. "Really? Really? How is it my fault that I'm not a shifter? That's like being fucked off at the sun for rising." Another thought occurred to me. "And if I was a shifter they were effectively bringing me into the danger zone by capturing me in the first place! If this disease is only here and in Somerset so far, then…"

"'So far' being the operative words, Mackenzie," said Corrigan from the door.

Damn it, he was as quiet as a ninja. Or a cat. Figures.

He moved into the room with silent feline grace. "The disease is spreading. There are already reports from Gloucester. Rogue shifters are of particular concern because they're nomadic. If one happens to catch this disease and then decides to wander around the country then the results could be catastrophic."

"So why in the hell don't you just warn them? Put something out on the Othernet, and tell everyone."

"'First of all, we'll create a panic. Second of all, do you really think they'd believe us? The entire shifter world – and that includes the local packs – seem to think that we're the boogiemen. Some of them," he looked at me pointedly, "even seem to think that we'd go so far as to destroy entire localities because a single human knows of their existence."

"Oh," I muttered. "So you definitely aren't going to…"

"No, you feckless harpy, I definitely won't."

"Why are you telling me this? You could have kept me stringing along so that I'd stay here without you forcing me."

Corrigan looked momentarily at Tom and Betsy, who were both watching our exchange with slightly astonished expressions on their faces. "I rather thought that someone would have told you the truth already by now."

"My Lord Alpha, I…," Tom began nervously.

Corrigan held up a hand and he fell silent.

I cleared my throat. "Actually, Tom suggested it but wouldn't go so far as to tell me everything. It appears that loyalty around here is in abundance," I said pointedly, taking a dig at him for his previous remarks.

The Lord Alpha didn't even glance in their direction, he just stared hard at me before continuing in a lighter tone. "Besides which, kitten, I don't think anyone could really hold you against your will."

He stepped over to me and hooked his hands under my armpits, pulling me up to my feet. I hoped that he didn't come away with any old sweat of mine against his manicured hands. He turned me around and I felt him undoing the cuffs that bound my wrists together. His body was close to mine and his warm breath was scalding my neck. I felt the bloodfire rise in response. Fucking hell, what was wrong with me? I was not, most definitely was NOT, attracted to this overbearing lump of brooding masculinity. Praying that he couldn't hear my heart thudding, I tried to keep my voice calm.

"You're letting me go?"

Corrigan finished uncuffing me and turned me around to face him. He took a step backwards and stared at me unfathomably. "We have enough here to deal with without some non-human non-shifter trouble-maker hanging around. I've decided it's better for everyone if we just let you leave."

I tried to tell myself that I did not feel a little flicker of disappointment at that. "After all that trouble?" I taunted him gently. "What happened to 'if the mages want you then I want you too?'"

The muscle in his cheek ticked again. "I believe that you are a lady of your word. Promise me that you won't do anything to hurt any shifter and I will let you go."

"I can't promise that, Corrigan," I protested. "What if a shifter comes after me? I have to be able to protect myself."

He growled, annoyed. "I will make sure that you are left in peace."

"You can't assure me of that! You can't expect everyone in the whole wide world to jump to your bidding."

He raised his eyebrows, the green in his irises becoming more pronounced. "Actually, kitten, I'm the Lord Alpha. Yes, I can."

"Yes, but…," I began to splutter.

"Fine," he sighed. "Do you promise not to intentionally hurt without provocation any shifter?"

"Uh, okay, I promise," I said, still baffled by Corrigan's abrupt volte-face. What had happened to change his mind?

He gestured towards the door with a flourish. "Then you are free to go."

Without waiting for me to respond, he turned on his heel and walked out, motioning for both Tom and Betsy to follow him. On the way out, Betsy turned and shot me a look, "Kitten?" she hissed. "What on earth, Mack?"

I just shrugged at her, trying not to look as shocked as I felt. I rubbed my wrists where the cuffs had chafed and looked at the open door. Okay, then. I shrugged again and headed out after them.

CHAPTER 23

WALKING BACK UP THE SPIRAL STAIRCASE THAT I'D SO unceremoniously been carried down, I still felt very puzzled and slightly hurt. I mean, it was good that Corrigan was letting me go, but it just didn't make any sense.

Once I rounded the top of the stairs, I was faced with a large ornate chamber. A glass dome covered in different shades and colours of stained Tiffany styled panes glimmered in the dying afternoon sun. There was a group of shifters to my right, clearly Brethren by their dark suits and vaguely superior countenances, but for all their airs they appeared to be incredibly worried about something. I wasn't particularly surprised. Whatever this disease was that was ravaging the pack, it was clearly something not to be taken lightly.

No-one stopped me and, in fact, virtually no-one even bothered to glance my way. It was as if I'd somehow ceased to exist. I was sure I'd not imagined the buzz that had occurred as I'd been brought in, even if I'd been blindfolded. At yet now, no-one was interested. Why had Corrigan given up trying to find out what I was? Didn't he care about the whole green fire shooting from fingertips bit? I was pretty sure that I wasn't just in need of my ego being massaged and that there was something else up.

Spotting Staines striding across the room with the loping and limbering stride that gave away his alter-ego as a were-bear, I took a deep breath and walked up to him, grabbing onto his arm. He spun around and snarled at me.

"What the fuck do you want?"

"Staines, I know you don't like me very much, but what the hell is going on?"

He yanked his arm away and glared. "Get lost, human. You've caused enough damage."

"Staines, come on," I insisted.

His yellow sheened eyes narrowed. "If you must know, the Lord Alpha has got it."

"Got it?" I asked in confusion.

"Got the fucking disease. The one we can't control or cure. The old woman just confirmed it not long ago. We're going into shut down."

My stomach dropped with a lurch. Corrigan? But he was too fit surely to be ill. "But he looked fine! Well, a bit tired and pale but I just saw him."

"Well, he'd hardly tell you what was going on, would he? You're not one of us."

The spite and venom in Staines' voice was staggering. I barely noticed though, still reeling as I was from the information about the Lord Alpha. I thought back to his appearance just now but all I could remember was how I'd felt being in such close proximity to him.

"What happens now?" I asked in a dull voice.

"Now?" Staines looked at me disbelievingly. "Now piss right off and don't bother us again."

I forced myself to refrain from reminding him that it hadn't been me who'd been doing the bothering.

"I mean, what happens to Corrigan?"

He looked at me balefully. "If it's anything like the others, then he'll get gradually weaker and weaker. There are already indications that his temperature is rising. Shifting just makes it worse. This disease seems to affect the liver and the kidneys. His skin will start to turn red with hot flushes, he'll get thirsty and then…" Staines shook himself and seemed to remember who he was talking to. "Now fuck off, girlie, we don't need you here."

He jerked his head towards one of shifters in the group to the right. He broke off and came over.

"Sir?"

"Escort Miss Smith off the premises. See to it that she doesn't return."

The shifter moved to take hold of my arm but I side-stepped away from him. "I can make my own way out, thank you very much."

"Then make it," snapped Staines, turning away.

The shifter next to me put his hands on his hips. I looked him in the eye, daring him to try to touch me again. He looked away. Hah. Pulling my shoulders back, and trying to ignore the sick feeling inside me at the news that Corrigan was ill, I walked out towards the entrance and into the street.

I'd forgotten how cold it was outside and shivered almost immediately. I turned and looked at the now closed door to the Brethren's headquarters. I chewed on my lip for a moment and then made my decision.

Corrigan?

There wasn't an immediate answer. A squat dirty looking truck barreled past me in the road, disappearing out of sight. I tried again.

Corrigan? Are you there?

For a moment I thought he wasn't going to answer but then his Voice popped into my head, sounding tired.

What is it, Mackenzie?

Staines told me. That you've got it. I didn't think that I needed to elaborate on what 'it' was.

And? Are you going to gloat now?

Upset that he thought so little of me, I sat down heavily on one of the steps leading away from the building. Now wasn't the time to fight back. *I'm sorry, Corrigan. There must be something you can do. Julia knows a lot of stuff about a lot of herbs.*

She hasn't been able to do anything more so far than ease of the pain of those suffering.

Do you know where it came from?

Only that it originated in Somerset as far as we can tell. The first victim was an older shifter. Nobody realised how serious it was until the others around him started to get ill also.

I thought of Betsy, Tom and Julia, along with all of the other shifters inside, just feet away – Staines' comment that they were going into shutdown. *What's going to happen to the Pack?*

Why do you care? You left, remember? He didn't sound annoyed, which worried me more than anything. He just sounded as if he'd had enough. I wished now that I was back with him; the urge to give him a hug was overwhelming. Perhaps it would be worth wangling my way back inside. I didn't have long before I had to get back to the mages, but under these circumstances they might be a bit understanding. Not that understanding and compassion was something I had yet noticed was a trait of any of the magic wielders, but you never knew.

Are you sure it just affects shifters?

What – are you worried about yourself now? There was a slight tinge of irritation flitting back into his Voice now, which gladdened me immensely. *Besides, I thought you were in a rush to go off and play student with the mages.*

It might be dangerous letting me out on the street, Corrigan, I could be a carrier. Maybe I should stay with you. Uh, I mean, with the Brethren.

We know that humans aren't affected. In fact, no species other than some animal ones and shifters are affected by the red fever. We're not entirely stupid, kitten, we did check.

I doubted very much that any of the Brethren had thought to

check whether that included dragons, but wisely didn't say anything. Then I paused suddenly in mid thought.

What did you call it?

Mackenzie, I've got things to do. There are plans that need to be put into place in case the disease spreads further.

Corrigan, this is important. What did you call it?

The red fever. The symptoms start off with just a temperature and headache. A bit like the flu, I suppose. But a day or two in the afflicted shifter's skin starts to flush red. If they shift, then their eyeballs turn red also. It's really all downhill from there. One of our doctors has come up with some kind of blood test that detects whether someone has it or not. We were all tested this morning, before you were brought in. Nine of us are already infected. She expects that the first symptoms will start appearing in the next few hours.

My mind was suddenly whirling. I tried to think and focus.

Mackenzie?

Uh, Corrigan, I've got to go.

I'd expect nothing less. Look after yourself, kitten.

His Voice left with his final words ringing in my head with an air of depressing finality about them. I pushed them out of my thoughts and pulled myself up off the cold step. I needed to get to Scotland and time was of the essence.

With no money, and no identification, flying was out of the question. The train or the bus would take too long. What I really needed was Solus, but clearly he was playing hard to get. I tried calling out his name, just in case he'd now decide to hear me, but my voice just bounced around the empty street. This was clearly not a very efficient way of getting in touch with him. I thought about the troll in the weapons shop. I didn't think I could trust that creature as far as I could throw him – and that wouldn't be far given how squat and heavy looking he'd been. But Solus hadn't paid for the knives – and I certainly hadn't paid for the knives – and the troll had certainly seemed to know the Fae already. So, even though it seemed like a long shot, it was just possible that he would have a way of contacting Solus, if only to bill him.

With sudden purpose, I took off. I figured I was at least five miles away from the shadowy little alleyway where the troll's shop had been and I didn't know this city at all. My weak sense of direction would probably not hold up well amongst the maze of concrete buildings. But I didn't have to actually go there in person. All I needed was a computer.

There were no shops – and certainly no internet cafes – anywhere nearby. As I ran, I listened for the buzz of people and traffic. The streets were fairly quiet but there was a distant hum coming from over to my right hand side. As soon as I could, I turned off into that direction.

Before too long, I passed a homeless guy sitting at the side of the road with a brown paper bag covering whatever the tipple of the day was. I slowed down and bent over to talk to him.

"Hey, where's the nearest internet café?"

He gazed up at me with unfocused eyes. "That's a hell of a fight you've been in, sweetheart," he slurred.

"I'm not your sweetheart," I snapped. "Internet café? Where can I find one?"

He pursed his lips and then jerked his head up to the right. "Over there. On Bewer Street."

I threw out a quick thanks, dropping the last of my crumpled up money from Alex into his hand, and sprinted off. He shouted something after me, but his words were lost in the wind. I dodged a few rubbish bins and skirted down a small side street, my eyes scanning the area. There was a graffiti laden street sign on the other side of the road so I jogged over and tried to make out the words underneath the black spray paint. Bewer Street. Outstanding. I glanced up and down, trying to work out which direction to take. There appeared to be a cluster of shops up ahead so I ran off in that direction, the cold wind whipping at my face.

I slowed when I started to near the shops. I passed a liquor store and a 24 hour convenience shop that clearly wasn't very convenient nor was it 24 hours because it was all shut up. The next shop front along was an internet café. I tried the door but it was locked. Cursing, I jiggled the doorknob pointlessly, but the café wasn't going to open miraculously just because I wanted it to. I peered inside the grimy windows. There were several desktop monitors dotted around. I couldn't make out anyone inside.

Jogging around the back, I looked for a way in. There was a back door with a plate of glass covered with wire mesh set into it. I cast around for somewhere a key might be hiding, turning over a few stones that were lying around and kicking over a rubbish can that was filled to the brim with sour smelling rotting waste. Nothing. Fuck it. I picked up one of the stones and threw it at the door but it bounced harmlessly off. The shop might look like it was falling apart but getting through the wire mesh was going to take more time than I really had to spare. I'd missed the lockpicking part of my education but figured it really couldn't be that hard. If I could just get hold of a credit card or a bobby pin then I could try that. Looking down at the upturned bin, I wrinkled my nose in disgust. There was nothing else for it, however.

I knelt down and began rummaging through, wondering what diseases I'd be picking up myself by doing this. There were remnants of old mouldy bits of bread, plastic wrappings and bits of cardboard. Everything I touched seemed to have some horribly foul gloopy stuff covering it. Eventually I came across a scrunched up pile of papers that seemed to be photocopies of letters addressed to the local council complaining about the poor rubbish collection procedures. Their complaint was my gain in more ways than one, however, because they were bound together with a paper clip. Wiping the gloop off the little piece of metal first by swiping it over my jeans, I straightened it out and then crouched down beside the lock to try my luck. I stuck the clip inside the rusty lock wondering what the hell I was doing. With my free hand, I gripped the door knob, intending to twist it as I fiddled around trying to catch the lock. Without warning though, the knob turned and I was falling headlong through onto the back porch.

"Fucking hell!" I swore aloud. The bloody door hadn't been locked at all in the first place.

Scowling in irritation, I picked myself up carefully. Either the café owner was careless or someone was still inside, so I quietly made my way through to the front, keeping my senses alert in case I was discovered. It appeared, however, that they were simply just not as careful about security as they should have been as the whole place was silent. Briefly sending up a prayer of thanks to the god of fortuitous breaking and entering, who definitely seemed to have been on my side of late, I jogged over to one of the computers and turned it on. As it slowly creaked its way into life, my gaze fell on the small bar at the side. There were shelves filled with dubious looking plastic wrapped cakes and a small display fridge. And there was a state of the art coffee machine with a green light blinking next to it. Sighing in happiness, I jumped over and found myself a mug, flicking on the machine to pour a shot of sticky black caffeine goodness, then I made my way back to the computer, gulping thankfully as I went.

Once the machine was turned on, I made my way onto the internet and typed in the address in the search bar that would take me to the Othernet gateway. Before too long, the familiar glow of the otherworld's search engine blinked at me. I typed in troll, weapons and London, immediately coming up with a list of possible sites. I clicked on the first one and the unsmiling face of the troll stared out at me. Perfect.

There was a tab detailing contact information so I clicked on that and ended up with various bits of information, including a phone number. Memorising it quickly, I moved over to the café's front desk and picked up the phone there, dialing the number. It rang several times before a familiarly gruff voice answered.

"What?"

"You might want to work on your customer service there," I commented.

The troll hung up. Fuck. I had to stop pissing people off with my big mouth. I rang it again. Again the troll answered.

"What?"

"I'm sorry about before. I'm calling because I was in your shop yesterday. Maybe you remember? I was with my friend and we picked up a couple of daggers."

"No refunds," growled the shop owner.

"I don't want a refund," I said hastily, before I annoyed him any further. "I just need to check that you have the right details for payment."

"Lord Sol Apollinarus. Care of the Ritz Carlton, same as always."

Yahtzee. Although 'Lord' again? Solus clearly was more important than I'd given him credit for. Despite that, it was a great start. I doubted that he checked into the hotel under 'Lord Sol Apollinarus' though.

"Er, and the name you have registered at the hotel is...?"

"Who is this?" demanded the troll suddenly as my luck started to abruptly run out. I was about to try to pacify him to see if I could wheedle Solus' other pseudonym out of him, when I heard voices coming from the back door through which I'd entered.

Shit. I slammed the phone back onto its cradle and ducked down behind the coffee bar, heart thudding. I'd have to hope that whoever it was had just forgotten something – like locking up properly perhaps - and wasn't going to hang around. Then I remembered the computer. The page I'd left it on was linked to the Othernet. That was not good. I was pretty sure that no-one, be they mages or shifters or even trolls, would be particularly happy with me if I left that particular gateway open to prying human eyes. I vaulted over the wooden bar, somersaulting in a roll to the computer and quickly disconnecting and clearing the history, before curling up under the desk and pulling the swivel chair in front of me to try to cover myself.

The voices grew louder. "Jesus, Tina, you need to lock that door every time we leave."

"Yeah? How about you need to lock that door? Not everything is my fault, you know."

The couple continued bickering to each other. I, meanwhile, tried to make myself into as small a ball as possible and prayed they didn't enter the actual shop front. For once, my luck was holding and the voices drifted away and up stairs to where I assumed there was a small apartment. I began to extricate myself from under the desk when I realised that my hair was caught on something. Without really thinking about it, I tugged my head away and almost yelped at the sharp yank on my scalp. Reaching up, I gave a grimace of disgust as I realised that I'd managed to attach myself to someone's discarded chewing gum on the underside of the desk. That was seriously gross. I picked with my fingers, trying to release myself, eventually pulling free but with half of the gum coming with me. Feeling up to my hair with my fingertips, I scowled at the large amount of sticky gunk that had now attached itself to my scalp. On the grand scale of things it was a small matter, but I was pretty vain about my hair. Pulling my fingers away and wiping them on my jeans, I sighed. It would just have to wait till later. I cast a forlorn look over at the coffee machine and clambered out from under the desk, then exited quietly through the back door. 'Tina' had helpfully left it unlocked again.

Once outside, I considered my options. Somehow I was going to have to get to the Ritz-Carlton hotel to find Solus. I hadn't had time to get onto the normal human internet and find out exactly where the hotel was. It had to be in central London, however. I had an idea in my head, I guess from having seen it in pictures or on the news, of what it looked like, but its specific location was a bit of a mystery. I didn't have any money left now so I couldn't jump into a cab to get there. I thought for a moment about flagging one down anyway and making Solus pay for it at the other end – let's face it, it would be the least he could do after not answering my previous requests for his presence - but there was no guarantee that Solus would even be at the hotel and I didn't want to cause any more potential trouble. There was nothing else to be done, I'd just have to try and run my way there. I hoped it wouldn't take too long; my time must surely be starting to run out.

I jogged back down to the main road and looked up and down. There seemed little point in going back the way I'd come, so I figured I'd continue to head away from the Brethren and hope that it was the right way. It occurred to me as well, that for my plan to work, I'd have to somehow get back to the Brethren too. Hopefully by then I'd have Solus back on my side and helping. I could remember Bewer Street but stupidly hadn't thought to pay attention to what street I'd started from. It wasn't like I could ask for directions. I imagined that conversation in my head with a random passerby. 'Yes, um, hello, sir? Can you tell me where all the dying shapeshifters are holed up?' No, that probably wouldn't work.

Setting off yet again, I tried to look up at the skyline for tall, recognisable buildings. It kind of stood to reason that they would be in the centre of the city where the hotel was. The angles must have been all wrong, however, because all I could see were telephone wires and grey skies. I was just pulling my gaze away from the heavens when I careered straight into a hard, warm body.

"What the fuck?" There hadn't been anyone in the street a moment before.

"I might ask you the same question, dragonlette," drawled the object of my search.

I began to pummel Solus on the chest. I wasn't trying to hurt him and he didn't move away but he equally didn't look massively impressed either.

"Where have you been? Solus, I've been calling and calling you!"

The Fae folded his arms and glared at me. "I'm not your servant and neither am I at your beck and call. I think we need to re-define the parameters of our relationship."

"Solus," I groaned, "I don't think you're at my beck and call at all but I thought that maybe we were kind of friends and that I could count on you. I needed your help. I know you're a Fae and you don't like humans but I thought maybe you liked me a bit." I realised as soon as the words were out of my mouth just how pathetic that sounded.

"You're right," he said. "I don't like humans. But you aren't human, are you? And that, not that I owe you an explanation, is where I've been."

I was a bit confused. Solus elaborated. "The Summer Queen is none too impressed that I have not yet explained why I have been spending so much time on this plane. I could, of course have told her that I have a living breathing Draco Wyr with me, but it occurred to me that might not be the best idea just yet so I have been prevaricating about you on your behalf. Neither is she particularly happy that there is a comatose Scottish witch on her land."

I freaked out. "You almost told her what I was? You prick! Solus, you're the one who told me that I couldn't tell anyone at all! Well, clearly I don't need to because you're doing all the blabbing for me!"

"Dragonlette, she's my Queen. And I didn't tell her YET, but I might have to."

Jesus, what was it with all these otherworld idiots and their chain of command?

"Anyway," Solus continued, "you'll be pleased to know that I have gained you somewhat of a reprieve. She's agreed to allow your Mrs Alcoon to stay for the time being, providing that you travel to Tir-na-Nog in the near future to meet her so she can determine your true nature for herself."

"She's going to have to get in line," I growled.

Solus raised his eyebrows at me questioningly. I filled him in on the events of the last forty-eight hours, from what had happened at the Ministry up till I'd left the Brethren. I wasn't entirely sure if it was a good idea broadcasting the fact that the shifter world was becoming incapacitated by a disease, especially to someone who I clearly couldn't really trust, but if my plan worked, then I figured it wouldn't really matter. And if my plan didn't work, well then it wouldn't really matter.

"How did you know I was here?" I questioned, suddenly. I had given up on calling for Solus ages ago and wasn't massively keen on the idea that he could find me with a snap of his fairy fingers whenever he wanted to.

"I received a very strange phone call from Balud about someone trying to track me down. He said the call came from this area."

Oh. Balud must be the troll. He must either have some mad tracking skills of his own or some outstandingly good tech to have pinpointed my location. I decided that either way I didn't really want to know. There were other things to worry about for the time being.

I softened my voice and looked hopefully at Solus. "So, will you help me now?"

"I don't quite understand, dragonlette. What help do you require? I do not see that there is anything you can do, unless you have a medical degree tucked up in your sleeves somewhere."

"Don't you get it? I thought you were all-knowing and wise. One of the things Mrs Alcoon had me do was collect some blisterwort from the Cairns for her to help her friend."

"To help her friend get over some mild illness," Solus said, confused.

"Well, yeah, but she also said that it had been used in the past to cure other things, including something called blushing disease."

Solus' expression cleared. "And you think this blushing disease might be what your pack is suffering from."

"They're not my pack, Solus," I said absently. "But, yes."

"There is one other thing that you've not really thought about," he added.

"What?"

"You're a Draco Wyr. This Iabartu woman..."

"Uh, demi-goddess, thank you very much."

He ignored me. "She wanted your blood, according to you, so that she could use its properties. And those properties include healing. Maybe all you need is to get your Lord to suck on your blood, vamp style, and then all your problems are solved." He clicked his fingers with a snap for effect.

"It's a possibility, Solus, but I don't know what my blood can do. Neither do you for that matter. I don't know if it'd end up making things worse, not better. And besides, it's also addictive. I don't want to turn the pack into a bunch of drug addicts."

"They might want to know why you are giving them blood in the first place too, of course," he surmised.

"Yes, and I'm trying to keep that a secret." I glared at him to let him know how pissed off I was that he'd been telling others what I didn't want anyone to know.

He gazed back innocently. "Hey, you can trust the Summer Queen. She's one of the good guys."

I refrained from commenting that I didn't think the Fae were ever truly going to be classed as the 'good guys' but decided it wouldn't exactly help my cause. Instead I returned to my original question. "So, will you help me?"

"If you promise me that when you're done with all this daft magic training stuff, you come to Tir-na-Nog and meet the Queen."

"Yes, yes. I promise," I said rashly. "You know it might be five years though?"

He shrugged. "Time is not a problem."

I snorted. "Not for you. I'm on a clock." I peered at him

anxiously for a moment. "You will keep Mrs Alcoon safe until then?"

Solus bowed dramatically and grinned at me. "You have my word." He held out his arm and the air started to shimmer purple. I held my breath waiting for the inevitable flood of nausea to hit and closed my eyes tightly.

CHAPTER 24

SEVERAL MOMENTS AND SEVERAL RETCHES LATER, I WAS PICKING myself up off the dark mossy ground at the Clava Cairns. Unlike the last time I'd been here, there wasn't a soul in sight. In fact, other than a patch of blackened grass from someone's abandoned campfire, there was no trace of the winter solstice festivities that, for me, now seemed half a lifetime ago.

Solus was standing a few feet away, hands on hips, and head slightly cocked. He looked vaguely amused.

"Don't say anything," I growled at him.

The corner of his mouth lifted slightly. I glared at him in further warning and he shrugged and wandered off to inspect some of the standing stones. Spitting on the ground to rid myself of the taste of bile, I began to cast around for signs of the blisterwort. There appeared to be a cluster over to my right so I strode off, ignoring the Fae further.

I figured that I'd probably require a great deal of the stuff. While it was by no means indigenous to Inverness, I had absolutely no idea where else I'd be able to procure some so it made sense to get as much as I could right now. I was careful to dig into the cold hard ground with my fingertips and uproot the plants completely however. At least that way Julia would be able to make proper cuttings to encourage it to grow elsewhere – preventing any future outbreaks of the disease. As I did so, I entertained myself with visions of Corrigan falling at my feet in abject gratitude at my having saved the entire Pack from oblivion.

"I will never call you kitten again, Mack, my savior," I grunted, scrabbling into the earth while on my knees. "Neither will I have my minions capture you and throw you into a cell. Instead I am clearly out of my league as leader of the Pack. You must take my place and I will become your servant."

An image flashed into my mind of myself draped over a chaise longue and Corrigan, wearing nothing more than a loin cloth, dropping grapes languidly into my mouth.

"What are you muttering about?" asked Solus from right behind me.

I started, blushing involuntarily as my daydream immediately evaporated. "Uh, nothing." I cleared my throat. "Make yourself useful, Solus, and help me get as much of this as I can."

The Fae moved round in front of me and knelt down, waggling his fingers in my face. "Do you see these?"

"Yes, you have fingers. Congratulations. Now put them to use."

"Dragonlette, you fail to see what is right in front of you. It takes considerable time and effort to maintain such perfectly manicured and groomed fingers as these. I am not about to ruin such good work by shoving my hands into some frozen Scottish dirt for a shapeshifter. In fact, truthfully, I don't really understand why you are doing it either. We are talking about the people who threw you out because you weren't furry enough to be one of them and from whom you've been hiding for the last six months."

"Well, by the sounds of things I didn't have to be hiding from them at all. I had kind of got that wrong. They were only worried that I might have gone rogue, not that I might be a human." I shoved the blisterwort I'd already collected up at Solus. "Here. If you're not going to help dig it up, then the least you can do is hold the bloody stuff."

He reluctantly took hold of the plants, with the faintest expression of someone who'd been asked to carry nuclear waste. "That still doesn't explain why you're so keen to help them. What have they done for you?"

I sighed and moved over to another patch. "Life isn't all about quid pro quo, Solus. Sometimes it's just nice to be nice." I tried conveniently to forget that I'd just been fantasising about exactly what quid pro quo I could get from Corrigan.

"Bullshit," he said mildly. "You're not nice."

I began to splutter, pausing from my digging. He waggled his eyebrows at me. "Oh, come on, dragonlette. You have an outrageous temper. And when was the last time you were nice to someone?"

"I'm nice all the time!"

"Go on. Name the last time you were nice."

I stared up at Solus, slightly open-mouthed as I tried to think. Surely there must be lots of times in the last few days? I rocked back on my heels. "Oh god. You're right. I'm a horrible person. I can't remember the last time I was nice. I'm a bitch."

Solus laughed at my mournful epiphany. I shot him a look filled with daggers, then realised that probably wasn't very nice. "Dragonlette, you're not a bitch. You're just a dragon. You have a bad temper and a strong sense of survival but you're so much more than *nice*. Relax." He grinned at me. "And stop changing the subject."

"What do you mean?"

"You're not helping the shifters because you're nice. You're helping them because you want them to like you. Or rather because you want a certain black haired, green eyed cat to like you at least."

"Corrigan? You think I'm doing this because I want Corrigan to like me? I can't stand him! He's a total arse. In fact, he's a megalomaniac who has done nothing but cause me trouble."

"And?" prompted Solus.

"And what?"

"Oh come on. You clearly fancy the pants off of him."

"Fuck off! I do not!"

I pulled myself up to standing and eyeballed Solus. He just calmly looked back at me. "It's okay, dragonlette, you can say it."

I shook my head at him in glum confusion.

"Say 'Solus, you are always right'."

I stared at him. "I do not fancy Corrigan," I enunciated.

He smirked. "Sure."

My mouth was suddenly dry. I thought about the Lord Alpha and the last time I'd seen him, with his green gold eyes roving irritably over me, and the ridiculous disappointment I'd felt when he'd turfed me out, as well as the way his muscles had rippled under his shirt despite the tiredness that was no doubt caused by the red fever.

"Oh God," I whispered.

"There you go," said Solus smugly. He licked his lips. "It's alright though, I can wait."

It took me a moment for his words to register and for me to find my voice. "Wait for what?"

"Till you work it out of your system." The Fae leaned in towards me and lowered his voice. "It's because he's so unattainable that you have, what do you humans call it? The hots for him? You'll get over it and I'll be here."

My eyes narrowed. "You'll be here? Solus…"

"Shhh," he said, placing a long finger against my lips. "This is a discussion for another time."

I opened my mouth to speak again but realised I had no idea what I would say, and shut it again. Solus might be right that I had a tiny crush on the Lord of all shapeshifters and he was probably right that it was just because I couldn't have him. However I knew deep within that there was not even the faintest flicker of attraction inside me for the Fae. I shifted uncomfortably, hoping that the reason he'd helped me so much had not been because he thought he might get something out of it by the end, before remembering that he was on the point of giving me up to the Summer Queen. It was probably more curiosity about shagging a dragon that had piqued Solus' interest, rather than any real emotion. I relaxed.

I moved away from him and changed the subject. "It's getting light. I need to get back to London to give this to Julia and then return to the mages."

Solus cocked his head and sketched a quick bow choosing not to remark on my sudden volte-face. "As you wish, dragonlette."

I began to snap at him not to call me that but the air was already starting to shimmer and the all too familiar nausea was rising in my stomach. I felt the Fae press something into my hand and dully registered that it was the cluster of blisterwort. My vision started to go blurry and the night sky swirled around in dizzying clouds. And then I was back in the entrance hall of the Brethren's hide-away, on my knees, nails clutching into the cool decorative floor tiles while around me I heard ripping clothes and the growls of changing shifters. Why Solus couldn't have picked a less conspicuous spot was beyond me. I looked around for the Fae, forcing down the nausea, but he was nowhere to be seen.

A tawny wolf took a step towards me, teeth bared. A sliver of drool hung from its mouth.

"Careful," I said slowly, trying to get control of my stomach and getting up to my feet, "you'll mess up the pretty floor."

From behind me I felt something snap at my calves. I sighed. I wasn't quite sure I was up to another fight just yet. As more shifters came into the hall, some already transformed, I knew that the odds would be massively against me anyway. I just had to get hold of Julia and pass her the blisterwort.

"I'm not trying to cause you any trouble," I shouted out. "I have something to help you."

The growling around me got louder. Goddamn shifters and

their hardheadedness. I caught sight of a familiar figure, her body lowered and ready to pounce.

"Lucy! Look, you know me." I coughed slightly. "Well, sort of. I need to give this to Julia. It's for the red fever. It'll cure it, I think. Please, just let me…"

Before I could finish my sentence a giant paw cuffed me on the side of my head and I went sprawling back onto the floor. The familiar flames answered the ringing pain in my head and, without thinking, I jumped to my feet and prepared to defend myself. I saw through narrowed eyes that the attack had come from Staines. I was going to enjoy this. Tingling heat ran through my veins and I felt my fingertips prickle. Interesting, that meant that the green fire was returning. I made a mental note of how long it had taken the strange magic to recover and hastily stuffed the blisterwort down the back of my jeans so that it didn't get singed. It rubbed irritatingly against my skin and I inwardly cursed the stupid shifters who I was actually trying to help.

I concentrated on my hands, damping down the fire before it got started in one rational moment as I decided that I'd make this a fair fight, and then kicked out at the bear, not quite connecting, and rolled immediately to my left and back onto my feet. The other shifters around me moved back, clearly allowing the Lord Alpha's right hand man the chance to take me down on his own. Fine, if that was the way they wanted to play it then I'd rise to the occasion.

Staines leapt towards me, with more lithe grace than I would have expected from his lumbering form. I managed to spring out of the way in time, however, and jumped up in to the air, scissoring out a hard kick and connecting with his shoulder. I landed back on the floor in a crouch as he began to barrel towards me. His right flank was vulnerable though and I saw my way in to slapping him down for good. I shifted my weight, preparing myself, and then stopped as I abruptly remembered the promise I'd made to Corrigan. Goddamnit. Although Staines had made the first move, I supposed that I had materialised rather dramatically in the middle of their home.

I jumped out of the way and turned, straightening up and holding my palms out in the universal language of surrender. "I don't want to fight you, Staines."

He snarled at me in bare acknowledgement of my words.

"I mean it." As much as it galled me, I forced myself to completely relax. "I've just come to bring you this."

I reached behind me to pull out the herb. The muscles in Staines' shoulders tensed.

"For fuck's sake," I spat, "I'm just trying to help you. These," I produced the blisterwort out with a flourish, "will help you."

He sprang forward, knocking me to the ground, until he was on top of me with his muzzle in my face.

"Jesus, you lumbering oaf. I'm one of you."

Staines snorted to show just how much he thought of that statement and opened his jaws to reveal sharp teeth. I twisted my head to the side to avoid his unpleasant hot breath and gasped. "Way Directive 14, you idiot."

He paused, dark eyes staring at me unblinking. Way Directive 14 stated that no shifter could attack another creature who surrendered without prejudice. I had to hope that he was a stickler for the rules. He growled and leaned back, still in bear form. I raised myself up to my elbows.

"I give myself and my loyalty to the pack," I intoned formally. "And if you'll just give these to Julia she can use them to cure the red fever." I pulled at the blisterwort that I was still clutching tight in my hand and waved it in his face. I softened my voice. "Please, just try it."

"Oh, yeah?" came a sarcastic voice from the side of me. It was the were-tiger, un-transformed, who'd carried me in so unceremoniously earlier in the day. "How do we know that's not some kind of poison?"

"Oh, for God's sake," I hissed. "You know what I can do." For a split second I let the green flames flicker on, and then off again.

"Do you really think I couldn't hurt you if I wanted to? I lived with the pack for most of my life. I wouldn't harm a shifter unless I had to."

"You went rogue."

"I can't go rogue if I'm not really a shifter now, can I?" I was trying to keep reason in my voice. "And the only reason I left was because I thought that you – the Brethren – would be pissed off enough that I was human to kill my pack. I wasn't to know that that was just some kind of myth."

"We did used to do that, Mack. It's just that nowadays that sort of thinking is considered a bit old-fashioned." It was Lucy, back in naked human form and speaking more softly than her were-tiger brother.

"It doesn't mean that we can't resurrect the old ways," snarled the were-tiger.

"Logan," sighed Lucy, "just leave it for now. She helped us alright? In Cornwall. I would have died if it wasn't for her."

"From what the evidence suggests, you wouldn't have been in danger in the first place if it wasn't for her."

I tried to move but Staines held me in place. "Look, I'm sorry, okay. Just take the plants. If you decide not to use them, then that's up to you. But I'm telling you," I added with a desperate note in my voice, "that they'll help you. They'll help Corrigan."

"Well then I suppose I'll have to try them, won't I?" Corrigan's voice boomed down from the landing of a grand staircase in the front of the hall.

I swallowed and tried to shift over to see him. He still looked good. A bit pale around the edges and there was the hint of a red flush rising from under his collar. But he wasn't bedridden just yet. I felt a wave of relief flood through me. Thank God.

Staines finally moved off of me so I was able to scramble to my feet. I ignored the large circle of shifters that was around me, many of them still in were form and staring at me with wary malevolence.

I stuck out my hand and shook the herbs in the air. "It's called blisterwort. Someone once told me that it was good for something called blushing disease or red fever. It sounds like what you've got. I really do think that this will help." And, I thought silently to myself, I can always get you to suck my blood as a last resort, as Solus had suggested.

"Fetch the Cornish woman," Corrigan instructed one of the shifters near him who took off at a dash. He surveyed the whole scene before him and made a dismissive wave with one elegant tanned hand. The shifters in the hall almost immediately melted away. Jeez, it didn't matter how often I saw his control over the Brethren, it always astonished me.

Staines made an odd guttural noise, still in bear form. Corrigan looked at him and some sort of unspoken communication passed between them. I tried to see if I could make use of my own meagre Voice powers to listen in but it was to no avail. Staines lifted his large body up into the air for a moment and then slunk away.

Corrigan gazed down at me, his green gold eyes entirely expressionless. My knees felt slightly weak. "Uh, thanks," I muttered.

"I spend months searching for you and then once I find you and let you go, you don't seem to want to leave, kitten."

My insides squirmed. "I'll leave, my Lord," I said quietly, "but, please, first take this." Yet again, I stuck out the blisterwort and waved it around. "I really do think it'll work."

"Why?"

"Why? Because Mrs Alcoon, the woman that I need to go back to the mages for, told me about it. Honestly, it sounds like it cures exactly what you've got."

"No," he murmured. "Why did you come back with that? Why are you helping us?"

Nonplussed, I stared up at him. "The pack is my family. Of course I'd do whatever I could."

"I'm not your family."

"No," I said softly, "you're not. But, I…" I took a deep breath. "I don't want you to be hurt. I think you're alright, Corrigan."

My cheeks were burning and I looked away, sure that he could see right through me. He gave a short bark of laughter and started moving unsteadily down the stairs. Alarmed, I ran up beside him and put an arm around his very broad shoulders to support his weight, telling myself that it was only because I didn't want to see him topple forward and down the stairs because if he did Staines would probably have my head. Heat was emanating off his skin and betraying the strength of his illness but he smelled so very good, a mixture of citrus spicy goodness. I inhaled deeply.

"My Lord, I think you should sit down."

"I prefer it when you call me Corrigan," he said gruffly. "And before I sit down I want you to explain to me what you mean by saying that I'm 'alright'."

He turned his emerald green eyes towards me with the flecks of gold flickering within their depths. I licked my lips.

"Mackenzie, dear, you've come back! What's this about a herb?"

"Good timing, Julia," I muttered under my breath.

Corrigan's eyes turned sharp but he didn't comment.

"Pardon, dear?"

"Nothing." I carefully extracted myself from under Corrigan's arm, making sure that he wasn't about to fall over, and trotted back down the stairs to where Julia was waiting. I stuck out the cluster of herbs. "Here. I think this will cure the red fever. It's…"

"Blisterwort, yes, goodness. I haven't seen it in years." Julia peered up at me. "What makes you think it'll provide a cure?"

"A little bird told me. I'm sure it'll do the trick, Julia. And if it doesn't…," my voice trailed off, not wanting to put into words the idea that the Pack could bleed me dry and then they all might quite possibly be completely cured. Fortunately she didn't really seem to notice.

"Yes, yes!" Julia's eyes were gleaming in sudden excitement.

"This might work. If I brewed it up with some lemon to make it palatable. Mackenzie, you may have just saved us all."

Before I could be embarrassed at her words, Corrigan interrupted. "Aren't you being just a little premature?" The skepticism in his voice was slightly galling.

"Perhaps not, my Lord. Blisterwort is an ancient remedy and something that I simply hadn't thought of. I suddenly feel really quite optimistic." She beamed at me and patted my hand. "I'll go and try it out now."

She wheeled round and sped her way out of the hall. I watched her go and then turned towards the door.

Where do you think you're going?

I didn't look back. *I've done what I came here to do. The blisterwort will work, I'm sure of it.*

You seemed to have another suggestion if it didn't.

Damn him, he didn't miss a trick. *It will work.*

"You should stay in case it doesn't, Mack."

It occurred to me that his words were the first time in what seemed like forever that someone had used the name I actually liked to be addressed by. I gave him credit for the thought and finally turned. "Thank you."

He looked surprised. "For what?"

"Calling me by my name."

His eyes gleamed at that. "What? You don't like kitten?"

I scowled at him, but he just grinned. "You know, *Mack*, I'm feeling a bit shaky up here. Perhaps you should come up and steady me again."

"A few hours ago you couldn't wait to push me out of the door."

He shrugged. "That was before you told me that I was alright. So, I'll ask you again, what did you mean by that?"

He was looking at me much like I imagined a cat looked at a mouse before it chomped its head off. I was tempted for a moment to tell him that it turned out I thought he was more than alright. That it took all of my willpower not to start drooling whenever I was in his presence and that his scent made me weak at the knees. And despite his illness, his flirting left me in little doubt that he'd be happy to oblige my fantasies. I thought about the pictures on the Othernet of him with other women that I'd seen and wondered if I was prepared to be nothing more than a notch on the Lord Alpha's bedpost. Probably.

"I suppose I meant that I like you." I took a deep breath and watched his reaction.

"You are the most infuriatingly unfathomable woman I think I've ever come across."

My bloodfire stirred in nervous irritation. "What the hell do you mean by that?"

"Just that, kitten. One minute you are purring and begging to be stroked and the next you're hissing and spitting at me. Is it that you're just high maintenance?"

"High maintenance?" I sputtered. "How dare you!"

I stomped up the staircase to look him directly in the eye. When I reached his level I opened my mouth to show him exactly just how much spitting and hissing I could really do, but he grabbed me instead with both hands.

"Got you." He said it lazily, in a very self-satisfied manner, but I caught a shaky inflection in his voice. I looked at him closely and realised in alarm that the whites of his eyes were turning red. Oh shit.

"Julia!" I shouted down the stairs. "Julia! It's Corrigan, you need to come quickly!"

"You need an old woman in a wheelchair to come and rescue you from the big bad Lord Alpha?" He wobbled slightly, only just managing to steady himself.

"For fuck's sake, Corrigan." I extricated myself from his grip and began to lead him down the stairs. His skin was starting to feel clammy. I swallowed and tried not to panic. He leaned on me, making me realise that if he was prepared to show me that amount of weakness, then he must be feeling very bad indeed. There was still no sign of Julia so I tried a different tack.

"Staines!" There was a high pitched note to my voice that I didn't like. I was starting to feel uncomfortable heat flaring inside, but my bloodfire wouldn't help Corrigan this time. Fortunately, the bear appeared, transformed back into a human – and clothed, thank goodness. He took in the scene at a glance and bounded up the stairs to take hold of the other side of Corrigan. Between us we got him down the stairs and onto a nearby wooden bench that was elaborately carved with different animals.

"We need to get Julia. The blisterwort will help him," I gasped.

Staines stared at me with mistrust in his eyes.

"Staines, please. She can help. You might not be able to trust me but you know you can trust her."

He grunted in grudging acquiescence. "She's on her way."

The words were barely out of his mouth when Julia came bustling in with Betsy right behind her carrying a cup of something steaming. The smell of the brewed blisterwort immediately reminded me of Mrs Alcoon and the debt I still owed her. I watched anxiously as Staines knelt down and put the cup to Corrigan's lips. I was running out of time to get back to the mages and work on getting her released so this had better work. Corrigan drank down the tea, unfocused eyes on me the whole time. Once he was done he closed his eyelids.

"I'm going to need to get him upstairs to his rooms," said Staines to no-one in particular. "The last thing the rest of the Pack needs is to see him like this." He turned to me and fixed me with a steely gaze. "You do realise that if this doesn't work, and that it hurts him instead, I will rip you from limb to limb, Way Directives be damned."

I barely acknowledged him, instead keeping my own eyes trained on Corrigan. I had no idea how long the blisterwort could take to act. I'd been so sure that it would work, but if it didn't...

"I need a knife," I said, softly.

"A knife? Do you really think that we would give you a weapon?"

I turned to Staines with baleful eyes and pointed at my arm. "Then cut me."

"What?"

"Make me bleed, Staines."

"You're fucking crazy."

"Staines…"

Will you two shut up?

We both turned and stared at Corrigan on the bench. His eyes were open and, I noted, his eyeballs were back to their normal shade of brilliant white. Julia was by his side, checking his pulse.

"Still a bit fast," she said calmly, "but the blisterwort already seems to be doing its job. It works unbelievably fast."

"Get it to the others, Julia," said Corrigan, sitting up a little more.

"Yes, my Lord." She was unable to keep the smile of relief out of her voice but as she turned to go out she shot me a look that I knew well: one that said she wanted words with me. Oops. I probably shouldn't have been so quick to bring up the whole blood thing. Despite the fact that the plant I had brought was going to save the whole Pack from the red fever, wanting to open up my veins would still look more than a little odd.

Staines turned to me. Here we go, I thought. "Thank you," he said gruffly.

I almost fell over. "What was that? Can you speak up a bit? I didn't quite catch it the first time." I waggled a finger in my ear to emphasise my point.

"Fuck off." His gratitude was clearly short lived. He went back to ignoring me and turned to Corrigan. "My Lord, we should get you to bed."

"No. I need to check on the others." He stood up and shook himself slightly. Staines moved away to give him space while I watched him warily. Pulling his shoulders back in an unmistakably feline manner, he blinked slowly and looked over at me. "I suppose I owe you a thank you."

I waved a hand dismissively in the air and sketched a dramatic bow. "I am here but to serve you, oh Lord and Master."

He snorted loudly, and then abruptly stumbled against me, the weight and warmth of his body suddenly heavy against my shoulder. I staggered a bit, but Staines was there immediately, hooking one of Corrigan's arms round his hefty shoulders to take the weight. "You are going to bed to rest, my Lord Alpha."

"Staines, I said I would check on the others and that is what I am damn well going to do," Corrigan growled.

"And what good is it going to do them if you keel over on top of them?"

"It is my duty."

"Shut up, my Lord."

I was watching the two of them with my mouth slightly agape. This was a side to Lord Shifty and his minions that I had most definitely not experienced before.

Staines clucked like a mother hen and continued. "A few hours' rest and you will be raring to go and fighting fit."

I hadn't taken Staines to be a cliché man up till now and I just couldn't resist throwing in one of my own. "As right as rain."

The pair of them turned to stare at me as if they'd forgotten that I was even there. Good God, they were like an old married couple. Staines bowed stiffly to me, which was no mean feat given that Corrigan's weight was still slung round his shoulder. "As the Lord Alpha stated, again, thank you."

I couldn't help myself from grinning cheekily back at him and winking. He rolled his eyes and turned to move away but Corrigan resisted. "Mack?" He spoke softly but there was a persistent question to his voice. "Will you stay?"

I held his gaze for a moment, before shaking my head regretfully. "I have to go, my Lord. I have a prior appointment that I must keep. I'm sorry." I realised that it was true. I wanted like nothing more than to stay there, with him, with the other weres, where I felt as if I belonged, even if only slightly.

"Don't call me that."

"Err…what?"

"My Lord. Don't call me my Lord. You aren't one of us."

I felt a stab of pain and hurt through my chest. I swallowed, trying to ignore the pricking of tears behind my eyes. "Of course."

He sighed. "The two of us seem to live in a world of constant misunderstanding. What I mean, Mack, is that you aren't one of my subjects. In fact, after having saved my life and quite potentially that of the entire Pack's, you are most definitely my equal."

Staines sucked in his breath at that but it barely registered.

Corrigan leaned forward slightly. "Whatever manner of creature or mage you might be." He grimaced for a moment and then reached out with his free hand to clasp mine. His skin was cool to the touch, but his grip was strong and reassuring. "I don't just owe you a thank you. We all owe you a true debt of gratitude. I would like you to keep in touch, Mack. And, know this, if you ever need help of any shape or form, then the Pack will be at your side. Do you need intervention with the mages?"

"I…" Lost for words, I swallowed and tried to regain my composure. "No. Thank you. I gave them my word that I would return to them. They won't hurt me, they just want to help me." Well, by making me spend five stupid years in their stupid school, I thought ungratefully. I looked regretfully up at Corrigan and reached out to brush his cheek with my hand. Then I thought better of it and let my hand drop to my side. Something in his eyes flickered a moment and then disappeared.

Staines coughed. "I can have someone drop you back at the Ministry."

I was about to retort that I didn't need his damn help before remembering that I was still completely penniless. "Okay.

Thanks. Can you say goodbye to the others for me? Julia and Betsy and Tom?"

"You don't want to say goodbye to them yourself?"

"I, uh, no. It's best this way. I'm going to be gone for a long time."

Corrigan stared at me unfathomably for a moment, before pulling shakily out from under Staines' arm. He leaned forward until his face was scant centimetres away, then pressed his lips to mine with such a feather light touch that I wasn't even sure whether it had really happened or not. "Then I'll be seeing you, kitten." He turned back to Staines, who gave me a brief stiff nod, and then they both left.

I stared after them for a moment, drinking in the lingering male scent that Corrigan had left behind him. There was a knot in my chest that didn't seem to be going away and that had nothing to do with my blood fire. I clenched my fists and glanced down. A tinge of green light surrounded my hands, reminding me that time was short.

* * *

THE PACK'S limousine pulled up outside the Ministry's imposing metal gates. Unlike the last time I'd been here, there was now a rather scary looking guard posted at the front. I allowed myself a small smirk at the mages' renewed energy for security. The window in the front rolled smoothly down and the driver murmured something inaudibly to the guard, who nodded briskly and gestured with one hand. The ornate gates opened and the car slowly drove in and up the short drive.

Once we came to a complete halt outside the front door, I moved to get out, not waiting for the driver to come round and open the car door. This didn't seem to make him very happy because he rushed out and almost sprinted round the car. A weredog, I thought. It figures. He bowed deeply to me and doffed his cap. What a difference a day makes. I smiled at him absentmindedly and made my way up to the front door. Before I had a chance to knock, however, it swung open with a dramatic motion.

The Archmage was standing in the hallway, with a crowd of others behind him, none of them looking particularly thrilled to see me. They'd probably been hoping I wouldn't show up so they could flex their magic muscles in a fit of retribution. I shrugged. Bully for them.

"Ah, Miss Smith," intoned the magician. "So good of you to join us."

I snorted "You didn't exactly give me much choice now did you?"

"I hope that's not bitterness in your tone. You do realise that by receiving this opportunity to study with us and control your gift, you are privileged beyond what most mortals could ever dream of? " He paused for a moment and gazed at me assessingly. "Although I doubt that if you were truly mortal I'd have had both the Lord Alpha and the Seelie court demanding that I guarantee your safety."

I raised my eyebrows slightly. The Seelie court? That didn't bode too well. I mentally cursed Solus and his big blabbermouth and hoped that it was just him looking out for me, and that he'd not given away my heritage to all his fairy buddies. I also tried to ignore the little thrill that Corrigan showing interest in my well-being gave me.

The Arch-Mage held out his hand. "Well? Are you ready?"

I wasn't going to roll over that easily. "You promise to release Mrs Alcoon?"

He looked irritated for a moment. "As we have already stated."

I attempted to eyeball him for a moment but he just looked at me implacably. I shrugged and then clasped his hand in mine. "Then I guess I'm good to go." The air began to shimmer and my stomach started to lurch in familiar anticipation. Damnit. I closed my eyes tightly and hoped for the best.

ABOUT THE AUTHOR

After teaching English literature in the UK, Japan and Malaysia, Helen Harper left behind the world of education following the worldwide success of her Blood Destiny series of books. She is a professional member of the Alliance of Independent Authors and writes full time, thanking her lucky stars every day that's she lucky enough to do so!

Helen has always been a book lover, devouring science fiction and fantasy tales when she was a child growing up in Scotland.

She currently lives in Devon in the UK with far too many cats – not to mention the dragons, fairies, demons, wizards and vampires that seem to keep appearing from nowhere.

OTHER TITLES

A werewolf killer. A paranormal murder. How many times can Emma Bellamy cheat death?

I'm one placement away from becoming a fully fledged London detective. It's bad enough that my last assignment before I qualify is with Supernatural Squad. But that's nothing compared to what happens next.

Brutally murdered by an unknown assailant, I wake up twelve hours later in the morgue – and I'm very much alive. I don't know how or why it happened. I don't know who killed me. All I know is that they might try again.

Werewolves are disappearing right, left and centre.

A mysterious vampire seems intent on following me everywhere I go.

And I have to solve my own vicious killing. Preferably before death comes for me again.

* * *

A Charade of Magic series

The best way to live in the Mage ruled city of Glasgow is to keep your head down and your mouth closed.

That's not usually a problem for Mairi Wallace. By day she works at a small shop selling tartan and by night she studies to become an apothecary. She knows her place and her limitations. All that changes, however, when her old childhood friend sends her a desperate message seeking her help - and the Mages themselves cross Mairi's path. Suddenly, remaining unnoticed is no longer an option.

There's more to Mairi than she realises but, if she wants to fulfil her full potential, she's going to have to fight to stay alive - and only time will tell if she can beat the Mages at their own game.

From twisted wynds and tartan shops to a dangerous daemon and the magic infused City Chambers, the future of a nation might lie with one solitary woman.

Book One – Hummingbird

Book Two – Nightingale

Book Three – coming in 2023

* * *

The complete *Blood Destiny* series

"A spectacular and addictive series."

Mackenzie Smith has always known that she was different. Growing up as the only human in a pack of rural shapeshifters will do that to you, but then couple it with some mean fighting skills and a fiery temper and you end up with a woman that few will dare to cross. However, when the only father figure in her life is brutally murdered, and the dangerous Brethren with their predatory Lord Alpha come to investigate, Mack has to not only ensure the physical safety of her adopted family by hiding her apparent humanity, she also has to seek the blood-soaked vengeance that she craves.

Book One - Bloodfire

Book Two - Bloodmagic

Book Three - Bloodrage

Book Four - Blood Politics

Book Five - Bloodlust

Also

Corrigan Fire

Corrigan Magic

Corrigan Rage

Corrigan Politics

Corrigan Lust

The complete *Bo Blackman* series

A half-dead daemon, a massacre at her London based PI firm and evidence that suggests she's the main suspect for both ... Bo Blackman is having a very bad week.

She might be naive and inexperienced but she's determined to get to the bottom of the crimes, even if it means involving herself with one of London's most powerful vampire Families and their enigmatic leader.

It's pretty much going to be impossible for Bo to ever escape unscathed.

Book One - Dire Straits

Book Two - New Order

Book Three - High Stakes
Book Four - Red Angel
Book Five - Vigilante Vampire
Book Six - Dark Tomorrow

* * *

The complete *Highland Magic* series

Integrity Taylor walked away from the Sidhe when she was a child. Orphaned and bullied, she simply had no reason to stay, especially not when the sins of her father were going to remain on her shoulders. She found a new family - a group of thieves who proved that blood was less important than loyalty and love.

But the Sidhe aren't going to let Integrity stay away forever. They need her more than anyone realises - besides, there are prophecies to be fulfilled, people to be saved and hearts to be won over. If anyone can do it, Integrity can.

Book One - Gifted Thief
Book Two - Honour Bound
Book Three - Veiled Threat
Book Four - Last Wish

* * *

The complete *Dreamweaver* series

"I have special coping mechanisms for the times I need to open the front door. They're even often successful..."

Zoe Lydon knows there's often nothing logical or rational about fear. It doesn't change the fact that she's too terrified to step outside her own house, however.

What Zoe doesn't realise is that she's also a dreamweaver - able to access other people's subconscious minds. When she finds herself in the Dreamlands and up against its sinister Mayor, she'll need to use all of her wits - and overcome all of her fears - if she's ever going to come out alive.

Book One - Night Shade

Book Two - Night Terrors

Book Three - Night Lights

* * *

Stand alone novels

Eros

William Shakespeare once wrote that, "Cupid is a knavish lad, thus to make poor females mad." The trouble is that Cupid himself would probably agree...

As probably the last person in the world who'd appreciate hearts, flowers and romance, Coop is convinced that true love doesn't exist – which is rather unfortunate considering he's also known as Cupid, the God of Love. He'd rather spend his days drinking, womanising and generally having as much fun as he possible can. As far as he's concerned, shooting people with bolts of pure love is a waste of his time...but then his path crosses with that of shy and retiring Skye Sawyer and nothing will ever be quite the same again.

Wraith

Magic. Shadows. Adventure. Romance.

Saiya Buchanan is a wraith, able to detach her shadow from her body and send it off to do her bidding. But, unlike most of her kin, Saiya doesn't deal in death. Instead, she trades secrets - and in the goblin besieged city of Stirling in Scotland, they're a highly prized commodity. It might just be, however, that the goblins have been hiding the greatest secret of them all. When Gabriel de Florinville, a Dark Elf, is sent as royal envoy into Stirling and takes her prisoner, Saiya is not only going to uncover the sinister truth. She's also going to realise that sometimes the deepest secrets are the ones locked within your own heart.

* * *

The complete *Lazy Girl's Guide To Magic* series

Hard Work Will Pay Off Later. Laziness Pays Off Now.

Let's get one thing straight - Ivy Wilde is not a heroine. In fact, she's probably the last witch in the world who you'd call if you needed a magical helping hand. If it were down to Ivy, she'd spend all day every day on her sofa where she could watch TV, munch junk food and talk to her feline familiar to her heart's content.

However, when a bureaucratic disaster ends up with Ivy as the victim of a case of mistaken identity, she's yanked very unwillingly into Arcane Branch, the investigative department of the Hallowed Order of Magical Enlightenment. Her problems are quadrupled when a valuable object is stolen right from under the Order's noses.

It doesn't exactly help that she's been magically bound to Adeptus Exemptus Raphael Winter. He might have piercing sapphire eyes and a body which a cover model would be proud of but, as far as Ivy's concerned, he's a walking advertisement for the joyless perils of too much witch-work.

And if he makes her go to the gym again, she's definitely going to turn him into a frog.

Book One - Slouch Witch
Book Two - Star Witch
Book Three - Spirit Witch

Sparkle Witch (Christmas novella)

* * *

The complete *Fractured Faery* series

One corpse. Several bizarre looking attackers. Some very strange magical powers. And a severe bout of amnesia.

It's one thing to wake up outside in the middle of the night with a decapitated man for company. It's another to have no memory of how you got there - or who you are.

She might not know her own name but she knows that several people are out to get her. It could be because she has strange magical powers seemingly at her fingertips and is some kind of fabulous hero. But then why does she appear to inspire fear in so many? And who on earth is the sexy, green-eyed barman who apparently despises her? So many questions ... and so few answers.

At least one thing is for sure - the streets of Manchester have never met someone quite as mad as Madrona…

Book One - Box of Frogs
SHORTLISTED FOR THE KINDLE STORYTELLER AWARD 2018

Book Two - Quiver of Cobras
Book Three - Skulk of Foxes

* * *

The complete *City Of Magic* series

Charley is a cleaner by day and a professional gambler by night. She might be haunted by her tragic past but she's never thought of herself as anything or anyone special. Until, that is, things start to go terribly wrong all across the city of Manchester. Between plagues of rats, firestorms and the gleaming blue eyes of a sexy Scottish werewolf, she might just have landed herself in the middle of a magical apocalypse. She might also be the only person who has the ability to bring order to an utterly chaotic new world.

Book One - Shrill Dusk

Book Two - Brittle Midnight

Book Three - Furtive Dawn